THE SOKOI

~by~

Alan McDermott

Also by Alan McDermott

Gray Justice
Gray Resurrection
Gray Redemption
Gray Retribution
Gray Vengeance
Gray Salvation
Gray Genesis

Trojan

Run and Hide
Seek and Destroy
Fight to Survive
When Death Strikes

Motive
Fifteen Times a Killer

When I started writing this work of fiction in the spring of 2021, there was nothing to indicate that Vladimir Putin would have designs on a full-scale invasion of Ukraine. Although I make brief mention of it in my novel, I never imagined it would come to be.

This book is dedicated to the brave people of Ukraine.

Chapter 1

Alex Mann pulled the heavy coat collar around his ears and once again cursed his government for not being in a cold war with Jamaica. Even with his thermals underneath the tuxedo, the piercing cold seeped into his bones. In a grey sky, laden clouds shed their load.

Traffic was light as he walked down Theatre Square towards the Bolshoi, Moscow's iconic theatre and opera house. It wasn't the place he would have chosen to meet Helena, but he'd been given no choice in the matter. The location and time had been left at the dead drop, and he hadn't had the opportunity to make alternative arrangements. He'd had two days to prepare, however, so he'd visited the theatre the night before and made a note of all entry and exit points. He'd also arranged to meet his latest customer there this evening.

Mann stamped the snow from his feet as he reached the entrance and joined the queue waiting to get in to see an opera by Modest Mussorgsky. Once inside and out of the biting wind, he fixed the parting in his short black hair, presented his ticket and made his way to the box on the fourth floor.

Anatoly Kirov was already there. The Russian was a sweating mound of a man, dressed similarly to Mann in a black tuxedo, but his strained to contain the body it concealed. Dripping off Kirov's arm was a young woman wearing a gown straight from the catwalk. She rose when Mann entered the box, and he kissed her gently on both cheeks.

'Ludmila, you look stunning,' he said as he removed his overcoat, and he meant it. Her long blonde hair flowed over her shoulders and she wore just the tiniest hint of make-up. Ludmila was in her early thirties but looked ten years younger.

Ludmila smiled appreciatively. She placed her hand around the back of his neck and kissed him on the cheek, then pulled back and straightened his collar. 'You don't look too bad yourself.'

Kirov clasped Mann's hand in his. 'How is my boat coming along?' the Russian asked. 'No problems, I hope?'

'Everything is on schedule, Anatoly. You have nothing to worry about.'

'Just as long as it is ready for the Monaco Grand Prix.'

The highlight of the Formula One calendar, held in the tiny principality, drew yacht owners from around the world. Kirov had made it clear he wanted the biggest boat there come May next year.

'I can guarantee that you'll be the envy of the world,' Mann assured him with a smile. 'The designer has already been round to measure up for the mink wall trimmings in the master bedroom.'

Kirov grimaced at the mention of the décor, and Mann shared his revulsion. Ludmila had been responsible for that detail, and even a man as rich and powerful as Kirov wasn't going to argue with her.

They took their seats in red velvet chairs as the auditorium below began to fill. Mann used the opera glasses to scan the great hall.

'I've heard great things about tonight's performance,' Kirov said. 'The tenor is going to be a big star one day.'

Mann couldn't care less about the show, but he kept up the appearance that he was there to be entertained. All he really wanted was the file Helena Federova had brought with her. There was a new Russian nuclear missile in development—codename Pyotr after Peter the Great—that was said to be faster than anything in the NATO arsenal. It also had a stealthy profile, making it extremely difficult to intercept.

The British government was desperate for a copy of the plans.

Mann checked his watch. 'If you'll excuse me, I must visit the toilet before the curtain rises.'

'Of course,' Kirov said.

Mann left the box and walked down the curved hallway to the rest rooms. As he neared them, a woman with short black hair walked towards him. She wore a cream dress that fell just below the knee, and a string of pearls hung around her neck.

Helena, right on time.

Her work in the Russian Ministry of Defence gave Helena access to a lot of classified material, and she'd been passing most of it to the British for the last three years. In days gone by, she would have been run by an agent working out of the British Embassy, but the staff there were under so much surveillance that it simply wasn't feasible anymore.

It was up to people like Alex Mann to make contact and collect what Helena had to offer.

Mann's cover was that of international businessman. He purportedly worked as the personal account manager for a company selling yachts to the very wealthy. It was a legitimate business, backed up by a silky website, professional marketing material and an office in Mayfair, London. Every few months, he would fly to Moscow with a view to entertaining one of the many oligarchs with money to waste on frivolous toys.

If Helena came across anything that couldn't wait for Mann's next visit, she would write an email on a Gmail account and leave it in the draft folder. She had been asked to upload the documents rather than having to go through the whole spy rigmarole, but she never had access to electronic copies; the only way she could get them out of the building was by converting them to microfilm. The Gmail account was checked daily by staff at Vauxhall Cross, the home of the Secret Intelligence Service. If a message was found, Mann would call up one of his Moscow clients and arrange to visit them to provide an update on the build of their recent purchase. Once there, he would leave a sign to let Helena know that he was in town—a chalk mark on the side of a drainpipe outside a coffee shop that Helena passed on her way to work each day. When she saw it, she would drop off coded instructions at a bookstore, slipping a piece of paper between the pages of an obscure Finnish art book. It was a simple way to communicate, but the downside was that Mann was at her mercy when it came to the meeting arrangements.

This time it hadn't been so bad. Helena had already booked the box in Mann's name, and all he had to do was convince his client to tag along. If Kirov had refused, it wouldn't have been the end of the world. Mann could have attended the show alone, but Kirov had been delighted to accept his generous offer. Mann would have to endure a few hours of what he considered torturous music, but he'd been through a lot worse in his time with MI6.

Mann kept his left hand down by his side ready for the brush, a manoeuvre where two people walk past each other and hand over intel. It could be in the form of a slip of paper, a flash drive, a coin with a secret compartment, anything. In this case it was a capsule less than an inch long that unscrewed in the middle. It could be mistaken for cold relief medicine, except that it was made of ceramic. Inside would be the microfilm containing everything Helena could dig up on the new missile.

The handover didn't go as Mann had expected. Instead of brushing his hand, Helena stumbled on her high heels and fell into him. They stood there for a couple of seconds, like lovers in an embrace, as Helena whispered to him, her voice trembling.

'Find Sergei Belyakov. Stop him.'

She straightened up and apologised profusely in Russian, ensuring her hair was in place and flattening out her dress.

Mann assured her that it was no problem, then continued to the rest room. He'd felt her hands on his waist, and once he reached the toilet, he entered an empty stall and locked the door. He found the capsule in the outside pocket of his jacket. He unscrewed it, checked that the microfilm was inside, then screwed it back together tightly. He put it in his mouth and swallowed it. There was little chance of him being frisked at the airport on the way home, but he wasn't about to take any chances. Once he got back to England, it would simply be a case of waiting for Mother Nature to do her bit. He could always help things along with a dose of laxative if needed.

With his main task complete, Mann turned his attention to Helena's breach of protocol. She wouldn't have made such a risky move if it weren't of the utmost importance.

Who the hell is Sergei Belyakov?

He couldn't do a search while he was in Moscow. The Russians had sophisticated electronic intelligence—or elint—capabilities and would easily pick up any internet searches he performed. Instead, Mann would have to get back to London before he could look into the question.

It was time to cut the mission short.

Mann flushed the toilet, then washed his hands and returned to the box. Kirov had ordered champagne and canapes, and the plate was already half-empty. Below them, the auditorium was filling quickly and the orchestra was warming up. Mann took his phone out.

'I must get a selfie for my Instagram account,' he said, standing.

Ludmila got to her feet and pressed herself against him so that she could be in the photo. Mann looked at Kirov, but the Russian sipped his champagne and waved him away politely.

Mann took a few snaps, selected the best one and uploaded it to the social media account that was being monitored by a team of operatives back in London. The Instagram post was a signal that he wasn't compromised but needed an excuse to get out, and Mann knew they'd be checking the next available flights as part of his cover story. Each social media account had a different meaning. If he posted a random BBC News article on Facebook, the mission had gone well and he was returning home. A three-word post on Twitter—any three words—meant the shit was flying and he needed an out.

Mann took his seat and looked out over the opera buffs below him. He spotted Helena's cream dress. She was seven rows from the back, browsing the programme.

Mann's phone rang, and he saw from the caller ID that it was the office of the yacht manufacturer.

'Stuart Davenport,' he said, using his cover name.

'It's Elaine. I'm afraid we have a problem with one of the builds,' the voice said. 'How soon can you be in Amsterdam?'

Mann pretended to be annoyed at the intrusion, then promised to be on the next flight out.

'I'm so sorry, Anatoly,' he said to Kirov as he put his phone away. 'I have to go and sort out an urgent issue with one of the boats we're building. You stay and enjoy the performance, and I'll try to get back as soon as possible.'

Kirov assured him that it wasn't a problem, but Mann's attention was on the auditorium below. Specifically, the men in dark suits who were converging on Helena. They had FSB—Federal Security Service—written all over them. There was one at either end of the row she was sitting on, and both were talking into microphones on their cuffs.

Mann knew he should leave, but like a car crash, he couldn't take his eyes off the scene playing out below. He saw the men walk along the row, ignoring the protests of the seated patrons, and when they reached Helena simultaneously, they leaned in and spoke to her. Helena seemed to be protesting, but the men quickly put an end to that. They took an arm each and marched her to the aisle, then out through the exit.

Mann knew he'd outstayed his welcome. 'I'll see you soon,' he said to Kirov as he threw his coat on. He flashed a smile to Ludmila, then walked out of the box just as the orchestra burst into life.

Mann headed for the rear exit. If the FSB were onto Helena, they would no doubt be looking for him, too, and if that was the case, there were bound to be operatives covering the lobby.

Mann pushed through the wooden doors to the street, straight into two men who were clearly waiting for him.

'He's here,' one of them said into his cuff in Russian.

They both walked towards Mann, who turned and started walking in the opposite direction. He heard their pace quicken.

'Mister Davenport,' one of them said.

Mann continued walking, listening to the sound of their footsteps, and when he sensed they were within range, he planted his left foot and lashed out with the right. He caught one of them in the chest, sending him sprawling into the snow, then rounded on the other and delivered a spinning hook kick to the head. He joined his companion on the floor, and Mann took off.

He was blown, there was no doubt about it. How, he didn't know, but there was time for that later. For now, he had to get away from the immediate area, then find a way out of the country.

Mann ran past a neighbouring theatre and onto a one-way street, not easy in a tuxedo and dress shoes on the slick streets. He took a right, following the traffic, then a left into a pedestrianised area. He sprinted as best he could past bars and cafés, coffee shops and burger houses, and when he reached an eight-lane highway he ducked into the underpass.

Mann shucked off his coat as he spotted a beggar. The man was sitting with his head down, but he looked up when Mann approached him.

'Swap?' Mann asked in Russian.

The beggar touched his light raincoat and then looked at the heavy replacement on offer. His face lit up as he took off his stinking coat and handed it to Mann.

Mann's nose wrinkled at the smell of the garment, but if it saved his life he would have gladly eaten it, never mind worn it. He gestured to a grubby hat the beggar had on.

'How much?' the beggar asked, smiling to show several brown and broken teeth.

Mann took out his wallet and removed a thousand-rouble note. The beggar shook his head and held up five fingers. Mann sighed and handed over five grand, about a hundred pounds sterling. The hat and cash were exchanged in a flash.

Capitalism had truly come to Russia.

Mann carried the foetid garments through the underpass, then put them on before emerging into the night. He walked with a slight limp to alter his gait, his head down as he thought about his exit strategy.

The British Embassy was about three or four kilometres away, a forty-five-minute walk. The trouble was, if the FSB knew his name, they no doubt knew his nationality. The first thing on their to-do list would be to cut off that avenue of escape. They would have a ring of men circling the building on the bank of the Moskva River.

Mann had no option but to call it in. He took out his phone, opened Twitter and typed in a brief tweet.

It's snowing again.

London would see the message and plan a way out. All Mann had to do was get to one of three pre-arranged meeting points and wait for the cavalry to arrive. The nearest was the Ascension Church on Bol'shaya Nikitskaya Ulitsa, a fifteen-minute walk away.

Mann began to shiver. His disguise might keep the FSB at bay, but not the cold. He upped his pace to get his circulation moving, and he prayed that the church was heated at this time of night.

As Mann approached the meeting point, he sensed danger. The street was relatively clear and no one appeared to notice him, but the feeling wouldn't go away. He started to jog. The building was in sight, just a couple of hundred yards ahead on the right.

The squealing tyres told him he wasn't going to make it.

A car raced ahead and stopped abruptly in the street. Two heavy-set men got out and ran towards Mann, who turned and tore away. Another car shuddered to a halt as he crossed the street, this one disgorging three men. Mann barged into the nearest one with his shoulder, knocking him off his feet, then sprinted down a side street. Footsteps pounded after him, and even though Mann was running at full pelt, he could hear them closing. He waited until the last second, then jammed on the brakes and leaned forward. His pursuer couldn't stop and went flying over Mann's back, landing heavily. Mann turned to face the others, panting. He was as fit as he'd been in his life, but there was no way he could outrun these guys. There were three of them, then two more appeared behind them. One was holding his injured arm, while the other strode confidently to stand in front of the muscle.

'Mister Davenport,' he said in heavily-accented English. 'Or should I say, Alex Mann. Save yourself some pain and come with us.' He was about fifty, with grey hair cut so close to his scalp that he appeared bald at first glance. A scar ran down his left cheek.

Mann was shocked that the Russian knew his real name. He tried not to show it. Instead, he sought to put a name to the face. He'd seen it before, but the name wouldn't come. *Kolarov? Kunyet…Kuznetsov! That's it. Maksim Kuznetsov!* 'Why should I?' He asked the second-in-command of the FSB. 'You attack me for no reason and now you want me to go with you willingly?'

Kuznetsov shook his head slowly. 'Let us not play games. We know who you are and you know who we are. Just get in the car.'

'And if I don't?' Mann asked, trying to stall them in the hope that he could spot a weakness in their ranks.

'If you don't, then Yuri will shoot you in the face.'

One of the heavies took a Makarov pistol from a shoulder holster and let it hang by his side, his finger flexing near the trigger. Mann could see he was itching to pull it.

Unarmed, and with no way of escape, Mann had little option. He raised his arms. 'Lead the way.'

Chapter 2

It was a short drive to the yellow neo-baroque building on Lubyanka Square. Formerly the headquarters of the KGB, it now housed the FSB and still had a prison on the top floor. There were no windows at that level, which historically led many prisoners to believe they were being held in the basement.

Alex Mann was under no such illusion. He knew the history of the place, and it was one landmark that he'd never wanted to see the inside of.

Maksim Kuznetsov was about to give him the abbreviated guided tour.

They went in the back way. Yuri had applied cuffs to Mann's wrists before relieving him of his possessions and placing him in the car, and now two men took an arm each and walked either side of him. Thankfully, his captors had discarded the beggar's hat and coat.

They reached an ancient-looking elevator, but when the doors parted the interior appeared new. Mann wasn't surprised to see Kuznetsov press the button for the top floor.

As they rode up in silence, Mann tried to project a calm exterior. Inside, though, his heart pounded like a jackhammer. Few things scared Alex Mann, but of all the scenarios he could have imagined as an MI6 operative, this was the one he dreaded the most.

He wasn't without hope, though. As soon as his superiors learned of his situation, they would get to work on a solution. It would probably involve a prisoner swap, perhaps even the lifting of sanctions on certain Russian individuals, then Mann's replacement would arrive and the game would continue.

When the elevator reached the prison level, Mann was led down a grey concrete hallway, where mould grew on the unpainted walls. At the end of the passage was a steel door, and above it a CCTV camera. Mann heard a *whirr* and *clunk* as they neared the door, and it swung open from the inside, pulled by a man in a green uniform. Like the previous corridor, there were no windows here. It was much shorter, though, just a few metres long before another metal door barred the way, and two cameras covered the small area.

They were buzzed through into the prison proper. Here the flooring was dirty white tiles with a black diamond pattern, and the walls were painted two shades of green. At least, they had been many years earlier.

The group stopped in front of an open cell door. Mann's cuffs were removed and he was shoved inside. He turned to see Kuznetsov standing in the opening.

'We will have a little chat soon,' the Russian said. 'It is in your best interest to be frank with me.'

Kuznetsov made to close the door.

'Wait!' Mann said. 'I want to speak to my embassy.'

Kuznetsov smirked. 'I don't think so.'

The door closed with a bang that sent a shudder through Alex Mann. He took a seat on the wooden bench that was probably once a bed. There were two of them in the room, one on either side, as well as a sink and a bucket with a lid on it. It wasn't the Ritz.

Questions flooded Mann's mind as he sat, staring at the wall: how did they know his real name? How did they find out about his connection to Helena? And how did they know where to look for him?

The first was the most concerning. Helena didn't know his name, nor did the staff at the embassy. In fact, the only people who knew his real identity were in England. Did that mean there was a mole in MI6? He tried to come up with an alternative explanation, but none made sense.

Mann put that question aside and moved on to the next. How did they know about his relationship with Helena? That had to have been down to a mistake on her part. She must have slipped up somewhere, perhaps when copying the classified data she'd been sharing.

The last mystery was how they knew to find him near the church. If they'd tracked him on CCTV he could understand it, but he'd been wearing the disguise and affected a limp. Surely they hadn't seen through that.

At least they wouldn't find anything incriminating on him. The capsule Helena had given him was designed to be swallowed, and it would be at least another day before it would make a reappearance.

As he circled back to the first question, a key turned in the lock and the door swung open on grumbling hinges. Two men in army fatigues stood in the hallway, and one of them gestured with a baton for Mann to leave the cell. He complied, to find two more Russians waiting. The quartet escorted him along the passage and through yet another steel door.

Mann suspected they were taking him to his initial interrogation. Beyond that, he didn't know what to expect. Spying on Russia used to be such a civilised game. You tried to get their secrets while they tried to catch you. If they succeeded, you might get roughed up a little, but then the pieces were reset and the game restarted.

That had been before Igor Sokolov took over. Russia was fast becoming a totalitarian state, where dissenters were silenced and opposition parties were outlawed, their leaders imprisoned. Emboldened by these successes, Sokolov turned his attentions to his neighbours. Russia annexed Crimea, invaded Ukraine. Backed by the world's largest nuclear arsenal, Sokolov gambled that the international community would do little beyond issuing strong condemnations and imposing a few toothless sanctions. He'd been right.

It worried Mann that he was the first British operative to be captured under Sokolov's reign. Russia didn't have a death penalty—at least, not officially—but there was no telling what other plans Sokolov had for him before an exchange was made.

He was sure he'd soon find out.

They stepped into a similar corridor, this one with just two metal doors facing each other. Mann was taken into the room on the left, which was empty apart from a long table against the far wall with an orange item of clothing on top.

'Strip,' one of the guards said in Russian, tapping his baton against his leg.

Mann spoke the language fluently, but pretended not to understand. It was a bad move.

One of the guards standing behind Mann kicked him in the back of the knee, and as his leg gave way, another brought his baton down on Mann's head. Lightning blazed in his skull as Mann collapsed to the floor. Boots laid into him, kicking him in the thighs and ribs, and Mann could do nothing but curl up into a ball to protect his vital organs.

'Enough!' a voice shouted.

The assault ended abruptly, but Mann remained where he was in case it was a ruse.

'Get up,' the voice said in English, and this time Mann recognised it as Kuznetsov's. He uncurled himself and made sure the guards had retreated a safe distance, then got gingerly to his feet. It felt like at least one of his ribs was cracked.

'You might do as you wish in your own country,' Kuznetsov said, 'but here you would be wise to follow instructions. Now get undressed.'

Knowing that refusing was just going to invite another beating, Mann slowly took off his clothes. The room was cold, and by the time he was down to his underpants he was shivering.

'Those, too,' Kuznetsov said.

Mann turned and removed his underwear. The moment they hit the floor, the guards pushed Mann up against the table, forcing him to bend over. They stuck their batons under his arm and across his back, pinning him down and enraging his rib injury, and as Mann looked to his side he saw one of them applying a rubber glove. Mann bucked, but the restraint technique neutralised his efforts. His legs were forced apart, and the guard was none too gentle with his internal examination.

Mercifully, it was over quickly.

'Clear,' the Russian said as he removed his glove.

Mann was released. He collapsed to the floor, not because of the trauma, but because he wanted them to think he was weak, fragile. If he appeared defiant, resilient, they would be wary of him, watching his every move. If he acted submissive, they may eventually let their guard down and offer him some chance of escape.

Rough hands pulled him to his feet, and the orange garment was thrust into his chest. Mann unfolded the one-piece jumpsuit and put it on. Once dressed, he was ordered to put his hands out in front of him. When he did, they reapplied the handcuffs.

They led Mann across the hallway to the room opposite. This one was painted in the same green motif, and in the middle of the room was a metal table with thick chain attached to a sturdy ring in its centre. The guards shoved Mann into a chair facing the door, looped the chain around his cuffs and secured it with a padlock.

Kuznetsov walked in and sat opposite Mann.

'Tell me about your meeting this evening with Helena Federova,' the FSB man said, his English clear and easy to understand.

The Russian wasn't taking notes, so Mann suspected the interview was being recorded.

'Who?'

'The lady who fell into your arms at the opera. The one who gave you the capsule that you no doubt swallowed. That Helena Federova.'

Any hopes that this might be a fishing expedition were now dashed. They knew about the exchange, even the manner of transfer. Few people were privy to that information, and Mann didn't think they could have got it from Helena so quickly. All he could do was stall for time and hope MI6 realised he was missing and get to work bringing him home.

'I think you have the wrong man. I was just enjoying a night at the opera with one of my customers.'

'Really?'

'Really,' Mann echoed, 'and I have nothing more to say until I speak to someone from my embassy.'

Kuznetsov looked blank for a moment, then shrugged. 'Okay.' He got up and told the guards to take the prisoner back to his cell before leaving the room.

Mann was surprised at the sudden end to the conversation. He was even more shocked that the Russian had agreed to let him see his people. As he was marched back to his cell, he wondered how long it would be before they were able to get him on a plane back to London.

Once again, his restraints were removed and the cell door slammed shut. The sound didn't seem so bad the second time around, especially now that there was a glimmer of hope. He sat down and began to mentally prepare his debriefing. His bosses would want to know what had gone wrong—lessons learned—so that they could mitigate the risk for the next person they sent in. The problem was, he still didn't know how everything had come unravelled.

Mann was still pondering that when the slat in the door sprang open and a tray of food was passed inside. He took it and sat back down. The surprises kept on coming. He had what appeared to be a steak, with potatoes and asparagus, along with bread and butter and a cup of water. Mann tried a small sliver of the meat, and it was melt-in-the-mouth good. Five minutes later, the plate was empty. He placed it by the door and curled up on the bench to try to fend off the cold.

In the windowless room, he had no idea what time it was. He thought it might be after midnight, but couldn't be sure.

Whatever the hour, it was unlikely the embassy staff would visit him tonight. Using his arm as a pillow, Mann tried to get some sleep.

Chapter 3

At just after one in the morning, Maksim Kuznetsov phoned his boss, General of the Army Dmitri Gudkov. They discussed the progress on the Alex Mann case, and then Gudkov had initiated a three-way conference call with President Sokolov.

'Do you have a confession?' was the first thing the leader of the Russian Federation asked.

'There's little point interrogating him. We have his contact in the MO,' Gudkov said, referring to the informal abbreviation for the Ministry of Defence.

'What about the Federova woman?' Sokolov asked. 'Did she pass on any information about Belyakov?'

'My people are questioning her as we speak,' Gudkov replied. 'Soon, she will tell us everything.'

Especially what she told the British spy about Sergei Belyakov, Kuznetsov thought.

Alex Mann and Helena Federova had come to their attention a year earlier thanks to a walk-in at the Russian Embassy in London. A mystery woman had handed over a photograph, a head shot of a man in his early thirties, with short black hair and a face that was easily forgettable.

'His name is Alex Mann—two Ns—but he travels to Moscow under the name Stuart Davenport,' she had said. 'He works for MI6.'

The woman had turned and left before she could be pressed for more details. The photograph had been dusted for fingerprints, but it had been wiped clean and the woman had worn gloves.

A junior staffer had been tasked with delving into the life of Stuart Davenport. It emerged that he was a regular visitor to Moscow, and as his clients were the extremely rich, there was already a small dossier on him. That grew considerably over the next twelve months. A team was assigned to him every time he landed at Sheremetyevo International Airport, and they followed him everywhere, noting who he met or even casually spoke to. The main thing they were watching for, though, was contact with a local.

That came on his second visit under surveillance.

To the casual observer, the exchange would have been nothing more than two people brushing past each other. To the trained surveillance team, it was confirmation that Stuart Davenport wasn't who he claimed to be.

They identified the contact as Helena Federova, an analyst at the Ministry of Defence, and monitored her every move from that moment on. The team installed a key logging program on her computer, allowing the FSB to detect every key stroke she made, and placed state-of-the-art cameras in her home. For the next nine months, they watched every move she made in real time, heard every word she uttered. They learned that she used a Gmail account to leave drafts for someone—probably MI6—and that she would leave messages for Mann in a bookstore. The code had been easy to break, allowing the FSB to place resources at the meet before Federova or Mann arrived. They also found several of the capsules in her apartment, which told them how she passed secrets to Mann.

The plan had been to give Federova access to disinformation that she could unwittingly pass to the British. One example was the Peter the Great rocket, a fictitious missile that would drive their boffins crazy as they tried to replicate it. The rest of the information she had access to concerned mundane activities dressed as secrets: troop movements near the Finnish border; invasion plans that turned out to be war games.

It was something that could have played out for many years, until Federova stumbled across something she shouldn't have seen. A mix-up by a new—and now ex— employee in a different department meant she had seen documents relating to Sergei Belyakov's mission. It was supposed to be sent to General Herve Federov's hfederov@mil.ru account, but a typo meant it went to Helena instead. It happened late in the afternoon, and by the time the error was rectified, Federova had left for the day. Her computer was checked, but according to the key logger there had been no commands to print or copy the information. However, she could have photographed the details on her screen.

The decision had been made to terminate the operation on Federova. Once she had passed on the latest file, they pounced. They had taken Helena immediately to an interrogation room, while Mann's capture had been more hectic. Thankfully, Kuznetsov had had the foresight to engage the services of Anatoly and Ludmila Kirov. He knew that Mann had arranged to meet the pair, and Anatoly had a looming tax evasion trial that Kuznetsov could make go away. All the Kirovs had to do was plant a discreet tracker on Mann, and the state would overlook his financial misconduct.

It was just as well. Mann had spotted the FSB operatives arresting Federova and had run, unaware that his every move was monitored. Now they had Mann, his contact, and in the next few hours they would have the capsule that he had no doubt swallowed. They would soon know what information Federova had passed to him.

'Then we just have to decide what to do with Mann,' President Sokolov said.

'If he knows anything about Sergei Belyakov, he can never leave the prison,' Gudkov said.

'Assuming he doesn't, is there anyone we can swap him for?' Kuznetsov asked. He knew that no Russian operatives were currently being held captive by the British, but there were some people the president would like to see back in the country. 'Perhaps Vasily Ivanov.'

Ivanov was a dissident and a fierce critic of the Sokolov regime. He'd fled to London two years earlier to escape a ten-year prison sentence for sedition, and still stoked insurrection from his new home. It was thought that the British government was helping him in his quest.

'It's a nice thought, but he is too useful to the British. They would never hand him over.'

Kuznetsov—like everyone else—rarely liked to contradict his president. This time, however, he was sure it was worth it. 'Perhaps if their man was in grave peril, they might change their mind.'

Kuznetsov could imagine Gudkov glaring at him for daring to suggest the president might be wrong. As the silence dragged on, he held his breath, wondering whether he'd miscalculated.

'What kind of peril?' Sokolov eventually asked.

'I thought perhaps life in prison,' Kuznetsov said, his heart pounding with relief. 'Specifically, the Widow Maker.'

It was Russia's most notorious prison. Penal Colony Number Thirteen had earned the name after over six hundred deaths in three years. Most prisons, such as the infamous Black Dolphin, housed inmates in their cells a large percentage of the day, only allowing them to exercise in a cage for an hour a day. There was strict discipline, with the prisoners forbidden from sitting or lying on their bunks for sixteen hours of the day, and they had to respond, 'Yes, sir!' to every command from the guards. Beatings for failing to adhere to the stringent rules were common.

The Widow Maker was different. It housed the worst criminals to pass through the system, from mass murderers to paedophiles, rapists and even cannibals. Each morning, after roll call, they were put into a communal area and left there for most of the day. Some long-termers were given jobs such as cleaning or cooking and were left alone by the rest of the population, but anyone else was fair game. Fights were commonplace, many of them fatal. Other times, it was straightforward murder. An inmate would be selected by the toughest prisoners and would be killed for any number of reasons. They might be seen as a threat, but most often it was because of the crimes they had committed. Rapists and paedophiles didn't last long in the Widow Maker. There were rumours that inmates and guards gambled on how long each victim would last.

'Alex Mann wouldn't make it through the first day,' Gudkov said. 'We might as well put a bullet in his head now.'

'I'm not saying we send him there,' Kuznetsov said, 'but if we tell the British that we're *going* to send him there…'

'…they'll do all they can to prevent it.' Sokolov added. 'I like it.'

'And if they refuse to trade?' Gudkov asked. 'We would have no choice but to send him there anyway. Otherwise we would look weak.'

'That's right,' Kuznetsov said. 'If it turns out to be an empty threat, we weaken our position for the next exchange. We must commit to a course of action.'

'I agree,' the president said, 'but do we have enough proof for a conviction?'

Lack of proof had never been a barrier to jailing those who displeased Sokolov, but Kuznetsov didn't comment on it. 'We will have the microfilm that Federova gave him by the morning. That will be sufficient.'

'Then it's settled,' the president said. 'Arrange a trial immediately. Once convicted, we'll announce that he'll spend three days in a local jail before being transferred to Penal Colony Thirteen. The short window of opportunity will give the British all the incentive they need. Let me know when it's over and I'll inform the ambassador in London to initiate talks with their foreign office.'

'If I may,' Kuznetsov said. He'd already contradicted his president once and hated to do so again, but he'd thought about how this would play out, and he believed he had a way to strengthen their hand. 'I suggest we say nothing to the British. If we do, it may look like we were angling for a deal all along. It might be better if we sentence him and let them make the first move.' If a trial involved a foreign national, a communique was routinely sent to that person's embassy or consulate. That would be enough to get word back to London.

'A valid point,' Sokolov said. 'I'll schedule some time tomorrow to take their ambassador's call.'

Sokolov abruptly left the call, as he was known to do, and Kuznetsov felt his star rise a little higher.

* * *

Kuznetsov arrived at the FSB building at seven that morning. He'd only had three hours of sleep, but that wasn't uncommon in his position. State security wasn't a nine-to-five deal.

He made straight for the office of the commander of the night detail.

Captain Nikolai Zaitsev was in his thirties. He'd spent ten years in Spetsnaz before transferring to the FSB, and it showed. There wasn't an ounce of fat on his body, and his face had the look of someone who'd spent a lot of time in harsh conditions. The skin had a texture like old leather. Zaitsev was sitting at his desk with his feet up, reading a copy of the morning newspaper. He quickly cast it aside and jumped to attention as Kuznetsov entered his office.

'Colonel, I didn't expect to see you here so early.'

'Evidently,' Kuznetsov said. He flicked off a reply to Zaitsev's salute. 'How are the prisoners?'

There were only two men being held in the building. One was Mann, the other a journalist who had been poking his nose into a senior politician's affairs.

'Bolyev still refuses to name his source,' Zaitsev said. 'We're upping the scale of the interrogation as we speak.'

Kuznetsov nodded. 'And the Englishman?'

'We fed him twice, as ordered, and we have looked in on him every fifteen minutes. He was still sleeping the last time we checked...' he looked at his watch... 'seven minutes ago.'

'Good. Wake him and give him his breakfast.'

Zaitsev smiled. 'Yes, sir.'

* * *

Pounding on the door shocked Alex Mann awake. He sat up, confused for only a couple of seconds before remembering where he was. The cell was still cold, and he hugged himself, rubbing his biceps to try to maintain what body heat remained.

The flap in the door clanged open and a tray appeared. Mann rose and took it, then returned to his seat. They'd given him some kind of pastry, along with coffee, a sealed pot of cream and a sachet of sugar. There were also slices of cheese and cold meats next to a plate of bread. Despite having eaten twice in the last few hours, Mann wolfed them down. They might be treating him decently now, but that could change at any moment. Better to take all the sustenance he could while he had the chance.

When he was done, he put the tray back on the open slot and ducked down to see the guard standing outside. 'What time is it?' he asked the Russian.

There was no reply. The tray was removed and the hatch slammed shut.

Mann took his seat again.

After ten minutes he got up to pace and get some movement in his muscles, but something didn't feel right. The chill going through him was nothing to do with the temperature. It was something he'd encountered once before on a mission in the Middle East.

Food poisoning.

Mann threw off his boiler suit and tossed the lid off the bucket. He managed to squat just as the first explosion shook his body. Seconds later, the cell door opened and two new guards stood looking at him. One was a few inches taller than the other. Mann lazily christened them Lofty and Shorty.

Mann was about to ask for some privacy, but realised that they weren't there for the entertainment. They wanted the capsule he'd swallowed, which was why they'd fed him so well. The last meal must have contained a powerful laxative, and they were just waiting for it to appear.

Another wave escaped from him, and there was nothing he could do to stop it. His intestines felt like they were tying themselves in knots as they gurgled and spluttered in preparation for the next onslaught.

It was a full ten minutes before Mann was able to declare himself empty. He reached for the toilet paper, but the two guards grabbed him by an arm each and lifted him clear of the bucket. They threw him against the far wall, and Shorty picked up the bucket as they left. The door clanged shut once more.

Over the next hour, Mann cleaned himself up. A new bucket arrived just in time. Mann had three more bouts before the cell door opened again and the guards beckoned him out.

Mann stood wearily and immediately felt lightheaded. He knew he was dehydrated, but the tap in the cell wasn't working and his requests for water had gone unanswered. He suspected it was designed to keep him from thinking clearly. Perhaps it meant the interrogation was going to be ramped up in the coming hours. Not that there was much point. Innocent people didn't shit state secrets.

Lofty and Shorty cuffed him and led him through several doors to the elevator. Once on the ground floor, they took him to a black van and put him in the back. Three armed escorts dressed in combat gear rode with him.

The journey lasted only a few minutes. When the van stopped, the three escorts ushered Mann through the rear entrance of a building. They walked down a grey tunnel, then through a door that led to what looked like another prison.

Mann didn't understand why he was being transferred. It would have made more sense for the FSB to interrogate him in their own headquarters.

One of his escorts gave the jailer Mann's details, then…nothing. Mann expected to be given a cell, but the three men with him simply stood, waiting. There wasn't much Mann could do but join them.

After a few minutes a telephone rang. The jailer answered it, then nodded towards a set of stairs. The three guards took Mann up.

Mann was shocked to find himself in a Perspex box. It had one seat, which had been secured to the floor. Beyond the transparent screen, he could see the familiar layout of a courtroom.

'What the hell is this?' he demanded, but the guards simply thrust him into the chair and held him there.

There were several people in the court, most dressed in military uniforms, with more entering all the time. Two tables faced the bench. One was empty, the other manned by three men and a woman. Mann didn't have to guess which belonged to the prosecution and which was the defence table.

It didn't look good. He hadn't known what to expect after his capture, but he hadn't imagined anything close to this. It looked like he was going to be tried before he'd even been charged with a crime.

A man in a rumpled suit entered the room and made a beeline for Mann. He put his hands up on the Perspex screen.

'Alex! I'm Sloane, from the embassy. I'm going to try to get you out. Just stay calm and say nothing. I've got—'

Mann didn't hear what Sloane had. Four security personnel rushed into the room and dragged the protesting Sloane away from the screen. They took him to the far side of the courtroom, an area reserved for the public. Mann tried to get out of his seat, but his guards kept him clamped in position.

The next person to enter the room was Maksim Kuznetsov. He offered Mann a malicious smile as he passed, then took his place at the prosecution table. The moment he sat down, the door leading from the judge's chamber opened.

The judge looked to be in his eighties. He walked slowly to the bench and took his seat, then fidgeted with some papers before looking down at the bailiff, who gave the judge the details of the case being tried.

There was just one charge: Carrying out an act of espionage.

The judge waved a hand to Kuznetsov, who stood and began laying out the case against the accused.

'Hey! Aren't you supposed to ask if I plead guilty or not guilty?'

The judge banged his gavel a few times, and two of the guards surrounding Mann pushed his shoulders down into the chair.

'I haven't been charged with anything!' Mann shouted. 'I haven't even been interviewed!'

More banging came from the bench, and the judge leaned forward and spoke into his microphone. 'If he cannot control himself, take him out. We will continue without him.'

Mann was pulled to his feet. He tried to slip the guards' grasp, but they were experienced and held him firmly. They dragged him down the stairs and threw him into the first open cell, and the door clanged shut as Mann got to his feet. He grasped the bars of the cell and tried in vain to shake them.

'I want a lawyer!'

Mann was no longer fearful; he was downright angry. If they'd given him a few beatings before eventually handing him back to London, he could have accepted that, but to subject him to a sham trial was low, even for a tyrant like Sokolov.

'Hey! Dickhead! I want to speak to my embassy!'

The guards just stood chatting, ignoring his outburst, which infuriated Mann even more. He launched one last tirade, then kicked at the bars before sitting on a metal bench.

The fury bubbled up inside him, but it eventually boiled away to nothing as he forced himself to focus. Anger would get him nowhere. He needed to think his way out of the situation.

That did him no good, either. No matter which way he looked at it, he was screwed.

31

The door to the detention wing flew open and Sloane bustled in, accompanied by a uniformed guard who unlocked Mann's cell and let Sloane enter.

'What the hell's going on?' Mann asked. 'Why are they putting me on trial without going through the proper process?'

Sloane sat down and urged Mann to do the same. When he did, Sloane leaned in close. 'I have no idea what's going on, but they have a real hard-on for you, it seems.' He extended his hand. 'Dominic Sloane, by the way.'

Mann had never met Sloane, but knew of him, just as he knew all the players at the local embassy. He shook the proffered hand. 'What has London said? Can they get me out?'

'They're looking into it. When I got the fax to say you were going up before the judge this morning, I came straight here and called the foreign office on the way. We need to give them time to set things in motion.'

Something suddenly occurred to Mann. 'How did you know my real name? I've always travelled under a different ID.'

'The fax said Alex Mann AKA Stuart Davenport. We knew your Davenport legend, and I just assumed you told them.'

'No, when they picked me up, Kuznetsov knew my name already.' Mann tried to think who could have shared his personal details with the Russians. As Sloane had confirmed, no one local was party to that information. 'Someone in London must have told him.'

Sloane frowned. 'That's not good.'

A slight understatement, Mann thought. 'How much time do I have?' he asked. 'How long is this trial due to last.'

Sloane looked pained. 'It's already finished.'

'What? But I haven't been questioned, there was no defence counsel, nothing. I didn't even enter a plea.'

'Little of that matters here these days. There was a defence counsel. He turned up after you were brought down here, but he offered no evidence.'

'He didn't ask any questions at all?'

'Not one,' Sloane said. 'And it's not surprising. We know the judge is one of Sokolov's biggest supporters. The whole trial was a sham.'

'Sham or not, what was the verdict?' Mann asked, dreading the response.

Sloane bowed his head, then slowly looked up at Mann. 'Guilty.'

Mann stood and kicked the bench. 'So that's it? I'm gonna spend the next five years in some Siberian hellhole?' Sloane didn't say anything. He looked like he wanted to, though, which Mann took for a bad sign. 'Longer?'

Sloane swallowed. 'They gave you life.'

'*Life?*'

Sloane nodded slowly. 'In Penal Colony Number Thirteen.'

Mann collapsed on the bench, his whole world shattered. He'd heard about the Widow Maker, where prisoner deaths were an almost daily occurrence. He knew how to handle himself, having aced MI6's extensive unarmed combat training, but that wouldn't do him much good against a crowd of Russian murderers.

'The good news is, your defence lodged an appeal and the judge granted it,' Sloane said. 'You'll be held here until it's heard in three days' time.'

That sounded strange to Mann. 'He didn't ask any questions in this charade of a trial, but when he lodged an appeal, the judge said yes?'

'I know what you're thinking. My guess is, they're giving London a deadline to agree some kind of deal.'

Mann stared down at Sloane. 'And if the Russians don't get what they want?'

Sloane's silence was all Mann needed to hear.

He was screwed, big time. The Westminster wheels spun notoriously slowly, and three days was not a long time in politics. It certainly wasn't a huge amount of time when faced with what was effectively a death sentence.

'Who or what would they want in return?' Mann asked.

'There's no telling. We're not holding any of theirs, so it could be the lifting of sanctions on certain individuals or the unfreezing of assets. We'll just have to wait and see. In the meantime, can I get you anything?'

'Yeah, a pistol with one bullet.'

'Don't think like that,' Sloane said. 'London will do all they can to resolve this.'

Mann wasn't so sure. His capture was certain to embarrass the government, and while most people would want him back safe, others would view any deal as a sign of weakness, perhaps even tantamount to negotiating with terrorists. The Russians had, after all, performed high profile hits on British soil.

It was unnerving to know that his fate rested in the hands of others, all of them complete strangers, men and women who could never appreciate the position he was in. Any decisions made would be based on the political picture rather than out of concern for his wellbeing. *Yes, a man might die, but we have to consider how we would look in the eyes of our international partners.*

He did have one hope, though.

'Tell London that my contact, Helena, broke protocol to give me a name. She said I had to stop him.'

'What was the name?' Sloane asked.

Mann shook his head. 'They get that when I arrive home, not before.'

Sloane sighed. 'You know they'll want proof, otherwise they'll just see it as a desperate attempt to force their hand and get you out.'

It would seem like that, but Mann had no other choice. If he told Sloane about Sergei Belyakov, his bosses back home would have no incentive to move mountains on his behalf.

'Helena wouldn't have put herself at risk to tell me if it wasn't critical…and urgent.'

'Do you at least have a target?' Sloane asked. 'Is it going to happen here or in the UK?'

'I have no idea,' Mann admitted. He rubbed his rib. Thankfully it didn't seem broken, just bruised. It still hurt like a bitch. 'Just pass that along and let me know what they say.'

'I will, but they're going to want to know how things went pear-shaped.'

Mann wished he knew. He told Sloane everything that had happened from the moment he left his apartment the previous evening. 'They picked me up a few yards from the church, which was the closest extraction point. They must have known I was going there.'

'If that's the case, then you're probably right; someone within Six gave you up.'

Much as it pained him to think that the people he'd worked with for so long could betray him, there was no other explanation. 'That's what I was thinking. There's no way they could have followed me.'

'I'll let Horton know. If there's a mole, he'll find it.'

Mann hoped so, but that was a secondary objective. The priority was getting him the hell out of this mess.

Chapter 4

Roland Cooper put on his brown leather jacket and walked out of his flat in Camberwell. The wind sliced through him immediately, but Cooper had no intention of ever trading in his coat for something warmer. He'd bought it on a trip to Italy four years earlier, and wore it everywhere, rain or shine. The leather was scuffed in places and a hole had worn in the right pocket, but he reckoned it was still good for a few more years.

He headed north towards the river, employing the counter-surveillance skills he'd learned and used over the years. Happy that he hadn't picked up a tail, he stopped once to get a coffee and bacon roll before continuing to the office on the south bank of the Thames. Considered an architectural monstrosity by some, the building housed the SIS—Secret Intelligence Service—otherwise known as MI6.

Cooper's office was on the third floor, where his remit was planning and logistics.

It hadn't always been the case.

Until three years earlier, Cooper had been an overseas operative—or spy, in old money. Then a random act of stupidity changed all that. While Cooper had been driving through London, another driver who was texting on his phone blew through a red light and hit Cooper's classic Mini side-on. His car had none of today's safety features like side-impact air bags, and Cooper's right leg had been mangled, his knee pulverised. To this day, he still walked with a slight limp. That had been nothing compared to the damage it had done to his face. A twisted piece of metal from the crumpled door had sliced a deep gash that ran from his temple down to his jawline, narrowly missing his right eye. Although now fully healed, the scar would remain with him forever.

The office had an air of urgency as he entered. There were three other people in the department, and Cooper saw the team leader, Sharon Williams, talking to Mark Snow. Donna Mitchell was typing furiously on her keyboard.

Cooper took his jacket off and hung it over the back of his chair before approaching Williams. She was a small but full-bodied woman, with long black hair that was always tied in a ponytail. Her fiery personality more than compensated for her lack of stature.

'What's happening?' Cooper asked.

'We lost Alex,' Williams said. 'The night shift got a level three extraction message, then he went off grid.'

Cooper was stunned. Alex was the only person he counted as a true friend. The other members of the team were fond of Mann, too. They ran everything for Alex's missions, from monitoring his social media to providing support via the local embassy. They also helped maintain his legend—the false identity Mann travelled under. Alex was one of the best, and if he'd sent a level three, it must have been an emergency. They hadn't had one of those in years. 'Did they check the rendezvous points?' he asked.

'They did,' Williams said. 'They had people at all three within twenty minutes. There was no sign of him.'

Williams' mobile phone rang. She answered it and listened, then ended the call with, 'Yes, sir. Right away.' She turned to Cooper. 'Horton wants to see us.'

Cooper was surprised that the chief would want his presence, but didn't say so. When summoned by Horton, you didn't question it, you just went.

They took the stairs up to Horton's office. The chief was waiting for them in the doorway, and as soon as they entered, he closed the door behind them.

On joining MI6, Cooper had expected the chief's office to be something out of an old boys' club: mahogany wall panels, plush carpets, leather Chesterfields. In fact, it was a modern space with a functional desk, sideboard and one sofa next to a coffee table. The only thing that looked out of place was the fishbowl on the sideboard, which contained a tiny replica diver's helmet and two guppies. Horton said he used them as circuit breakers, staring at them whenever he needed to clear his mind.

'I just heard from the station chief in Moscow,' Horton said, resting his backside on the corner of his desk. 'Alex Mann was picked up by the FSB last night.'

'Shit!' Williams exclaimed.

'Shit indeed, but it gets worse. A trial was held first thing this morning. They've found him guilty of spying.'

'So soon?' Williams asked.

Horton nodded. 'They're up to something, but as yet we don't know what it is.'

'Has Sokolov made any demands?' Cooper asked.

'Not that I know of. I'm on my way to see FoSec in a few minutes. I just wanted to give you a heads-up first.'

39

FoSec—the nickname given to the foreign secretary—was the minister responsible for MI6, and the man Horton answered to.

The chief turned and picked up a folder from his desk. He handed it to Williams. 'This is the preliminary report. Take a look and give me your thoughts when I get back.' He walked past Williams and Cooper and opened the door, holding it for them. 'That's eyes only,' Horton said to Williams. 'You'll both see why when you read it.' To Cooper he said, 'You know Alex well. I'd be grateful if you could break the news to Debra.'

* * *

Willoughby 'Will' Horton strode into the foreign office building in Whitehall and took the stairs up to Geoffrey Taggart's office. He was greeted by Sandra, secretary to Taggart and several of his predecessors. She was in her sixties, the same as Horton, but was dressed like a frumpy thirty-something in a multicoloured dress that looked like a garden border. It was topped with a lime green cardigan. Whenever Horton saw her, the phrase, "mutton dressed as Spam" leapt into his head.

'Geoffrey said to go straight in,' Sandra smiled.

Horton returned the gesture and walked into the foreign secretary's office. It was a functional space, with just a large desk against the far wall, a pair of black leather sofas facing each other across a wooden coffee table, and a drinks cabinet that was rarely used by the teetotal minister.

'Will, good to see you,' Taggart said in his strong Yorkshire accent, and gestured to one of the sofas. 'Take a seat.'

Horton sat, and Taggart took his place across the table.

The foreign secretary was a squat man, five-seven and rotund. Horton often thought he was trying to make up for his lack of height by growing sideways instead. With his bald head, he looked like a black Buddha.

'What was so urgent that you had me cancel my working breakfast?'

Horton ran his hand across his own bald head, one covered with liver spots. It was a mannerism he was unable to control, and something he did whenever he was in an uncomfortable situation. It didn't get more awkward than this.

'It's about Alex Mann.'

'Ah, yes, the Peter the Great missile thing. What about him?'

The news about his disappearance obviously hadn't reached Whitehall. 'We lost him last night,' Horton said.

Taggart's smile disappeared. 'How?'

'We don't know the specifics, but he sent a level three alert late in the evening, which asks for immediate extraction. We lost contact with him after that. This morning, our embassy in Moscow was advised that Mann was due to appear in court. They dispatched someone to offer assistance, but by lunchtime Mann had been sentenced to life in prison.'

Taggart frowned. 'Have the Russians ever reacted this strongly before?'

Horton shook his head. 'The last man to go missing behind the curtain was over ten years ago, before Sokolov came to power. His name was Paul Barber, and he got five years. We managed to do an exchange a few months later. This is completely new territory.'

'Do we know what their end game is?'

'Not yet, but our man on the ground, Dominic Sloane, thinks they want a deal and have set a short timeframe to complete it. Mann will be held in a local courthouse for the next three days, after which he'll be sent to a penal colony where most prisoners are lucky to survive the first night. With his skills, Alex Mann might last a week at the most.'

Taggart chewed over Horton's words for a moment. 'Have the Russians told us what they want?'

'Not as yet,' Horton said. 'The sooner you make contact with them, the sooner we'll know.'

Taggart nodded slowly, then stood and went to his desk. He buzzed his secretary, who answered immediately. 'Get me the Russian ambassador.'

A minute later Sandra connected the call.

'Ambassador Stepanov, it's Geoffrey Taggart.'

'Geoffrey! It's good to speak to you again.' The Russian's English was excellent, but the accent still strong.

'If only this were a social call. I have recently heard about concerning developments in Moscow regarding one of our citizens. His name is Alex Mann.'

'I'm afraid I know nothing of this,' Stepanov said. 'Allow me to contact my superiors and get back to you.'

'Please do.'

Taggart put the phone down. 'He knows full well what's going on,' he said to Horton. 'The bastard just wants to make us sweat.'

Horton agreed. It was all part of the game, infuriating yet unavoidable. Diplomatic niceties had to be observed, even when a man's life hung in the balance.

Five minutes later, the phone rang.

'Bloody Russians,' Taggart swore, looking at his Rolex. 'You can set your watch by them.' He picked up and put it on speaker.

'I've spoken to Moscow,' Stepanov said. 'I think this is a matter we must discuss face to face.'

Horton had anticipated this move. It was designed to waste another couple of hours, bringing the deadline ever closer.

'I agree. When can you be at my office?' Taggart asked.

They heard the sound of pages turning, as if Stepanov was pretending to check his diary. 'Is one o'clock acceptable?'

'It is,' Taggart said. 'I'll see you then.' He ended the call and looked at Horton. 'That gives us three hours to brief the PM and find out how the hell this happened.'

Horton had been wondering the same thing. Alex Mann was too experienced to give himself away, and according to Sloane, the Russians knew Mann's real name. No one outside of London had that information, not even the station chief in Moscow.

As well as getting Mann back safely, they also had to find out who gave him up in the first place.

* * *

'I can see why it's eyes-only,' Cooper said to Williams once he'd finished reading the brief report. 'Someone gave Alex up to the Russians.'

Williams brushed a strand of wavy black hair away from her face and adjusted her round glasses. She was in her mid-forties, and had been poached from across the river—MI5, or counter-intelligence—a decade earlier. 'I agree. First thing we need to do is compile a list of all those who knew Alex was over there. There's the four of us, for a start, plus the night shift and the chief.'

Two people manned the office during the quiet hours, Peter Crane and Maggie Bentley. Cooper knew the whole team well, and didn't think it possible that any of them could be a mole. But then, if there was a Russian sympathiser among the ranks, they weren't likely to make it obvious.

Sharon Williams was one he could immediately cross off the list. Having worked with her for ten years, Cooper knew no one more dedicated to their country. She'd been the planning and logistics lead when Cooper had been in the field, and every mission had gone without a hitch. She also had a soft spot for Alex Mann. Not in a schoolgirl-crush kind of way, though. Alex may be handsome—though not in the conventional, striking sense—but Williams was happily married and doted on her three kids. No accusations of jealousy could ever be levelled at her.

As for the others, he was ninety-nine percent sure that none of them were traitors, but they would all have to be investigated.

The thought struck him that one more person had to be added to that list.

Himself.

He knew he hadn't betrayed Alex, but he had to prepare to have his private life ripped open. Someone would delve into every phone call he'd made, every text message he'd sent, every social media post he'd written or shared over the last few years. Everyone he knew would be interviewed, sowing seeds of doubt in their mind.

Cooper pitied the person who had to sift through all that personal information and disrupt so many lives. They were not going to be popular.

'I'll leave you to get on with that,' Cooper said, dreading his own task. 'I'd better go and break the bad news to Debra.'

Chapter 5

Alex and Debra Mann lived in a village a few miles northwest of Brighton, just off the A23. Cooper had been there a couple of times before at Alex's invitation, and easily found it again.

It was a red brick building, relatively new compared to its neighbours. Cooper knew that Alex had bought the place as a derelict, razed the old property and built anew, close enough to the original design to satisfy the local planning department.

Cooper parked in the driveway behind a two-seater sports car, then turned the engine off. Not for the first time that day, he wondered if he was the best person to deliver the news. He'd never been at ease offering words of comfort. They always sounded trite, and ultimately pointless. If someone had died, they weren't coming back, no matter what he said to the bereaved. He felt an asshole for thinking like that, but it was part of who he was. Life was tough, full of heartache and pain, and then you died. That philosophy was probably one of the reasons he'd been single for so long. His lack of empathy also meant he had few friends, but he counted Alex Mann among that number.

The least he could do was break the news gently to his wife.

Resigned to his task, Cooper got out and rang the front doorbell.

It had been over a year since they last met, but Debra Mann looked exactly as Cooper remembered her. Red hair cascaded over her shoulders, and green eyes twinkled above a slightly upturned nose.

'Roland! What a pleasant surprise,' she beamed.

Cooper offered a feeble smile in return. 'Hi, Debra. Can I come in?'

Her expression changed immediately. 'Of course.' She stepped aside to let him in, then closed the door and gestured down the hall towards the living room. Cooper walked in and stood by the large French windows which overlooked the garden.

'What's wrong?'

Cooper turned from the window and saw Debra standing with her arms folded across her chest. 'You might want to take a seat,' he said.

Debra remained standing. 'It's about Alex, isn't it?'

Cooper nodded slowly. 'We lost contact with him last night, and this morning we found out that he'd been arrested by the FSB—that's their secret police—'

'—I know who the FSB are,' Debra interrupted. 'My husband's a spy, remember?'

Cooper smiled awkwardly. 'I'm sorry.' He thrust his hands in his pockets and sighed. 'The FSB arrested him last night, and this morning they arranged a rush trial. Alex was sentenced to life in prison.'

Debra's mouth hung open for a moment, then she staggered towards the sofa and collapsed onto it. She stared down at her feet, her head shaking side to side slowly.

Cooper didn't know what else to say. Any words of condolence would sound hollow, just as it did when commiserating with someone on the passing of a loved one.

He was grateful when Debra broke the silence. She looked up at him, and it appeared the life had been drained from her body.

'How did it happen?'

'That we don't know,' Cooper lied. They had a pretty good idea, but it wasn't something they would share with a civilian, even if it was the wife of the man facing a potential death sentence.

'But what are they doing to get him out?' she asked.

'That's with the government now,' Cooper said, and saw her cringe as if she was about to be slapped. It clearly wasn't what she'd wanted to hear. 'I'm sure they'll do all they can to bring him home,' he added.

'Alex always said that if it came to this, if his hopes rested on the people in power, I should start picking out a casket.'

That sounded like Alex. He'd never put much faith in the government, especially when it came to foreign matters. They talked a good game, he said, but when it came to delivering on their words, they were toothless.

'It won't come to that,' Cooper said, delivering an empty promise of his own. It was preferable to agreeing with her.

Debra looked up at him and tried to smile, but it came across as a grimace.

He considered informing the press about Alex's situation. Once that was out in the open, the government would be under pressure to get him back. The only problem with that was that it would cost him his job, possibly even his liberty. He could plant the idea in Debra's head, but the authorities would have no trouble tracing it back to him. Even suggesting to someone that they go public with a matter of national security would destroy his career.

All he could do was revert to meaningless platitudes. 'Is there anyone you'd like me to call…' Cooper wanted to kick himself. He was truly hopeless at this kind of thing, no matter how much effort he put into it. Maybe they should have sent someone else. Williams, for one. Someone who cried at funerals and weddings, someone who could offer sincere and heartfelt consolation.

'I'll be fine,' Debra sniffed. She blew her nose on a tissue and balled it up. 'Please, just keep me updated on progress.'

'I will,' Cooper promised. It was the least he could do.

Debra stood and walked towards the front door. Suspecting she wanted to be alone to digest the news, Cooper followed.

'Remember,' he said as she opened the door, 'if you need anything, anything at all, call me.' He handed her his card, which showed just his name and a mobile phone number.

'Thanks,' she said. She seemed to have regained a little of her composure, which made Cooper feel better about leaving her on her own.

She closed the front door as he got in the car, and as he started the engine, Cooper prayed he'd never have to do anything like that again.

Chapter 6

Will Horton had only been to the PM's office once before. That had been to provide updates on terror threats that posed security issues for the Great Britain Olympic team. That meeting had been bland, and to Horton's mind, pointless. The information could have been sent in a memo. This time, however, he was glad to be there in person.

The office of the Prime Minister was disappointingly mundane, considering the history of the building. On the left side of the room the PM sat at a desk with his back to the door, while on the right side an oval mahogany table was used for meetings. It was here that Horton, Geoffrey Taggart and Henry Ward discussed the fate of Alex Mann.

Ward was just thirty-nine, the youngest PM in over two hundred years. He wore his brown hair very short, almost military, and his suits were the finest the tailors of Savile Row had to offer. Rumour had it that Ward started being prepped for the position from the day he entered kindergarten, and Horton believed it. Ward had joined his party as a teenager and stood for election at the tender age of nineteen. He'd been an MP ever since, holding three cabinet posts before taking part in a leadership contest two years earlier. The favourite—a fellow Etonian and incumbent chancellor of the exchequer—had dismissed Ward's chances, calling him naïve and lacking in personality. The other MPs didn't see it that way. Ward was elected as party leader in a landslide, and in the subsequent general election he'd run on a populist agenda, promising to cut the gap between rich and poor and to give everyone, no matter their background, a fighting chance in life. He'd secured a commanding majority in the house. His first action as prime minister was to appoint a new chancellor.

Horton hated him with a passion.

Suggesting he lacked personality was a disservice. As far as Horton was concerned, the PM had two of them: narcissist and autocrat. Everything in government centred around Ward, and his grab for absolute power had already begun. In his first Queen's Speech, Ward had set out bills that he wanted to get through Parliament in the coming year. They included clamping down on protests, making several parliamentary decisions nonjusticiable so that his actions couldn't be challenged in the courts, and watering down the powers of critical institutions such as the parliamentary ombudsman and the electoral commission. He'd even appointed loyal supporters to key positions on the committees that scrutinised the government and held him to account.

'I'm afraid I can't give you very long,' Ward said as his two visitors sat down. 'I've got a meeting at two, then I'm heading up to Scotland for a photo op. First thing in the morning, can you believe it? Apparently that's the best time to milk a cow. Who knew?'

Anyone with half an idea of how the real world works, Horton thought, but held his tongue.

'I'm grateful,' Taggart said, 'and I'll get straight to the point. The man we sent to get a copy of the plans for the Peter the Great missile was captured by the FSB last night.'

Ward didn't look particularly distraught. 'How did it happen, and did he send the information we wanted?'

'We're still trying to determine how he came to their attention,' Horton said. 'I'm afraid the data he was sent to retrieve is lost.'

'Naturally,' Taggart added, 'I initiated dialogue with the Russians first thing this morning.'

Ward simply stared at FoSec. 'And?'

'They put together a swift trial and sentenced him to life in prison. An appeal has been granted, but it takes place in three days.'

'Then perhaps we should wait and see what happens,' Ward said. 'You told me Alex Mann was a top operative. I'm sure he'll be okay.'

Horton had heard enough. 'I think what the minister means is that the appeal is the deadline to make a deal with the Russians. After that point, Alex will be transferred to a penal colony, one with a phenomenally high death rate.'

Ward was impossible to read, so Horton pressed on. 'If we don't get him out, he'll most likely be dead by the end of the week.'

'I see,' Ward said, showing absolutely no indication that he did. 'I take it Sokolov wants something in exchange for his safe return?'

Horton looked at the foreign secretary while crossing his fingers under the table.

'They want Vasily Ivanov,' Taggart said.

Ward laughed, a strange guffaw. When he saw he was the only one, his face immediately lost all expression. 'You're serious?'

'I'm afraid so,' FoSec said.

'Then I hope you told them in no uncertain terms that they can't have him.'

Taggart looked shocked at the idea. 'Well…no. A man's life is at stake. I thought we should at least consider their offer.'

'There's nothing to consider,' Ward said. 'Ivanov does crucial work in opposing the Sokolov regime. We can't just hand him back. You of all people know what they'll do to him.'

'If we don't hand him over, they'll do the same thing to one of ours,' Taggart said.

'It's not the same,' Ward insisted. 'Mann knew the risk going in. Ivanov simply wants democracy to prevail, and it's our duty to help him achieve his goal.'

Horton could see the argument was getting away from them. In preparing for the meeting, he'd gone through every eventuality in his head. This was the one that concerned him the most. He only had one card to play, and it was risky, but it was nothing compared to the danger Alex Mann faced.

Horton swallowed, knowing his career hung in the balance. 'If you take that route and the people discover that you chose a Russian national over one of our own, it could be devastating for the government,' he said, 'especially once it's pointed out that Ivanov recently donated over a quarter of a million to the party coffers.'

That information was already available to the public, and it wouldn't take long for the press to paint the obvious picture.

Ward's expression darkened. 'Is that a threat?'

'Not at all,' Horton insisted. 'I'm just pointing out the obvious. You more than anyone should know the harm that whistleblowers can do to a political party.'

Ward's predecessor had fallen to one of them. An online petition had gained over half a million signatures asking the previous PM to stop the practice of handing NHS contracts to private health firms. In a WhatsApp message to the health minister, the ex-prime minister had said that he wasn't about to be dictated to by the plebs. Once that reached the newspapers, the job of leading the country soon became available.

'This is totally different,' Ward said. 'Any decision I make will be in the interest of this country. If Ivanov manages to rally enough support to defeat Sokolov in the upcoming election, we will have eliminated one of the greatest threats to our freedom and security. If we hand him over, Sokolov will consolidate power and continue to attack us, whether it's cybercrime or hits on Russian nationals living over here. That would be the greater cost.'

Horton's hatred for Ward clicked up another notch. They both knew Ivanov had no chance of altering the Russian election. Sokolov had cruised to victory in both previous outings, and with the majority of opposition leaders either exiled or jailed, he was tipped to do so again. Ward's words might be enough to mollify the man in the street, but he wasn't fooling anyone in this room. London-based Russians had donated over three million to the party in the last two years alone, and if they got wind that Ward was willing to hand them to Sokolov, even the more generous ones, that funding would dry up.

'Then how do we get Mann out?' Taggart asked.

Ward shrugged, 'I don't know. Offer to lift sanctions on one of Sokolov's allies, or offer them a few million in aid, but they're not getting their hands on Vasily.' He looked at his watch, then stood and buttoned his jacket, signalling an end to the meeting.

Horton and Taggart rose, too. 'I'm not sure that will be enough,' the foreign secretary persisted. 'When I met with the ambassador, he was insistent that Ivanov was the only piece they were willing to exchange.'

'Then talk to him again,' Ward said, opening the door. He stood aside to let his visitors out. 'And keep me informed.'

* * *

Cooper knocked on the chief's door and was called in.

'Ah, Roland. Take a seat.'

Cooper dropped into one of the two comfortable chairs facing the desk. Horton sat opposite him.

'Nasty business,' the chief said.

'I agree. It can't be easy for Alex right now.'

Horton laced his fingers and rested his elbows on his desk. 'Yes, that too, but I was talking about the mole. You read the report Sloane sent. Kuznetsov knew Alex's real name when he picked him up. That could only have come from here.'

'There's no way the station chief in Moscow could have known?' Cooper asked.

'Not a chance,' Horton said. 'You know how it works.'

Cooper knew well. He'd spent a few years doing what Alex was doing, but in the Middle East. There, the local embassies and consulates only knew him as John Morgan, car dealer to the mega-rich. It was always a similar set up, with as few people as possible knowing the real names of the overseas operatives. They rarely ventured into the SIS building, and when they did, they assumed their legend. Mann was known as Davenport by almost everyone, and Cooper had been Morgan before the accident. Now that his travelling days were over and he was spending most of his time in the office, he reverted to his true identity.

'Then it's only a small number of people,' Cooper said. 'Ourselves, Williams, Snow, Mitchell and the night team, Peter Crane and Maggie Bentley. Shouldn't be too hard to find out who it was.'

'If only that were true,' Horton sighed. 'Add to that number the foreign secretary and the PM, plus whoever they told.'

Cooper hadn't considered the politicians. 'Was it really necessary to give them specifics?' he asked.

'Given the choice, I'd have said no, but the PM almost creamed himself when FoSec told him about Pyotr. He called a meeting with me and Taggart and demanded every little detail. Believe me, it was the last thing I wanted to do.'

'I can imagine,' Cooper said. He'd never heard a good word about Henry Ward, even from those who shared the PM's public-school upbringing. What he had heard was that Ward liked to micromanage every department, and that obviously extended to the security services. 'Does the PM know we had a leak?'

'Not yet, but he soon will. Once I've briefed him, you'll need to find out who he spoke to—'

'Me? You want me to find the leak?'

'You have a problem with that?' Horton asked.

'No. I just…surely I'm a suspect, too?'

'True, but I don't want this leaving the department, which is bound to happen if I bring in an outsider.'

Cooper saw the logic, but still wasn't sure he was the best person for the job. 'What about Sharon Williams? She's got the experience, she knows her team inside-out and has a better bedside manner than most people. Definitely better than mine.'

'I agree, but we've still got ops running in Asia and the Middle East. I need Sharon where she is. As for you being a suspect, I'm satisfied that it wasn't you. For one, the real mole would like nothing more to be the one looking for the leak. Your reticence reassures me.'

That was a fair point. Also, knowing that the person conducting the investigation wasn't the mole would have been his priority, too. If anyone else had done it, even Williams, there would always be the tiniest doubt in Cooper's mind.

'So how do I go about this?' Cooper asked.

'For now, concentrate on the team. Once I've spoken to FoSec and the PM I'll send you along to interrogate them. Nothing too harsh, please. Just get the names of anyone they spoke to about Alex's op, maybe ask them a few questions for the purposes of elimination.'

'You don't think it was Taggart or Ward?'

'Hardly. For one thing, if the PM was on Sokolov's side, he'd have handed Ivanov over without a second's hesitation. As for FoSec, I've seen the file Box created when he became an MP all those years ago.'

Box was one of the nicknames for MI5, which once had an address of PO Box 500.

'Is he clean?' Cooper asked.

Alan McDermott

'As the proverbial. Every FoSec goes through intense scrutiny, with all aspects of their lives put under the microscope. When someone's privy to such sensitive information, we'd be foolish not to.'

'And they don't object to the intrusion?'

'They might,' Horton smiled, 'if they knew. As for Taggart, he isn't married, so no chance of a honeypot sting, and he has more money than he needs. There's been no suspicious elint, and on the occasions he's been tailed, there was nothing untoward. I'm as sure about him as I can be.'

Cooper was sure that FoSec would be livid if he knew that elint—or electronic intelligence—surveillance was being carried out on him.

'It goes without saying that what I just told you goes no further,' Horton added.

'Of course,' Cooper agreed.

'Good.' Horton looked at his watch. 'I have a meeting with FoSec and the PM in half an hour. I'll let them know you'll be along to see them later this afternoon. Clear a space in your calendar.'

Chapter 7

Henry Ward was a sanctimonious prick, and that was fine by Cooper.

Horton had arranged to meet the PM and FoSec to let them know about the leak that had led to Alex Mann's capture. Instead of scheduling a further get together to allow Cooper to speak to them, the PM had insisted that the matter hadn't been discussed with anyone outside of FoSec and the chief. FoSec, apparently, hadn't been so taciturn. He'd told both of his aides about the ongoing mission.

Cooper sat in Horton's office with their names in front of him, Sarah Mulholland and Mark Ballam. They topped the list that included the entire planning and logistics team. He was glad that he hadn't had to prise the information from the ministers himself.

'The PM really said he didn't have time to meet with one of your underlings?' Cooper asked the chief.

'His exact words.'

'So much for "man of the people".'

'Well, quite.'

Cooper suspected Horton wanted to say more, perhaps share some of the other conversations he'd had with the PM or overheard, but the chief simply nodded at the piece of paper. 'You've got seven names to work with. Pop across the river at four and ask for Denholm Blake. He's got backgrounds on all of them.'

Including me, Cooper thought. He knew of Blake, but hadn't met him. Blake had been with MI5 for over thirty years and was one rung away from the top job.

'Any suggestions on how to play this?' he asked. 'I mean, it's not something I'm trained for.'

'There isn't exactly a handbook for this kind of thing.' Horton leaned forward and rested his crossed arms on his desk. 'The PM wants him or her found, and he's given you carte blanche. You have whatever means you need at your disposal. Short of buggering the Archbishop of Canterbury, you can do whatever you see fit.'

That was reassuring. Cooper would have to work with these people once this had concluded. Would they forgive him for thinking they might be traitors? He wasn't afraid of hurting their feelings, but there was a chance one of them might try to get their own back. Perhaps sabotage his work, or make accusations of bullying or harassment, anything to get him taken off the team, maybe even sacked. With a free pass from the prime minister, that base seemed covered.

'Will I have access to surveillance teams?'

'Blake has been instructed to give you whatever you need,' Horton told him. 'Only he and the DG know the nature of your task, and they've been instructed to keep it that way.'

'But surely any surveillance team they give me will know who they are watching.'

'They won't,' Horton assured him. 'I worried about that, too, but Blake said it'll be designated a training exercise.

Who better to tail in that situation than your rivals across the Thames?'

It seemed the chief had thought of everything. All that remained was to get cracking. He checked his watch and saw that he had an hour before he had to visit Thames House. Time to grab a bite to eat.

Cooper rose to leave.

'How did Debra take it?' Horton asked him.

'About as poorly as you'd expect. I asked if she wanted me to call anyone, but she insisted she was fine. She didn't look it.'

Horton rubbed his head. 'Give her a couple of days, then pop back and see how she's doing.'

Cooper hated the idea, but he'd already promised to keep Debra updated. Hopefully in a couple of days, some arrangement would be in place to bring Alex home and he'd be able to deliver some good news. 'Will do.'

'Okay. I'll let you get on.'

Cooper left the office and walked down to the street. At the nearest convenience store, he bought three sandwiches and a couple of chocolate bars. He had a feeling it was going to be a long day.

Chapter 8

Alex Mann opened his eyes and felt weary. He was unable to sleep in the barred cage, not with so many eyes on him and constant noise throughout the day and night. Other suspects came and went, held in one of three cages until it was their turn to appear before the judge. Thankfully he hadn't had to share a cell with any of them.

He was hungry, too. The decent food he'd been given in the FSB building was a distant memory. All he'd been given since arriving at the court building was two portions of borsht and plain bread.

He thought of the prime minister, the man who had the power to get him out of here. What was he eating today? Quail with truffles, girolles and celeriac puree, no doubt. The very thought made his mouth water and his stomach rumbled in agreement, so he turned his mind to other matters.

Debra.

She must surely know about his situation by now, and she was probably already preparing her 'I told you so' speech.

Debra hated his job as much as Mann loved it. Not because of the danger he faced, but because she was a fiercely jealous woman. She'd seen one too many Bond movies and assumed all spies were philanderers, hell-bent on saving the world one lay at a time. He'd done all he could to prove that she was the only one for him, but it hadn't been enough. When she discovered his Stuart Davenport social media posts, things got worse. In each one, he was with a local Russian and their wives or girlfriends. Debra would have screenshots ready every time he returned from a trip abroad.

Recently, things between them had deteriorated. Instead of worrying each time he was given a new assignment, Debra became angry, accusing him of having an affair. Why else would he keep going over there when he could find a respectable job in England, one that didn't require him to work away from home?

For the last eighteen months, she'd nagged him to find a new profession, but he'd pointed out that he'd been a spy when they'd met and it hadn't bothered her then.

He didn't see what the problem was. Their love life was great. At least, it had been. In the last year, things had admittedly cooled between them.

As he sat looking at the guards through the bars, Mann wondered if her behaviour had been a portent, a warning that something bad was on the horizon.

It didn't get much worse than this.

He jumped from his bench when he saw Sloane walk through the door. The attaché handed over a plastic bag for inspection and waited while two uniformed men examined the contents closely. They seemed satisfied that there were no weapons or explosives inside, and Sloane approached the cage door. A guard unlocked it, let Sloane enter, then locked it again. The guard stood outside, looking in, his hands behind his back.

'For you,' Sloane said, handing the bag to Mann.

It contained two sandwiches, an apple and a book. *Unleashed* by Karl Hill.

'Unleashed?' Mann said. 'Is that meant to be some kind of joke?'

Sloane squirmed. 'I'm sorry, I didn't…I read it a few nights ago and really enjoyed it. I thought it would take your mind off things. The author has created a top-notch character in Adam Black. I think it'll be right up your street.'

Mann put the book aside and opened one of the sandwiches. He pulled the bread apart and sniffed. Chicken and some sort of mayo. He took a small bite, chewed, then took a bigger one.

'I heard back from London,' Sloane said, dropping his voice.

Mann stopped chewing.

'The Russians want Vasily Ivanov.'

Mann swallowed. 'The dissident living in London?'

'The very same.'

'So when's the exchange?'

Sloane looked down, a sign that Mann was now familiar with.

'There's no exchange?'

Sloane shook his head. 'The PM doesn't think it'll look good with his international partners, though we suspect he doesn't want to piss off the rich Russian community back home.'

'So I'm screwed.'

'Not necessarily,' Sloane said. 'The foreign secretary is in constant discussions to see if there's anything else they can tempt the Russians with.'

'Then tell them to discuss harder, because I've only got about 48 hours before things start turning shitty.'

Not that they weren't shitty enough.

His appetite gone, Mann put the sandwich back in the bag. 'Has anyone told my wife yet?'

'Yes,' Sloane said. 'Someone called Roland Cooper went to see her.'

Mann couldn't help but smile. Of all the people, Roland was probably the best and worst they could have sent. He was a good friend—his best—but his brusque manner left many thinking he was cold, heartless. Mann knew that wasn't the case; Roland just wasn't one for showing emotions.

'I remember when Roland got his puppy. Said it would keep him company after his car accident a few years ago. I was with him when the dog ran out of his house and into the road, straight into the path of a car. Roland just picked it up, took it inside, wrapped it in a plastic bag and dumped it in the bin. No sorrow, no tears. I asked him if he was upset and he just shrugged. "It's a dog," he said.'

'I'm sure he won't have been that insensitive with your wife.'

Mann wasn't so sure. 'I can picture it now. "Hi Debra. Alex got caught and he'll probably be dead in a few days. The good news is, he told me you took out life insurance on him last year, so, silver linings and all that."'

'Really?' Sloane asked. 'He's like that?'

'Maybe not as bad,' Mann admitted, 'but he's no shoulder to cry on. He'll have done his best, though. He's a good man.'

'I'm sure he did,' Sloane agreed. 'Would you like me to get a message to her?'

There was so much that Mann wanted to say to his wife, but not through a third party. 'Just tell her I love her, and she was right. If I get out of this, she gets her wish.'

'What wish?' Sloane asked.

'She'll know.'

Mann had never entertained the idea of quitting the service, but now that he knew how little his paymasters valued his life, he wasn't going to risk it for them again. To make that work, he not only had to survive the Widow Maker, but escape.

'Next time you visit, bring me everything you can on Penal Colony Thirteen. Layout, previous escape attempts, number of guards, anything you can think of.'

'Are you sure that's a good idea?' Sloane asked. 'I mean, breaking out?'

'What are they going to do if they catch me?' Mann demanded. 'Put me in prison for life? They already did that, remember!'

'Yes, that was stupid of me. I'll see what I can do.'

A guard ran his truncheon along the bars of the cage.

Sloane got to his feet. 'Time's up,' he said. 'I'll be back later this afternoon with the latest. In the meantime, keep your chin up.'

Mann watched him leave, then dug into the bag to finish off the sandwich. His eyes fell on the novel, and he picked it up.

There wasn't much else to do.

Chapter 9

For the sake of convenience, Five had allocated Cooper a desk in a tiny room at Thames House. The files on the seven people he was investigating were all digitalised and could only be accessed from within the building. His request for printouts had been flatly rejected.

'Not a month goes by without government secrets being found by members of the public,' Denholm Blake explained. 'Left on train seats, at bus stops, in coffee shops. The only organisation that hasn't had such a breach is MI5, and I intend to keep it that way.'

Blake was mid-fifties, with neatly trimmed hair that was more salt than pepper. The DDG—Deputy Director General—was the only man apart from the DG to know why Cooper was in the building.

Cooper had spent nine hours poring over the files the night before, getting home just before one in the morning. He'd got back in at seven, keen to make a start on his prime suspect.

Sarah Mulholland was thirty-two. Her file photo, taken two years earlier, showed her to have shoulder-length black hair. She wore glasses with a clear plastic frame and stood five-eleven in her stocking feet. She wasn't strikingly beautiful, but there was something about her that appealed to Cooper.

Looks apart, what made her the stand-out candidate was the year she spent in Russia after she graduated from university.

The file said she spoke Russian and German fluently, handy attributes to have when assisting a foreign secretary— or a foreign government.

Cooper had to wait until almost nine to meet Aaron Duffield. The man from MI5 knocked on the door and introduced himself.

'Nice closet you've got here,' Duffield said, sticking his head inside the small room.

He looked young for a surveillance team leader. Cooper guessed his age at about twenty-eight, give or take. His short black hair was combed forward, and his nose looked like it had been broken at some time.

'Apparently this is the best they could offer.' Cooper stuck out his hand. 'Roland.'

'Aaron. Look, there's no way we can both get in here. Let's take this to my office.'

Cooper was glad of the chance to get out of the cramped room. He picked up a folder and followed Duffield along the corridor and up a flight of stairs.

'So whose idea was this?'

'The training exercise?' Cooper asked. 'No idea, mate. Well above my pay grade. I was told to give you a few people to watch and monitor your progress.'

They reached an office and Duffield unlocked it. He held the door open for Cooper and followed him inside.

'Maybe it's got something to do with the G7 coming up,' Cooper continued, 'and the PM wants to make sure we've got security screwed down tight.'

'Yeah, maybe.'

Duffield didn't seem convinced.

Cooper didn't care.

The office was much more suited to their meeting. Duffield had a desk big enough that they could both sit behind it and share the computer screen.

'So, what's the plan?' Duffield asked as they took their seats.

Cooper placed his folder on the desk. 'We're to pretend we've got intel that seven British nationals are planning an attack some time within the next three weeks. Target unknown. We need all the elint you can manage. Cameras in their homes, phones hacked, the works. One or more will have a burner phone, so you need to identify it and gain access.'

He wasn't sure that was the case, but if one of the suspects was talking to the Russians, that might be their choice of communication. It was unlikely, given how much security service personnel knew about electronic eavesdropping, but he had to consider every scenario. The most likely way they would pass intel to the Russians was face-to-face meetings or dead drops.

'We also want eyes-on around the clock. Record every person they come into contact with, even if it's a brush. Especially if it's a brush.'

'That's gonna take up a lot of personnel,' Duffield said. 'Don't forget, we've got active operations ongoing. They'll be severely impacted by this. Maybe we should hold off until we're better staffed.'

Cooper had anticipated this, but didn't let on. He knew he'd need around thirty people working the op, which was a sizable chunk of MI5's surveillance capability. 'I agree. Maybe go and have a word with Blake, see if he can kick this down the road a little, then we can both get on with some real work.'

'I will,' Duffield said.

Cooper stood. 'Great. Let's go.'

'Now?'

Cooper smiled. 'No time like the present.'

Duffield didn't seem as happy, but he led Cooper out of the room and down to the DDG's office.

Denholm Blake was reading from a sheet of paper when they knocked and entered.

'Sir,' Duffield began, 'We've discussed the requirements and it seems we're going to leave other operations severely understaffed. Perhaps it might be an idea to postpone this exercise until—'

Blake held up the sheet of paper. 'If you're worried that it'll detract from the ops you've already got in place, don't. I've just been reading the report from the training centre in Cobham. Twenty-three of them are on schedule to graduate next month. I see no reason why this can't be part of their training. Unorthodox, granted, but great experience for them.'

Duffield didn't appear enthusiastic. 'That's a lot of new blood, sir.'

'I agree, but as this is a training session, there's no comeback if they make a mistake.' He peered over his reading glasses. 'Or would you prefer to have them on live ops and use your existing team for the training?'

'No, sir. The trainees will be fine.'

70

'Excellent,' Blake said, and returned to his reading.

Back out in the corridor, Cooper had to suppress a smile. It had gone just as Blake had said it would. With that final barrier out of the way, they could get down to business.

They returned to Duffield's office, and Cooper could tell the team leader wasn't keen on babysitting so many newbies.

Duffield collapsed into his chair. 'Okay, who are the targets?' he asked.

Cooper handed him a list containing names and national insurance numbers taken from the suspects' personnel files.

Duffield brought their profiles up in separate windows, then frowned. 'Two of these are FoSec's aides,' he said.

'That's right. It was at Taggart's request, I believe. He said if they were all from Six, you'd have an easy job tailing them to work and back. This spreads you a little thinner. He and HoSec want to see how you handle that.'

HoSec—the Home Secretary—oversaw the domestic branch of the security service. In truth, all he knew was that a training exercise was being undertaken. The PM had cut HoSec out of the loop and gone straight to the Director General. The fewer people who knew, the better. That included Ward's own cabinet.

'How long is this going to run?' Duffield asked.

'Three weeks, tops. All overtime has been authorised, so no worries there.'

'Three weeks?' Duffield exclaimed. 'I thought it was going to be a couple of days at the most.'

It would have run indefinitely if Cooper had his way, but his superiors had cautioned against it. Too long, and people would start to suspect it wasn't merely a training exercise.

Cooper shrugged. 'Ours is not to reason why…'

Duffield sighed. 'I had tickets for the footie this weekend.'

'Who's playing?'

'Arsenal and Norwich.'

Cooper slapped him on the back and smiled. 'Then I just did you a favour.'

Chapter 10

'But they can't just sit around and do nothing!'

Cooper was beyond fury. When he'd entered Horton's office, he thought he'd been summoned to update the chief on the search for the leak. He hadn't expected to be told his friend had been left for dead.

'I'm sorry,' Horton offered. 'The PM insists that Vasily Ivanov is not going to be part of any deal.'

'So that's it? Alex is left to rot?'

It was wishful thinking. Cooper knew there was little chance of Mann lasting a week.

'There's still time to come up with a compromise before the deadline,' Horton said.

'And if they don't? What are our options?'

'Beyond a diplomatic solution, none that I can see. Ward isn't going to launch a rescue mission, if that's what you're thinking.'

'That's exactly what I was thinking,' Cooper said, arms folded tightly across his chest.

'Then get it out of your head. There's no way we're going to war with Russia over one man, even if it is someone we both know well.'

'I wasn't thinking war, just tit for tat. They've got someone we want, we snatch a close friend of Sokolov. See how he likes that.'

'Impossible,' Horton said. 'Even if the PM agreed to such a crazy idea, we've got no assets in country capable of pulling that off. By the time we insert them and find a viable target, it'll be too late.'

'I can be on a plane in two hours,' Cooper insisted.

'You?' Horton waved him away dismissively. 'Don't be ridiculous. You're trained in espionage, Roland. You're not Rambo.'

Much as it pained him to admit it, Cooper knew that Horton was right. He wasn't cut out for that kind of thing, especially after so long behind a desk.

'It just pisses me off when politicians treat people like pawns in a game.'

Horton sighed. 'It's called the big picture,' he said. 'They see it, you don't. Where you resorted to anger at the news, the PM looked to see what advantage he can gain from the situation. As there was none, it became a damage-limitation exercise. The smallest amount of damage he was willing to suffer was to leave Alex to his fate. They're a different breed, I'm afraid.'

'They're a bunch of heartless bastards, that's what they are.'

It felt good to get it off his chest, but Cooper realised he wasn't doing himself any favours. His spy career might be over, but he still had a good few years to offer the organisation. If he wanted to advance beyond planning and logistics support, he was going to have to show that he could act dispassionately in circumstances such as these. Besides, it wasn't the chief who'd hung Alex out to dry.

'I'm sorry,' he said, softening his tone. 'Alex is a good friend. I just hate to see this happen to him.'

'It's understandable, but we have to leave this to the PM. Taking matters into our own hands could spark an international incident. If that happens, it'll be more than just our jobs on the line.'

Cooper had to agree with the chief, though he didn't have to like it.

'Is the exercise up and running?' Horton asked, steering the conversation in another direction.

'Started this morning,' Cooper confirmed. 'I'll be spending most of my evenings across the river to get updates as and when they come in. I doubt there'll be much activity during the day as they'll all be working. Aaron Duffield promised to text me if they got any elint, though.'

'Good. Did they give you everything you asked for?'

'So far,' Cooper said. 'Aaron seemed to smell a rat, but that was expected. I was planning to give it a couple of days, and if nothing pops up, then maybe rattle some cages.'

'What did you have in mind?'

'A polygraph. Put them all through it and let them know they're suspects. It might cause the leak to panic and run to the Russians.'

'Sounds like a plan,' Horton said. 'As for Alex, don't lose all hope. There's still more than a day before the deadline expires. Apparently that's a long time in politics.'

Hopefully long enough, Cooper thought, as he left the chief's office.

He knew that Aaron Duffield was spending the morning getting his assets into position. He had thirty in total, with a third of them experienced personnel, the rest trainees. Not ideal, but better than nothing. Several had been posted around the SIS building, watching to see if any of the suspects left. This was vital, as Duffield had two teams setting discreet cameras and microphones in the houses of Sharon Williams and Mark Snow. The homes of the others would be surreptitiously kitted out over the next couple of days. Cooper had been desperate to see Sarah Mulholland prioritised, but to have asked for that would have raised eyebrows. Cooper's involvement was supposed to be limited to observing the results, not co-ordinating the operation.

As there was little to be learned until the suspected moles left work for the day, Cooper decided to pay Debra another visit.

* * *

Cooper hesitated with his finger over the doorbell. He'd spent most of the journey from London to West Sussex thinking about what to say to Debra, and he still didn't have it clear in his head. What *could* he say? There was nothing that would lessen the pain she was about to experience.

You've gotta try, he told himself. He owed Alex that much.

He had resolved one thing, though. It might cost him his job, but that was insignificant in light of what Alex was facing.

Cooper pressed the bell and heard the chimes coming from inside the house. Chimes, but nothing more. He looked at the driveway and saw Debra's car, which meant she probably wasn't out. Cooper tried again, but still no answer.

He suspected she'd gone for a walk or something. It was a decent day, considering the time of year. Rather than drive all the way back to London, he decided to sit in his car and wait for her to return.

As he unlocked his vehicle, Cooper heard a noise. It sounded like music, and it was close by. It came again, and he followed it around the side of the house and peered around the corner.

In the back garden, Debra was reclining on a sun lounger that was sandwiched between two portable garden heaters, their heating elements glowing red. She wore a bikini and sun hat, and one hand held a drink of some kind. Her eyes were closed as she listened to a Rihanna track that blared from her phone.

Cooper walked into view. 'Hi,' he said.

Debra jumped to her feet, her drink spilling on the patio. 'Jesus, Roland, you scared the shit out of me.'

'Sorry,' Cooper said sheepishly. 'I tried the bell a couple of times but there was no answer, then I heard voices.'

Debra picked up a towel and wrapped it around her body as she walked into the house.

Cooper followed, puzzled by her attitude. She must know that he was there to update her on Alex's situation, but she seemed genuinely put out, almost angry at his intrusion.

Debra sat down on the sofa in the living room. 'Are you here to give me the bad news?'

That's why she's pissed, Cooper thought. *She thinks I'm here to tell her he won't be coming home.* 'It's not really bad news, but then I suppose it's not what you were hoping to hear.'

Debra sighed and leaned forward, her hands clasped tightly together. 'Just tell me.'

Cooper cleared his throat. 'First of all, Alex managed to get a message out. He said he loves you, and he'll grant your wish, whatever that means.'

His words didn't seem to register. 'And?' Debra asked.

Just tell her, Cooper told himself. *Nice and quick, like ripping off a plaster.* 'The PM won't deal. The Russians are asking for one of their citizens in return, but Henry Ward won't hand him over.'

'Not even to save Alex's life?'

Cooper shook his head slowly. 'He's looking to see if there's anything else they can offer for Alex, but the Russians are standing firm.'

'So there's nothing we can do?'

There was one thing, but it was risky. 'If we can somehow put pressure on the government to get Alex back...' *I can't believe I'm doing this.* '...if public opinion was against the PM, that might create some wriggle room.'

'And how could we do that?' Debra asked. 'The public don't even know about him.'

Cooper raised one eyebrow, as if to tell her she was getting warm. 'But if they were to find out...'

He left the sentence hanging, the seed planted. He'd already said enough to warrant dismissal, perhaps even worse. But if it got Alex back, Cooper didn't care.

'I'd better get back,' he said. 'If you need anything...'

'Call you. I know. And thanks, Roland. Thanks for coming down again. I'm sorry I was such a bitch earlier.'

Cooper didn't want to agree with her, so he just offered an awkward smile and jerked his thumb towards the door.

Chapter 11

When Sloane entered his cell, Mann tossed the copy of *Unleashed* to him.

Sloane caught it clumsily, pinning it against his chest.

'You were right,' Mann said. 'It was a cracking read. Any more where that came from?'

'Three, I believe.'

'Let's hope I get a chance to read them.'

Mann could tell from Sloane's body language that the prospect was remote.

The attaché sat down on the bench. 'There's still no news from London,' he said.

'Nothing at all?'

'Nothing positive,' Sloane said, 'just the usual platitudes. They're doing all they can, getting you back is their top priority, that kind of thing.'

'What about here?' Mann asked. 'Have you spoken to anyone local to get a feel for the situation?'

'The ambassador had a meeting with a couple of officials this morning, but the Russkies are inflexible. They want Ivanov, nothing else.'

It wasn't what he wanted to hear, but Mann expected as much. He'd thought dispassionately about Sokolov's request and the PM's position, and there was no way Henry Ward was going to alienate his biggest donors.

That left him in a dire position. There was virtually no chance of him winning his appeal, so he had one more night in the relative safety of the courthouse cell before he was moved to the penal colony.

'What did you learn about the prison?' he asked Sloane.

'Not much. Structurally, it's a fortress. No one has ever escaped. It's estimated that there are forty guards on duty at any one time, but there's a garrison a few miles away that can send over four hundred men within twenty minutes.'

'Anything else?' Mann asked.

'There have been over ninety inmate deaths so far this year. That's almost one every three days. You're gonna have to watch your back in there.'

Mann already knew, not the number of deaths, but that he'd have to be on maximum alert day and night. What he needed was a weapon. There was no way he'd get a gun inside, and asking Sloane was out. He'd seen the way the man from the embassy was searched on every visit. There was no way he could sneak anything in, not even a knife.

He would have to improvise.

Mann stood and grabbed Sloane by his lapels, dragging him to his feet. 'If you don't get me out of here,' he screamed, 'I'll make it my personal mission to hunt you down and kill you!'

From the corner of his eye, Mann could see the guard fumbling for his keys. As the jailer looked down at his hands, Mann swiped the fountain pen from Sloane's jacket pocket and dropped it down the collar of his prison-issue jumpsuit.

The guard rushed in and clubbed Mann around the head with his night stick. Mann fell, expecting the blow but still blinded by the pain it brought. From his prone position, he saw Sloane shuffle out of the cell.

He knew that might be his last contact with a friendly face for some time, perhaps forever, and he was sorry that it had to end on that note. If he ever got out of this mess, he'd look Sloane up and apologise. His only other option—to ask Sloane to hand over the pen—would have been a mistake. The guard would have seen the transaction and Mann would have been robbed of his only chance of living to see the end of the week.

A thought occurred to him, and Mann cursed. He hadn't told Sloane about Sergei Belyakov. He'd kept the information to himself in the hope it would sway the prime minister to secure his release, but it wasn't to be. The least he could have done was warn London to watch for Belyakov. Mann had no idea what the Russian was planning, but if it was an attack of some kind, it might kill innocent people. Maybe it was something along the lines of the A-234 nerve agent used in Salisbury a few years earlier. If that was the case, it would be a real coup to capture Belyakov red-handed.

He would tell Sloane the next time they spoke, not as a gift to the British government that had abandoned him, but as a huge *fuck you* to his Russian captors.

* * *

Sloane walked towards the exit of the building in a daze. He'd never expected Mann to act so aggressively, and it had come from nowhere. One minute they were talking amicably, the next he was a wild man. Sloane hadn't known Mann long, but it seemed totally out of character.

Hardly surprising, though. Within a few hours, Mann would be transferred to a place full of murderers and thieves. It was enough to make anyone snap.

Sloane didn't have to like it, though. He'd been nothing but good to Mann, and this was how he repaid him? No, he could see out his remaining hours alone. When he got back to the embassy, he'd tell his boss to send someone else next time. If there was a next time. Unless there was crucial news to pass along, there seemed little point in another visit.

He got to the front desk and stood over the register. Some things never changed. In a digital age, the Russians still used pen and paper.

Sloane reached into his jacket pocket for his Mont Blanc fountain pen, a twentieth anniversary present from his wife. When his fingers couldn't find it, Sloane looked down and saw that his pocket was empty.

He turned to retrace his steps, then stopped. A grin slid onto his face as he realised what had happened to his pen.

Sneaky bastard!

Still smiling, Sloane picked up the government-issue ballpoint and signed out.

Chapter 12

Helena Federova knew she couldn't hold out much longer.

She had no idea how long it had been since her arrest. At least two days, she thought. With no windows in the interrogation room, it was hard to tell.

One thing she did know was pain. Indescribable and unrelenting, it came in waves and never really receded. They'd started almost as soon as she'd been strapped into the chair. Beatings and torture interspersed with questions.

She'd initially denied any wrongdoing, but that hadn't lasted long. They had proof, they said. Photos, recordings, physical evidence. They told her about the surveillance she'd been under: the software that recorded her every key stroke; the cameras and microphones placed in her home; the team of operatives who had followed her in public. Helena had thought it a lie, a trick to get her to confess, but once they showed her the photographs and played the recordings, she knew they were telling the truth.

So she told them almost everything. She admitted passing state secrets to Stuart Davenport, knowing he worked for the British government.

That wasn't enough.

Their focus turned to Sergei Belyakov. What had she told the British spy about him?

She knew they could have no proof. Her brief whispered warning to Davenport couldn't have been overheard, and she hadn't taken any physical evidence. No screenshots, printouts or photographs.

Helena denied mentioning it to the British agent. She said it appeared on her screen, but she hadn't read the document. She told them she didn't even know who Sergei Belyakov was.

That was a lie. She'd read it twice, the second time in disbelief. What he was planning was so monumentally diabolical that she couldn't imagine anyone concocting such a plan, never mind carrying it out.

Helena recoiled as the door opened. Every time someone came in, agony ensued. Punches to the head and body, kicks to her shins, a bamboo cane to her thighs. Recently they'd started pulling out her fingernails with a pair of pliers. The pain from that was unbelievable, worse than she could ever have imagined. Her body had been left bloody and bruised, her skin mottled purple and yellow.

And now they were back for more.

You can't tell them, she pleaded with herself. Davenport had to stop Belyakov. If not him, then he could at least pass word to London so that they could prevent the attack. If she told the FSB that the Englishman knew about their plan, they would alter it somehow, maybe postpone it, perhaps change personnel. They could replace Belyakov with someone else and the British would be vulnerable. No, Belyakov had to be stopped and his evil cargo exposed so that the world knew what Sokolov was capable of.

It was easier said than done. Her entire body was screaming for relief. Freedom was out of the question, but she would welcome death.

Her lips, cracked and swollen from dehydration and the constant assaults, formed the word *No* when she saw what they had in store this time.

The man who entered the room carried a blow torch. He placed it on the bench against the wall, alongside the bloody pliers.

'Tell me what you said to the English spy,' the man said yet again.

He was about sixty, his head bald on top with wispy white hair growing at the sides. He never showed any emotion, as if physically abusing another human being was no more of a chore than washing the dishes. Helena didn't know his name. She hadn't asked, he hadn't offered. What she did know was that failing to answer would invite more pain.

'I told him nothing,' she croaked. They hadn't given her food or water in the longest time.

The man simply nodded. He took a lighter from his pocket and clicked it next to the nozzle of the blow torch. A flame leapt out of the end, and he made small adjustments until it burned a fierce blue.

'Last chance.'

Helena tried to cry, but no tears would come. 'Please,' she begged.

Her torturer ignored her plea and held the pointed flame against her arm.

Helena screwed her eyes shut. At first she thought he was holding it too far away, just pretending to burn her so that she would answer, but then searing pain came in waves. Her brain felt like it was ready to explode, unable to cope with the messages it was receiving.

Helena Federova knew she couldn't hold out much longer, but she had to try.

'I told him nothing!' she screamed.

The man stood back. He turned off the blow torch and put it back on the bench. 'Why don't you just confess and save yourself all this trouble?'

Helena sobbed as the smell of burning flesh—*her* burning flesh—filled her nostrils.

The old man waited a moment for her to speak, then shook his head and picked up the torch once more.

'I can't tell you because there's nothing to tell!' Her throat hurt from the yelling, but it was nothing compared to the torment radiating from her arm. 'I brushed past him and handed him the file, that's it. There wasn't time for anything else.'

The old man studied her for a moment, then turned towards the door. He left the room and she heard the key turn in the lock.

Helena's head dropped onto her chest. How many more times would she have to endure moments like that before they stopped? She prayed it wasn't too many. She was close to cracking, her mind and body unable to bear any more punishment. But there would be no respite until she was either dead or her spirit broken.

You cannot tell them!

Easy to say when the danger was on the other side of the door. As soon as it opened, her mental defences would begin to crumble once more, as brick by brick they tore them down.

At least it would be some time before the next round of torture. They always left her alone, either to let her body heal or to let her reflect on how futile her situation was.

Or so she thought.

The old man had only been gone a couple of minutes when she heard the lock jangle once more. Helena tensed, anticipating his return, but the man who walked through the door was dressed in an army uniform. She recognised the colonel immediately. He stood before her, his hands resting on his hips.

'I can make the pain stop,' he said dispassionately. 'Just tell me what you said to Davenport.'

Helena looked at him with pleading eyes. 'I told him nothing. I've already explained that I didn't have time to tell him anything. You have to believe me.'

He drew his service pistol, a Makarov, and shot Helena in the foot.

She howled, bucking and twisting against her restraints, but they wouldn't give. 'I didn't tell him!' she cried. She looked down at her foot, unable to understand how such a small hole could create such agony.

Helena raised her head and locked eyes with the soldier. 'Please, believe me,' she begged.

'I do,' he said. He raised the pistol, pointed it at her head, and pulled the trigger.

Chapter 13

Sergei Belyakov strolled down The Mall towards Buckingham Palace, the early October sun on his back. He wasn't one for doing touristy things, but it was part of his cover, and if nothing else, he was a professional. His hair, which he'd had in a crew cut for the last twenty-plus years, was now two inches long, and he wore a baggy light jacket to hide his physique and military tattoos. Non-prescription spectacles completed the look. There was nothing about his appearance to suggest he was a member of the FSB. Instead, he just looked like a forty-year-old tourist who could have hailed from Austria, Australia, or anywhere in between.

Years earlier, two of his fellow agents had been sent to Salisbury to carry out an assassination, but they'd made the mistake of spending just three days there. When questioned later, they insisted they had been on holiday to see the cathedral. As if anyone would travel that distance to spend three days in a small, obscure town that few in Russia had heard of. It sounded about as plausible as someone from England flying all the way to Solnechnogorsk to look at the lake.

It helped that Belyakov's target was London itself, but even if it had been an outlying town or city, he would have insisted on at least two weeks in England to make his tourist claim sound reasonable.

So he wandered the streets, taking photographs of landmarks. Fountains, statues, buildings. He knew little of their history and cared even less.

This was his third day. Ten more to go until he could carry out his mission and go home. Ten more days of overpaying for substandard food. Ten more days in his pokey three-star hotel. Ten more days of abject boredom.

Then he would strike.

The venue was the capital itself. A march had been organised to protest the pay freeze for NHS workers and the continuing privatisation by stealth. The British government claimed the National Health Service was its most precious commodity, yet its workers claimed that they were being treated with contempt. The last time such a protest was held in London, an estimated quarter of a million people attended. This time, the crowd was expected to be four times the size.

A million people gathered in one place, plus everyone else who lived within a hundred miles of the city. Roughly ten million people, a sixth of the entire population.

It was ironic that the people were marching to protect the NHS, when they were all going to need it in the weeks to come.

Belyakov snapped a series of photos of the Queen's residence, then headed back towards the river. In his boredom, he found he was eating more than usual. At least all the walking helped keep his weight normal. At a coffee shop he ordered a double espresso and a sticky-looking confectionery. As he sat eating, he wished he had more to do, but he'd already determined the route of the march and the optimum place to strike. There was nothing to do but wait and pretend to be on holiday.

In seven days, he would gather the equipment he would use to launch the attack. It had all been prepared, except for the cargo. He would install that himself.

Belyakov felt no excitement, no adrenalin rush as he thought of his mission. The hard part was already behind him. If he was going to get caught, it would have been at the airport when he'd brought in the instruments of death, but customs agents hadn't even checked his luggage. He'd walked through the airport building unmolested and taken a cab to his hotel. Every time he went out for a walk, he used counter-surveillance techniques to ensure he wasn't being followed. So far, he'd seen no one.

He downed his coffee and stuck the last morsel of food into his mouth, chewing thoughtfully. He didn't know what he was about to unleash on the city, but he'd been told not to worry about being caught up in it. There would be no explosion, people wouldn't be collapsing on the streets, fighting for their last breath. Life would carry on as normal for a while, but come the depths of winter they would see the full extent of his actions. That ruled out nerve agents, which were fast-acting. He'd suspected it was some kind of virus, but quickly dismissed that idea. England—in fact, the entire world—had dealt with one recently, so they would be well prepared should another suddenly surface. No, it had to be something they weren't expecting, and he'd been told it couldn't be traced back to Russia. Belyakov had been curious as to what exactly he'd be carrying, but he'd simply been told to be patient. He would soon read about it in the newspapers.

He left the coffee shop and walked down to the River Thames, for no other reason than it reminded him of his beloved Moskva.

Chapter 14

Igor Sokolov poured two generous measures of vodka and handed one to Dmitri Gudkov. The head of the FSB took it graciously and thanked his president.

'You said you had good news,' Sokolov said, sitting down on a red leather sofa.

Opposite him, on an identical seat, Gudkov sipped his drink, then placed it on a coaster. 'Federova knew nothing of our ongoing mission in London.'

'You're sure?' Sokolov asked.

'As sure as we can be in these situations. I would say ninety-nine per cent of my own men would have cracked under the interrogation she went through. There's no way she could have held anything back. Besides, we had someone watching her at the opera. She stumbled into Mann, placed something in his pocket, then walked away. There wasn't time to pass on any information about Belyakov.'

Sokolov swirled the clear liquid in his glass. 'Question Mann, just to be certain. If he knows anything, find out who he told.'

He hoped Gudkov was right, and that Federova hadn't told the Englishman about Belyakov's mission. If she had, it would have to be called off. That would be a real shame. London was the perfect testing ground for Project Nightfall.

The real target was the continental United States, but Sokolov wanted to be sure his creation worked.

And what a creation.

The laboratory just outside Moscow was one of the world leaders in microbot technology, focusing on medicinal applications. Initially, the microbots—at three microns, half the size of a human red blood cell—had been developed to cure cancer by manipulating the Ras proto-oncogene protein. This protein is one of several switches in a cell's growth path, and it is either on or off. The idea was that by turning the Ras proto-oncogene protein off in cancerous cells, it would destroy them. Sadly, it didn't work. However, the developers discovered that they could cause the protein to be always on. This leads to the protein telling the cell it is okay to multiply, overriding the normal limits that control cell growth. This unfettered cell growth produced tumours in lab animals. Roughly half were benign, which meant the remainder were cancerous.

In searching for a cure for cancer, his team had unwittingly discovered a way to create it.

When Sokolov read the report, his first thought was to weaponise it. The more he mulled it over, the better it sounded in his head. A silent killer that takes weeks to act and produced natural results was the stuff of dreams. There had still been a few issues to iron out, though. If they could find a way to make it untraceable, it would be the perfect weapon. The ultimate weapon. They also had to find an effective method of delivery.

Alan McDermott

The latter was easy. Because of their size, the microbots could be made airborne. They were given tiny flagella as a means of locomotion, which they could use to ride air currents. Once they landed, they would deploy a tiny hook so that they weren't blown away, and could immediately tell whether they were sitting on animal or mineral. If the former, they would burrow into the skin until they reached a blood vessel, then ride it to the pancreas. Once there, they would get to work. If the latter, they retracted the anchor and waited for a gentle breeze to carry them away once more.

Making them untraceable was a different proposition altogether. For one, they acted independently, so there was no telling whether the victim was infected with just one microbot, or three million. Roughly five hundred microbots would fit on a pin head, so it was likely that each infected person would have multiple bots inside them. If just one was discovered at an autopsy, it would be disastrous. It was decided that the bots be given a maximum lifespan. Once they'd spent a week altering the Ras proteins of pancreatic cells, they would burrow to the nearest blood vessel and make their way to the stomach. There, they would be destroyed by the gastric juices, and whatever remained of them would end up in the toilet long before any cancer was diagnosed.

Tests performed in the laboratory produced better results with each iteration. After three years of development and continuous enhancement, over ninety per cent of rats developed tumours, with less than half being benign.

It was ready for human testing.

'And if Mann knows nothing about Belyakov?' Gudkov asked.

'Then we no longer need him,' Sokolov said. 'The British are never going to give up Ivanov, so there's no point waiting. Send him to the Widow Maker immediately.'

It would have been nice to have Vasily Ivanov back in Russia, where he could be silenced once and for all, but it wasn't to be. Instead, Sokolov could only hope that Ivanov was among the millions living in and around London who would develop cancer in the next couple of months. If not, then he would send a hit team to shut the man up for good.

Gudkov took his phone out and called Kuznetsov, passing along the president's instructions, then gulped down the remainder of his drink. 'Not long now,' he said to Sokolov. 'Ten days, and we'll know if the test is successful.'

'We'll know if the deployment is successful,' Sokolov corrected him. 'It will be a couple of months before we start seeing the results.'

'I apologise. You are right, of course.' Gudkov twiddled his empty shot glass, and Sokolov motioned with his head towards the drinks cabinet. Gudkov went to fetch another round, then sat down and put the generous measures on the table. 'How confident are you that the British will release the actual figures? They are by no means as transparent as they claim to be.'

'True,' Sokolov said, 'but they lack the will to crush dissenting voices. Once cancer rates start to soar, it will reach their department of health. If they don't release the figures, someone else will. Their NHS will be desperate for increased funding to deal with the anomaly, and if they don't get it, the media will be the first to hear about it. The opposition party will demand answers and the true figures, and that weakling Ward will provide them.'

'Then here's to a successful test,' Gudkov said, raising his glass.

Sokolov did likewise, confident that he'd chosen the right place to put the microbots through their paces.

He could have tested it in any number of places, but England was the perfect location. An island with a large population in its capital was far better than somewhere like Africa. There, the microbots his scientists had created would disperse over borders, and if that happened it would be impossible to know how well it had performed. Health monitoring was poor, and cross-border co-operation was lacking at best. The British, on the other hand, produced regular reports on all types of illnesses. The data would be robust enough to get a good idea of how successful Project Nightfall was going to be when launched against the United States.

The UK recorded around 370,000 cancer cases each year. In the next few weeks, Sokolov expected to see at least a ten-fold rise. If he did, and the results translated to the US, it would be a phenomenal success. America treated close to two million cancer patients each year. Nightfall would give them more than twenty million to deal with. They wouldn't be spread out over a year, either. Twenty million simultaneous cases would overwhelm their already fragile health care system. The recent coronavirus pandemic showed how little it took to shake the foundations. At its peak, over 130,000 people were in US hospitals being treated for the respiratory disease, and they were barely able to manage. It was impossible to imagine them coping with two hundred times that number of people suddenly demanding urgent cancer treatment.

The collapse of the healthcare system would just be the start. The pandemic showed how fragile the US economy really is, with businesses demanding trillions in bailouts just days after the most bullish stock market streak in history. Once the major cities were instantly deprived of millions of workers, businesses would be forced to close. Corporate and personal tax revenues would plummet and the government would have to borrow trillions—again—to bail out the big corporations.

As well as striking the biggest cities in each state, there would also be targeted attacks. Food production and distribution would be among the first hit. Pigs, cows and chickens were also susceptible to the microbots, so the largest farms would be attacked, as would the rural logistics centres that served the supermarkets. Once the stores started running low on essential foods, panic buying would grip the nation, followed by rioting for what was left on the shelves. Society would collapse, and the army would probably be called in to restore law and order, but that wouldn't last long. There'd be little food for the troops to transport, and what there was wouldn't go around. Prices would skyrocket, and in a country where forty per cent of the population already couldn't afford a $400 emergency, few people would be able to afford the basics.

America would be brought to its knees without a single bullet being fired.

'Are we on schedule for the summer? Gudkov asked.

'We are.'

Summer was the optimum time to strike the US, when more people were outdoors. They had over two hundred men and women ready to make the journey to America, and production of the microbots was on track. Each agent would carry two billion of the microbots with them, hidden inside normal personal hygiene cannisters such as deodorants, shaving foam and hairspray. They would purchase the rest of the equipment they needed once they arrived.

'It's a pity that history will not be able to hail you as the man who destroyed our greatest foe,' Gudkov said.

It was indeed a shame, but something Sokolov was reconciled with. Few people knew about Project Nightfall, and a tiny number of them would still be alive once it had been executed. The agents who would launch the attacks would come home to no fanfare nor celebration, but Sokolov already had something special planned for them. They would take a plane to a Russian resort on the pretence that it was a thank-you from their president, but it would never reach its destination. As for those involved in the development and production of the microbots, a tragic fire would silence them forever.

That left just Gudkov and a handful of others.

He would deal with them when the time came.

Chapter 15

Alex Mann slept fitfully. His dreams were of violence, perpetrated by him and against him in surreal scenes torn from the pages of a dystopian fantasy. He battled armies of men the size of bears, armed with only a piece of wood and the fountain pen he'd stolen from Sloane. One of his assailants came at Mann, dragging behind him a length of chain, and Mann jerked awake as the sound of it reached his ears.

The cell door opened to admit three men in heavy coats. They pulled Mann to his feet and slapped manacles on his wrists and ankles, then joined them with the chain he'd heard.

'What's going on?' Mann demanded. Through the window he could see that it was still dark outside, so they weren't taking him back to the courtroom to hear his appeal.

His escort remained silent. They took him along a couple of corridors and out into the freezing night, where Mann shivered uncontrollably as the cold hit him like a sledgehammer.

A large black van waited, its engine idling. When the rear door opened, Mann was only too happy to climb in. Once he was seated, he started to worry about where they were taking him. He asked the three men who had joined him on the benches in the back, but they remained stolid.

Mann soon learned his destination. The van stopped after just a few minutes on the road and the rear doors opened to reveal the back entry to the FSB building.

He wondered if they had changed their minds about the Widow Maker. Perhaps Downing Street had finally agreed to the deal. He was certain he'd soon find out.

The elevator took them to the top floor once more, and after shuffling through now familiar corridors, they finally stopped outside the room he'd been interviewed in on his previous visit. Mann stood facing the door, but they turned him around and pushed him into the room opposite.

It was a mirror image of the other room. It had the same faded green paintwork, but there was no table, just one metal chair fastened to the floor. Mann planted his feet. The restraints attached to the arms and legs of the chair were there for one reason only. His sudden stop earned Mann a punch in the kidney, and he was half-dragged, half-carried to the seat. He tried to lash out with his foot but the manacles prevented it. All he managed to do was unbalance himself, making it easier for the three men to push him into the chair. Mann bucked, determined not to be strapped in, but a club to the back of the head put paid to his struggles.

* * *

When Mann woke, the manacles were gone, but he wasn't free. His hands and ankles had been secured to the chair, thick leather straps that refused to yield when he strained against them. All he succeeded in doing was exacerbate the throbbing in his head.

'Relax, Alex. I just want to ask you a few questions.'

Mann looked up to see Maksim Kuznetsov standing a couple of feet in front of him. The deputy director puffed on a cigarette and blew the smoke up to the ceiling.

'Those things'll kill you,' Mann said, wondering what the hell Kuznetsov had planned. They already knew he was guilty, the trial was over, his sentence passed. What was there to gain from torturing him?

Belyakov.

They must want to know if he told anyone, or if Helena had mentioned the name.

Kuznetsov grinned. 'Trust me, there are worse ways to die.'

'Then do me a favour and try a couple of them.'

'I think not.' Kuznetsov stubbed out the cigarette on the floor. 'You, on the other hand, may soon experience one of them.' He walked over to a metal bench that was up against a side wall. 'Perhaps being stabbed in the belly with a shiv fashioned from a sharpened toothbrush handle. Or beaten to death with a sock filled with rocks. So many acts of violence in prisons these days.' He picked up a scalpel. 'You might even bleed to death from a thousand tiny cuts. *Lingchi*, the Chinese call it. People think it's just that, hundreds of small incisions, but that was rarely the case. Usually, they would carve out a big slice of meat, like a butcher preparing a pig. A bit from the leg, more from the back, the arms, the belly. Can you imagine how that must feel?'

Mann could, and it wasn't pleasant, but he wasn't going to let Kuznetsov know how anxious he was. 'Instead of the history lesson, why don't you just tell me what you want?' He hoped he sounded bored rather than scared.

'Of course.' Kuznetsov dropped the scalpel and returned to stand in front of Mann. 'What did Federova say to you when you met at the opera?'

'Nothing. Oh, she did say sorry, after she bumped into me. I'm sure you had people watching our exchange.' No harm in admitting he'd taken the microfilm from her, now that he'd been sentenced for it. 'Ask Helena. I'm sure she'll confirm it.'

'Unfortunately, Miss Federova is no longer with us,' Kuznetsov said. 'She met...an unfortunate accident.'

Mann's face darkened. 'You mean you tortured her to death.' He'd known that Helena would be in big trouble, but he'd hoped they'd treat her reasonably. Perhaps life in prison. To know she'd been murdered was a huge blow. He felt responsible for her death, but the time for reflection would come later.

Kuznetsov shrugged. 'Semantics. But if you must know, I made sure the end was quick.'

Anger boiled inside Mann as he stared at Helena's killer, 'What do you want from me? I've given you my answer and it's not gonna change.'

'It's not what Federova told me.'

'Then she lied,' Mann said, 'probably so that you'd end her misery. Torture is the most unreliable way to extract information—you should know that. People will say anything to make the pain stop, even if it means death.'

'We'll see.'

Kuznetsov turned and left the room. The moment he departed, two burly soldiers entered and closed the door.

Neither spoke. One stood against a wall and folded his arms while the other rolled up his sleeves.

When the punch came, Mann tried to roll with it, but his assailant knew how to deliver a blow. It felt to Mann like his cheek had exploded. He was sure there was damage to the bone, such was the ferocity of the strike. Before he had a chance to recover from it, another landed on the other side of his face, snapping his head sideways.

'I already told—'

Mann didn't have time to finish his sentence. A fist crashed into the middle of his face, and blood exploded from his nose. He didn't have to feel it to know it was broken.

'My turn,' the other soldier said.

'One more.'

The sledgehammer blow caught him on the side of his left eye, causing sparks to fly inside his skull. Mann thought his head was going to come off.

As the soldiers swapped places, Mann had a few seconds to think. He tried to imagine what Kuznetsov had in mind. Was this just to soften him up for more questioning, or did Kuznetsov intend to let them kill him with their bare hands?

The second soldier chased such thoughts from his head by delivering a round house kick. Fortunately, it grazed the top of Mann's head. Had it connected properly, it could have been fatal.

The first soldier laughed. 'Pathetic!'

'I'll show you pathetic,' the second said. He pulled back his arm and delivered a piledriver to Mann's mouth. His top lip split, and Mann felt a tooth loosen.

'You hit like a girl,' the first said.

Mann begged to disagree. He blinked, trying to clear the tears that clouded his vision. He desperately wanted to see the next punch coming, but his left eye was already closing, and the view from the right eye was like watching a poor quality video underwater. He saw the blur of an arm pull back, but all he could do was tense and await the next shot.

'Enough!'

Mann had never been so relieved to hear Kuznetsov's voice. Through a wet haze, Mann saw the two soldiers leave the room and Kuznetsov's slighter frame standing before him.

'Do you want to change your answer?'

Mann slowly shook his head and wished he hadn't. 'What can I tell you?' he asked, trying to sound petrified. It wasn't hard. If he remained defiant, the beatings would continue until he was dead. He could only hope Kuznetsov believed he was broken.

'You could start with the truth.'

I'm telling you the truth!' Mann screamed.

Kuznetsov put his hands in his pockets. 'I believe you.' He took out a pack of cigarettes and lit one. 'Much as I'd like to let my men tear you apart with their bare hands, my president wants to give you a fighting chance. He said you'd be sent to the Widow Maker, and he hates to go back on his word.'

How noble, Mann thought. The beating might be over, but he was under no illusion; what he faced next wasn't going to be much better. At least in prison, he'd be able to defend himself.

The two soldiers reappeared and untied the leather straps. They yanked Mann to his feet and pulled him out into the corridor.

'Goodbye, Alex,' Kuznetsov said as Mann was led away. 'I hope the next person they send proves to be more of a challenge,'

I hope the next person stomps on your balls and shoots you in the face, Mann thought. He wanted to say it out loud, but that might invite another stint in the chair.

When they reached the exit, Mann was disappointed not to see a van waiting. His escorts stamped their feet to fight off the elements. Mann would have given anything for one of their coats. As it was, all he could do was make himself as small as possible and pray that the transport arrived soon.

It was fifteen minutes before it turned up, by which time Mann was frozen to the bone. He'd endured many Russian winters, but this was the coldest of them, and it was the first time he'd been dressed in just a boiler suit. It wasn't something he wanted to experience again.

Not that he was likely to get the chance.

Inside the van, the temperature was bearable, but it wasn't going to be a comfortable ride. The chain that connected the shackles on his wrists and ankles was looped through a large metal ring set in the floor. Mann had to lean forward to let them secure it, and once attached he found he couldn't straighten up fully. He would have to spend the entire journey hunched over.

The escorts unzipped their coats but left them on, and Mann mercifully felt his body begin to thaw.

If they were taking him straight to the prison, it would be a long trip. Mann knew that the Widow Maker was located near a town called Yaroslavl, a four-hour drive. Plenty of time to prepare himself for what he was about to face.

Violence. That was a given. Violence, and spending every waking moment on his guard. Even when he slept, it would have to be with one eye open.

In short, he faced a nightmare.

The sheer number of deaths in the facility suggested the guards turned a blind eye to attacks. Perhaps they even encouraged them. It wasn't only his fellow prisoners that he would have to watch out for.

Mann was grateful to have the pen he'd stolen from Sloane. He was less pleased about where he'd had to hide it. Thankfully they moved him around in shackles, so they couldn't see his uncomfortable gait. That would change the minute they got to the prison. Once he was handed over, he would have to walk normally or the prison guards would suspect something. If he was lucky, they would put it down to the beating.

Mann touched his left eye. It was almost completely swollen shut. That would make self-defence a lot more difficult. The lack of depth perception and inability to track moving objects—fists and knives leaping instantly to mind—would make his first few days extremely hazardous.

Beyond staying alive, Mann knew he had to have a long-term strategy. Escape would be his priority, but it wouldn't be easy, especially on his own. Tunnelling would take years, and he wasn't prepared to wait that long. He needed to find some allies on the inside, people who know the layout of the facility and the routine of the guards. People who were as desperate to get out as he was. There should be plenty of them.

His eye would initially make him vulnerable, but he did have some advantages. For one, they wouldn't expect him to speak Russian. He also had the pen. The main thing he had going for him, though, was his ability to handle himself.

Mann had always been a fighter. He'd grown up on a London council estate, where he learned early on that you had to be handy with your fists to survive. From his earliest memories, he'd been getting into scrapes. It started in primary school, with fights at lunchtime. The first one ended in a beating, and when he got home with a torn shirt and swollen lip, his father had asked what happened. Mann explained that he'd been picked on, and the boy, Darren, had hit him half a dozen times. When asked if he'd hit him back, Mann shook his head. That angered his father.

'If someone hits you, you hit them back so hard, they'll never hit you again.'

His father taught him a few moves. How to stand, how to get power into a punch, how to block. Mann practised in his bedroom all weekend. When he got back to school on the Monday, Darren was waiting for him during the morning break. Mann remembered feeling calm. A little apprehensive, maybe, but that soon passed. The moment the bully aimed a punch and Mann blocked it, everything he'd practised that weekend flooded into his brain. Mann stepped aside and landed a punch on Darren's nose, knocking him onto his backside. While he was down, Mann kicked him twice in the ribs, then sat astride him and pounded the bully's face until his knuckles were bloody.

No one picked on Alex Mann for the next three years. It wasn't his last fight in that school, though. His father had taught him never to start a fight. *But if you get into one, you better damn well finish it.*

Buoyed by his victory over Darren, Alex had asked to join a martial arts club. His father had consented, on one condition: he was only to use his fighting skills in self-defence—never to be the aggressor. Mann had asked if he could help others who were being bullied, and Mann senior had agreed.

From that day on, Mann had seen himself as the saviour of the weak and downtrodden. Whenever he saw one of the known bullies in action, he would teach them a lesson.

In middle school, things went much the same way, except that he won his first fight convincingly. High school was different. The kids he'd grown up with had learned not to mess with him, but the high school drew students from a wider area, including three rough estates. Each one had its own leader, a champion, and none of them had heard of Alex Mann.

He soon rectified that. At fourteen, Mann was already close to six feet tall, but the bullies soon noticed that he didn't throw his weight around. To their mind, that made him weak, ripe for the taking.

Mann put his first and only challenger in hospital. He hadn't intended to, but Connor just wouldn't stay down. He kept coming back for more, even though Mann put him on his back three times. The third time he got up, Mann knew he was going to have to seriously hurt him if he wanted the fight to end. He warned the kid, who just snarled and ran at him in a rage. Mann waited for him, and as Connor threw a punch, Mann swivelled, caught the flying arm and threw Connor over his hip and onto his back. Mann followed him down and delivered two powerful strikes to Connor's rib cage, breaking four bones.

In the fourteen years since leaving school, Mann hadn't used his fists in anger until this week. He'd been through intensive training with Six, including regular refreshers, but now he was going to have to dig deep to remember each block, every kick, every punch.

Mann wondered whether he would have any use for those moves in the Widow Maker. Would it be a fair fight, one-on-one, or would a crowd jump him when he least expected it? Whatever they had in mind, he would employ the same tactic as he had at school: make them think twice about taking him on.

To do that, he knew he would have to do more than crack a few ribs.

One of the escorts took out a pack of cigarettes and handed them round. All three men lit up, and the interior of the van soon filled with a toxic cloud that only seemed to affect Mann.

With his hunched posture, swollen and bloody face, and now the polluted air, Mann didn't think his day could get any worse.

Fate laughed, and doubled down.

Chapter 16

When the van arrived at the prison, Mann was glad to get back out into the arctic night air. His lungs threatened to freeze as he gulped greedily, and he took in his surroundings. Not that there was much to see. They were in a small rectangular courtyard, with brick walls on either side and steel gates fore and aft. Above them, two men stood watching the proceedings, automatic rifles resting idly in their hands.

There was little time to recover from the journey. His handcuffs were removed and Mann rubbed his wrists, but the respite was short-lived. He was told to put his hands behind his back, and when he did, the cuffs were put on again. The moment they snapped shut, a black hood went over his head and one of the escorts grabbed the chain and pulled it high. Mann was forced to bend double as his shoulders screamed in protest and the pen in his anus made its presence felt.

Mann heard his escorts say their goodbyes as he was pushed towards the steel door ahead. He heard a lock turn and he shuffled along for another hundred or so paces before he felt a draft of warmer air. Moments later they were inside.

Mann expected to hear raucous noise from the prisoners, but then he realised it must be too early. He had no idea what time they'd woken him, but it was night when they set off and it was still dark, so he guessed somewhere around two or three in the morning.

When sound reached his ears, it wasn't what he'd been expecting. Death metal music blared from seemingly everywhere, the volume at maximum. Mann could feel the ground beneath his feet shaking. Being hunched over in the hood disoriented him. It was made worse when the blows rained down on him. Punches to the kidneys, a rifle butt to the back of the head, kicks to the shins. Someone landed an uppercut that caught Mann square on the nose, breaking it for the second time that night. They forced Mann to walk a gauntlet, and it seemed every guard on duty wanted to get in on the fun.

By the time he was jerked to a stop, Mann had no idea where he was. He'd wanted to memorise the path in so he might retrace it on his way out, but he lost track within moments of setting foot inside the building.

After one final punch to his ear, which stung like a bitch, the hood was pulled off his head and the shackles released. Mann was pushed forward into a tiny cell and crashed into the far wall. The door slammed shut, leaving him in complete darkness.

He waited for his eyes to adjust to the darkness, but after five minutes there was no difference. He put his back to the wall and walked heel, toe, counting the steps. It was eight feet long. He stretched his arms out and could just touch both walls.

On the one hand, he was glad to be alone. Conversely, if he had to spend the rest of his life in this tiny space, he was going to go mad very quickly. He didn't think this was his permanent new home, though. There was no bed, just the cold stone floor to lie on. No toilet, either. It had to be some kind of holding cell, or perhaps solitary confinement.

Mann felt his nose, and his fingers came away sticky. Even in the pitch darkness he could tell it was blood. He had to fix it or there was a chance he could develop a septal hematoma, which could lead to breathing problems later.

After one sharp crack and a stream of expletives, the bone was back in place. It still hurt like a bitch, but the pain would pass. It always did.

Mann was wide awake, but he knew he had to try and grab a couple of hours. The coming day was going to be tense, fraught with danger. He had to be on his guard and ready to tackle whatever they threw at him.

* * *

Mann's first full day in Penal Colony Thirteen began as the previous day ended. In darkness.

He was shaken out of a dream by the sound of keys in the lock, and the door opened to allow a burst of artificial light to assault his retinas. Mann squinted, trying to make out shapes, but all he could see were dark blobs.

'Get up!' a voice barked in Russian.

Mann put a hand down to push himself up before he remembered his instructions to himself: never respond to Russian. It was difficult when he knew the language so well, almost as hard as pretending not to understand English. He adjusted his position, but remained seated on the floor.

His ploy earned him a kick to the thigh, and Mann scrambled to his feet. His eyes were adjusting to the light, and he could make out two prison guards. One had grey hair cut in a flat top, so probably ex-military. The other was much younger, perhaps mid-thirties, with a long, hooked nose and a large mole on his right cheek. The men took an arm each and dragged Mann into the hallway. A third guard was waiting, and he thrust a pile of light grey clothes into Mann's arms, then topped them with a pair of old, military-issue boots and what looked like a wash bag.

'Move!'

Mann was pushed in the back, and he stumbled towards a steel door set at the end of the hallway. Mole Face opened it with a key, and the relative quiet was replaced by a cacophony of sound.

They were in a metal cage—similar to a chain-link fence, but much sturdier—the same dimensions as the hallway they'd just left. Every few yards there was a hole at head height, measuring five inches by twelve. The cage ran around the entire ground floor, and Mann could see another four levels above. The enclosure separated them from at least a thousand men, all wearing grey trousers and tops, the same clothes as Mann was carrying. They had congregated in a cavernous room that was about the length of a soccer pitch and twice as wide.

A small group was standing a few yards from Mann. One man in it was enormous, completely bald and carrying a lot of fat. He blew Mann a kiss, earning chuckles from his entourage. More prisoners noticed Mann and his escorts as they skirted the main hall, and soon the crowd was three deep at the cage, banging on the bars, shouting obscenities and death threats.

'You're very popular,' Flat Top said with a grin.

'Pretty boys always are,' Mole Face laughed. He looked at Mann. 'Better keep that ass clenched.'

'Nah, he won't last that long,' Flat Top said. He jerked his chin towards an area containing gym equipment. 'Gregor wants this one.'

From the corner of his eye Mann saw four men, one of who stood with his arms crossed across a huge, bare chest covered in tattoos. The man was a foot taller than anyone else, with a thick head of hair and bushy black beard. Unlike many of the men in the communal area, he wasn't carrying an ounce of fat. An imposing figure. He had his thumb pointed at his own chest in the international symbol.

Mine.

Mann had heard tales of British prison life. All prisons had an alpha male. He was the man who ran things, arranged for phones and drugs to be brought in. He was also the man you didn't fuck with. When a new prisoner entered the system, Alpha would send one of his posse to check them out. If the new guy caved under mere threats, he became one of Alpha's bitches. If he fought, then Alpha had a good idea how much of a danger they posed. Mann had been hoping that his first engagement would be with one of those peripheral figures, but it seemed the Russians did things differently.

He could add another item to his list of advantages, though. He now knew exactly who would be coming after him. Mann just hoped he had a couple of days to recover from his beating before battle commenced.

Mann was led up to the second floor and along a similarly caged gantry, past steel doors set every three yards. He looked down to take in the area below him. It had been laid out in three sections. The largest covered half the floor space and was filled with tables and chairs, and running along one side wall was what appeared to be a buffet service. Next came the gym, with weights and a row of static bikes. The other end of the room was clear, with a set of double doors in the corner. Mann saw someone come out drying his hair with a towel, so that was probably the shower.

There was something odd about the scene, and it took him a minute to work it out. There were no guards among the prisoners. There were plenty spread out over the first two floors, though. Each had a semi-automatic rifle and stood near one of the five-by-twelve holes in the grille. Mann suspected the large slits were designed for shooting through. He counted around twenty guards, but there were probably more stationed out of view above him.

What he could see when he looked up was just two more floors reaching up to the ceiling.

The guards stopped at a door halfway along the gantry and one of them held out an arm, indicating that Mann should enter.

The cell was better than expected. There were two bunks, a toilet with a rudimentary screen, a sink, and a table and chair. The top bunk was made, the bottom one just a bare mattress with bedding folded neatly on top. Pictures were stuck to the wall, a visual timeline of someone's daughter. They started with a photo of a baby in a crib, a poor-quality snap faded with time. The most recent picture appeared to have been taken at a graduation ceremony. There were eighteen in all, and Mann surmised it was one for each year of the girl's life. A battered transistor radio sat next to some kind of journal on the desk.

'Change. Now.'

Mann looked at Flat Top, his face displaying incomprehension. The guard grabbed Mann's orange coverall, shook it, then slapped the pile of clothes in his hand.

'Ah.' Mann swiftly changed clothes. The new uniform was a little large, but the trousers had an elastic waistband and clung to his hips. There were two sets of each. Thankfully, the boots were the right size.

Once Mann was dressed, Flat Top gestured for him to hold out his right arm, palm up. Mann did so, and Flat Top secured a band around his wrist, similar to the ones worn by patients in hospitals. Instead of a name, it simply had a bar code.

The elder guard gave instructions to Mole Face, who disappeared and shouted a name to the crowd below. A couple of minutes later a prisoner appeared outside the door, jumping to attention.

'Prisoner Kuzmin reporting as ordered, sir!'

Flat Top spoke to him, then turned and walked away, followed by the rest of the guards. Kuzmin entered the cell and stood before Mann.

He was in his sixties, with a balding pate surrounded by grey bristles. His face was thin, weaselly, and there was a gap between every tooth as he smiled.

'American?'

'English,' Mann corrected him.

The Russian thrust out a hand. 'Vladimir Ilyich Kuzmin, at your service.'

Mann took the hand and shook. 'Alex Mann.'

Kuzmin turned and climbed a metal ladder that was welded to the frame of the bunk. Once on top, he sat with his feet dangling over the edge. 'Mr Petrov told me to explain the rules to you as you don't speak Russian.'

'Not a word,' Mann lied.

'No problem. First rule is, whenever a guard speaks to you, you come to attention. If you don't, you get put down for selection. If you—'

'What's selection?' Mann interrupted.

'That's a punishment, but the guards never do it themselves. They've had too many go to prison for beatings and killings, so now they just get the other prisoners to carry out their dirty work. Gregor is given a list of those who have been selected, and he chooses one to go up against either himself or one of his gang. It's usually a death sentence.'

'Gregor being the one who looks like a bear.'

'That's right,' Kuzmin said. 'Gregor Belsky. Looks like a bear, fights like a bear.' He gestured for Mann to come closer and lowered his voice. 'Even smells like one.'

'What if no one is selected for punishment by the guards?'

'Someone is always selected,' Kuzmin said with finality. 'The guards bet on how long the selected prisoner will last. So do the other inmates. There's just too much money to be made not to have a fight at least twice a week.'

'So the fights are orchestrated?'

Kuzmin nodded. 'Anyway, enough of that. Each morning the doors are unlocked at five. You take your wash bag downstairs and log yourself through the gate using your wristband. You stay there until nine in the evening.'

'I was going to ask about the wristband.'

'You just hold it up against a scanner and it beeps to let you through a turnstile. That way the guards know when every prisoner is in the common area. Only then will they come out.'

'So the inmates and guards are never in the same room at the same time?' Mann asked.

'Never.'

That wasn't good news. One of the escape plans he'd considered was to take a guard or two hostage. That idea was out the window now.

'What if someone's ill, or they die in their cell? What happens then?'

'If someone fails to clock in by half past five, they send in a riot team to investigate. Four men, heavily armed, in case it's a trap. No one has been stupid enough to fake it, trust me. That's instant selection.'

'And once we're downstairs?' Mann asked.

Kuzmin shrugged. 'You just stay there. Breakfast is at six-thirty, lunch at twelve, dinner at five. There are toilets, showers, the gym.'

'What about unscheduled fights between prisoners?' It would be good to gauge the level of violence to expect on a daily basis.

'Never. That automatically gets you selected, too. You go right to the top of the pile. Same goes when you're locked up. Nothing ever happens in the cells unless the perpetrator wants to face Gregor, and none do.'

That was some comfort. Gregor seemed to have his eyes on Mann, but if he stayed out of trouble, then perhaps he could avoid a confrontation.

Selection sounded like a double-edged sword. On the one hand, it got you a date with a bear, but on the other, he felt confident he could walk freely among the population without getting a shiv in the kidneys or attacked in the shower.

He wanted to ask if anyone had ever escaped from the Widow Maker, but Kuzmin wasn't the right sounding board. Mann had only known him for a few minutes, and for all he knew, the Russian could be a snitch for the guards.

'Speaking of cellmates, who have I got?'

'Balakin. He's harmless enough.'

'What's he in for?' Balakin might seem harmless to Kuzmin, but if his crime was murdering someone in his sleep, it made the world of difference.

'He killed his wife in a drunken rage.' Kuzmin looked at the photographs on the wall. 'His daughter had just been born. His sister looks after her now. She sends him a picture every year.'

They chatted for another few minutes, with Mann learning that the laundry was done three days a week. He was to leave his dirty clothes in a pile outside the cell door and they would be collected on Mondays, Wednesdays. and Saturdays. Visits were once every three months and had to be booked weeks in advance, even for legal representation.

'Tell me about Gregor,' Mann said, thinking it would be wise to know about his foe.

Kuzmin's face darkened. 'He's bad news.'

'I guessed that much. What's his story?'

'Gregor was the right-hand man of a feared mafia boss. The police raided the boss's night club looking for him, but he managed to escape while Gregor held them off. He killed four cops before they took him down. Gregor arrived here five months ago, and on his first day he sought out the toughest prisoner and killed him. Since then, he's killed nearly forty men.'

'Does he use a weapon?' Mann asked.

'He doesn't need one. Sometimes he just beats them to death, but his favourite move is a bear hug. Apt, don't you think?'

'Very.'

'He grabs you from behind and squeezes…' Kuzmin demonstrated the move on an imaginary victim, making a face to show how much effort Gregor put into his manoeuvre.

'…until they can't breathe and they suffocate. I get it.'

Kuzmin relaxed. 'No. He keeps going until your ribs crack. Then he squeezes some more so that the broken bones penetrate your lungs, like daggers. Only then does he stop. He stands over you and watches your final, ragged breaths, like it's a joyous spectacle.'

Gregor sounded like a complete psychopath. 'These fights, when do they take place? Is there a set day each week?'

'No, it's just when Gregor feels in the mood. That's most days, if I'm honest. He killed a man just yesterday, but the next one could be today, tomorrow, it's anyone's guess.'

Mann hoped he had at least a week to recover from the battering he took in Moscow. Gregor had his eye on him, and it all depended on how long the bear could control his lust for death.

'I'm surprised the high death rate in here hasn't been investigated,' Mann said.

'Oh, they are, each and every killing. The trouble is, no one sees anything. Not the prisoners, not the guards. Why would they? If an inmate talked to the authorities, they'd be selected. If a guard does it, he'd suddenly find himself alone in the common area with the prisoners and no weapon. You can imagine how that would end.'

It was an easy scene to picture, but not a pleasant one.

A silence descended as Mann ran out of questions. In truth, his mind was too focused on his upcoming bout with Gregor to care about such mundane matters.

'Your English is excellent.' Mann could tell he was Russian speaking English, but he detected a hint of the home counties.

'Thank you. I studied in London and lived there for many years. In 2012 I came back to Moscow, just as Sokolov came to power. Biggest mistake I ever made.'

'What did you do to end up in here?'

Kuzmin grinned. 'I'm innocent, of course. Me and everyone else in this place. The charge, however, was being a member of a subversive organisation. What I actually did was run against Sokolov for the presidency. For that, I was sent here for ten years. What about you?'

'Spying for the British,' Mann told him. He could have lied, but word would reach the other inmates eventually. Might as well get it out in the open.

The smile disappeared. 'That won't make you very popular in here.'

'Kuzmin!'

Flat Top's voice immediately jolted Kuzmin to attention, even though the guard was nowhere in sight.

'We must go,' the elderly prisoner said. 'Bring your wash bag. Now.'

'What about a towel?' Mann asked.

'You get one in the shower room. Come, we have to go.'

Kuzmin raced through the door and stood rigid on the gantry. Mann followed and took his place next to him as Flat Top and Mole Face appeared.

'Get him downstairs, right now!'

Kuzmin tapped Mann on the hand and they walked briskly to the stairs. They jogged down two flights to the ground floor, then along the caged corridor to a turnstile. Kuzmin held his wristband over a scanner and a green light appeared. He pushed through and waited for Mann to do the same.

'That's the only way in and the only way out,' Kuzmin said. 'When you hear a loud buzzer, stop what you're doing and get over here as fast as you can. Any dawdling—'

'—and I go on selection.'

The inmates nearest the turnstiles had stopped what they were doing and were staring at Mann and Kuzmin. An eclectic bunch, to say the least. The identical clothing apart, some looked like ordinary people you'd pass in the street. Bankers, janitors, doctors, waiters. Others fit the stereotype of the hardened criminal: shaved heads, crude tattoos, bodies conditioned from hours spent in the prison gym.

None of them seemed keen on making a new friend.

Kuzmin led Mann through the crowd. Most parted to avoid any kind of confrontation that might see them on Gregor's *To Do* list, but a few stood their ground, forcing Mann to brush past them. Threats were growled, but Mann ignored them. No one was going to try anything, not when they would face selection, and ultimately, Gregor.

Kuzmin took Mann past the gym to the seating area. All the tables were identical, set to seat six people on benches screwed into the ground, like something from a pub garden.

These were made from steel, though, not wood. They found an empty one and Mann sat opposite his elderly guide.

Mann could feel eyes on him, but he kept his focus on the man in front of him. 'So what else should I know?'

'I think we covered everything,' Kuzmin answered. 'Wake up, come down here, obey orders, eat, go to bed. That pretty much sums up life in here.'

It wasn't much of an existence, and Mann wondered if he was destined to see out his life within the confines of these walls. If it was down to his government to facilitate his release, he knew he'd be waiting a long time. His boss, Will Horton, would undoubtedly be putting pressure on the PM to get him out, but that might not be enough.

There would be time to reflect on that when he got back to his cell, though. For now, his rumbling stomach signalled a new priority.

'What time is it?' Mann asked Kuzmin.

The old man pointed to a clock on the wall behind Mann's head. 'Almost time for breakfast.'

The huge crowd had started making their way towards the buffet bar, where a team of cooks were setting up for the morning service. A line had already formed, running the length of the shorter wall and around the corner. The longer wall was rapidly filling up, too.

'Come,' Kuzmin said. 'We don't want to be last.'

They tagged onto the end of the line. There were at least five hundred people ahead of them, with Gregor at the front of the queue. Mann expected them to be standing in line for at least an hour, but the Russian prisoners running the buffet had service down to a fine art. They dealt with an inmate every two seconds, ladling food onto metal trays and handing them out to the passing prisoners.

'When you get your food, just take it and move along. You won't be popular if you hold up the breakfast line.'

Like I'm ever gonna make friends in here, Mann thought.

Fifteen minutes later, Mann was handed a dollop of what looked like porridge along with a slice of black bread and a flimsy plastic spoon that would have proven completely useless as a weapon. He resisted the temptation to ask what he'd been given. Instead, he followed Kuzmin in search of a table. The prisoners who had been served first had already finished, so there were plenty of seats to choose from. They settled at an empty table, and Kuzmin dived into his food.

Mann sniffed his suspiciously. 'What is this? It smells like chicken.'

'It's kasha. Buckwheat cooked in chicken stock.'

Mann took a tentative spoonful and tried it. It was better than he'd expected. The black bread was actually dark brown, made with rye flour which made it dense. Mann had eaten plenty of it in his time.

They finished in minutes. Kuzmin rose to take his tray to the cleaning station, but he got halfway to his feet before he froze. His face registered fear.

Mann turned to see Gregor standing behind him. The Russian looked huge from afar, but he was much bigger close up. His biceps were the size of Mann's thighs, his chest almost a yard across.

Gregor walked slowly around the table and pushed Kuzmin slowly back down into his seat before sitting next to him.

'So this is the Englishman who would spy on my beloved Russia.'

Gregor's teeth were brown, his hair and beard thick, dark and unkempt. Not only did he carry the stench of a bear, he smelled like one had shit in his mouth.

Mann fought the instinct to answer him directly. Instead, he looked at Kuzmin, who offered a stuttered translation.

'Allegedly,' Mann answered. 'My trial was a sham and I'm waiting for the appeal.'

'Once you reach the Widow Maker, there are no more appeals, only Gregor.'

Mann waited for Kuzmin to finish speaking. 'So I have to face you, is that what you're saying? You're my judge?'

'And executioner.'

Mann waited for Kuzmin to translate, then smiled. 'Thanks for the offer, but I think I'll take my chances with my legal team.'

Kuzmin looked pleadingly at Mann, perhaps looking for a more favourable answer. Mann ignored him and held Gregor's gaze. With a resigned sigh, Kuzmin passed on the reply.

Gregor's face darkened, his eyebrows furrowed, eyebrows as thick as a man's finger.

'Lunch is at twelve,' the powerful Russian said. 'Enjoy it. It will be your last meal.'

Mann had expected this, but not so soon. Taking on Gregor was going to be a gargantuan task at the best of times, but in his current condition it would be over in seconds. Pleading for extra time to heal was going to be pointless, so Mann took a calculated risk. He looked at Kuzmin. 'Tell him I didn't figure him for a coward.'

'I'm not saying that,' Kuzmin said through clenched teeth.

Mann added a note of menace to his own voice. 'Tell him,' he said, his eyes still fixed on Gregor.

Gregor gave Kuzmin a gentle tap on the arm to hurry him up. It almost knocked the old man off the end of the bench.

Kuzmin mumbled in Russian, and Gregor looked like he was about to go nuclear. His jaw clenched, his hands formed into fists the size of melons.

'Only a coward would take on a man with just one good eye,' Mann continued, hoping to make his point before Gregor exploded into action. 'If he was a real man, he'd wait until I was healed and take me on in a fair fight.'

Kuzmin hastily translated.

'Or are you too scared?' Mann added.

When Kuzmin passed this on, Gregor leaped to his feet, leaned over the table and grabbed Mann by the front of his shirt, lifting him clear of his seat.

'I'm scared of no man,' Gregor growled, his breath making Mann's eye's water.

Mann had the sinking feeling that he'd miscalculated. For all his worries about spending the rest of his life in the Widow Maker, it might just end in the next few seconds.

'I'll give you one week,' Gregor spat as he thrust Mann back onto the bench, 'then I'm going to gouge out both your eyes and feed them to you.'

Gregor stood and faced the crowd that had gathered. 'No one touches him. He's mine.'

With that, the giant ambled over to the gym section, the throng parting to let him pass.

Kuzmin swallowed hard and caught his breath. 'You are either very brave, or very stupid.'

Mann wasn't sure which it was.

'At least you have seven days to prepare for your impending death,' Kuzmin said. 'Now would be a good time to make peace with your god.'

Alan McDermott

Chapter 17

Roland Cooper sat in the back of a van that had been adorned with a British Telecom livery, one of four such MI5 vehicles utilised for the exercise. Next to him was Aaron Duffield, and on a stool closest to the driver's seat was Michelle Lawson. She was in her early twenties, a year out of university where she'd earned a Masters' degree in behavioural science. Michelle was one of the stars of the training programme.

'Not too close, Tango Three,' Michelle said as she watched the livestream from a body cam.

There were four members of the ground team, three men and one woman. Each wore a discreet forward-facing camera. Audio was provided by microphones hidden inside shirt collars, which were activated by a pressel hidden in the cuff of a jacket or jumper.

The target for Tango team was Sarah Mulholland. She'd left her house, a three-bedroom semi in Twickenham, at a quarter to nine and driven her Mercedes saloon to a car park just off Oxford Street. From there she'd joined the Saturday shopping crowd. Sarah's current location was the lingerie section of Selfridges, with Tango Three—real name Dana Carpenter—keeping tabs on her.

Duffield took out his phone and hit a pre-set number. 'All clear. You should have an hour.'

The electronic surveillance team was standing by, parked up a couple of streets from Sarah's house. Dressed as British Gas engineers, they would enter the house and set up the cameras that would catch every moment of Sarah's life for the next few weeks. If challenged by a neighbour, they would say their remote sensing equipment had detected a gas leak at the property.

'Not the red,' Michelle mumbled. 'Too slutty.'

Cooper looked at the monitor and saw that Sarah was admiring a crimson bra and panty set.

'What colour would you recommend?' he asked.

'With her skin? Definitely white. Neutral, unassuming.'

'Not black?'

Michelle shook her head. 'It suggests power, but that doesn't fit with the rest of her wardrobe. Jeans, T-shirt, trainers. She's dressed for comfort, nothing else.'

Cooper was surprised that she could tell so much from what a person was wearing. It certainly wasn't part of his own training all those years ago.

'What about me?' he asked. 'What can you tell from what I've got on?'

All it took was a glance, then Michelle returned her gaze to the monitor. 'You're missing something,' she said. 'A part of your life that you can't get back. The jacket is a connection to the past, a time you still yearn for.'

Cooper was stunned. She couldn't have been more accurate. He did yearn for the past, to be out in the field instead of providing logistical support from a pokey office.

He missed the tension before a meet, the surge of adrenaline every time he walked into the enemy's lair, the lifestyles that his legends afforded him.

But that ship had sailed. His accident, a year after buying the jacket, had put paid to his plans. He'd argued that one day he'd heal and would be able to return to active duty, but the chief had kyboshed the idea. They needed an agent in the field immediately, not in a year or eighteen months. Cooper's slot had been assigned to someone else, and he'd been put in the support team while he recuperated. In the last year, despite numerous requests for a new posting, he'd been passed over time and again. It wasn't as if he was over the hill. At thirty-five, he still had many good years to offer.

Cooper had pressed Will Horton for a valid reason for not offering him a place in the field, and eventually the chief had relented. It was the ugly scar on his face. It wasn't a look that the rich clients of John Morgan would be comfortable with.

Cooper knew exactly what he meant; he wouldn't be able to seduce the clients' wives as he had in the past.

Horton floated the idea of Cooper joining the training department. He had a wealth of experience to pass along, and he'd be making a real difference. Logistical support was an integral part of any mission, but as the chief pointed out, it wasn't exactly rocket surgery. Anyone with a decent high school education could fill the role quite easily.

Cooper had passed. *Those who can, do,* he'd said. *Those who can't, teach.*

In truth, Cooper was still undecided on his future. He didn't see himself staying in support for the rest of his life, but he couldn't nail down a new path. He was leaning towards joining the police, not as a beat officer, but undercover work with the National Crime Agency. If he had the look of a criminal, he might as well exploit it.

'Actually, the jacket was a gift,' Cooper lied, uncomfortable that this young woman could read him so easily. 'I haven't replaced it because it's comfortable. Have you any idea how long it takes to break in a new leather jacket?'

'You could always drag yourself out of the eighties and switch to another fabric,' she grinned.

Cooper smiled back, but there was no way he was ditching the coat.

Sarah Mulholland paid for the red underwear, then walked out of the shop, down the road and into a coffee house.

'Tango Three, drop back,' Michelle said over comms. 'Tango One, you're up.'

'We regularly switch the tails so that the mark doesn't see the same person more than once,' Duffield explained. 'Tango Three will be changing her appearance now. She'll turn her jacket inside out or put it in her shopping bag, lose the glasses and put her hair in a bun. If we have to send her in again, Sarah won't recognise her.'

Cooper already knew this, along with the other tricks of the trade. Overseas operatives were prime candidates to pick up a tail, and as such he had been taught surveillance and counter-surveillance techniques. He didn't let on, though. As far as Duffield was concerned, Cooper was just a Whitehall bod.

They watched Sarah order a drink and sit at a table. She took out her phone and began to scroll. For thirty minutes she barely glanced away from the screen, then suddenly put it in her bag, downed the last of her coffee and walked out of the shop.

So far she'd made no contact with anyone, and it looked like she was heading back to the car park.

Duffield called the team at her house to warn them that she might be on her way home soon.

'All done,' he was told. 'We'll be gone in a couple of minutes.'

Cooper hoped to get something from her home life, because the shopping trip was a bust.

He waited until she got in her car and started driving towards her house, then called it a day. If she did or said anything of interest, Duffield was under strict instructions to call him. Until then, all he could do was head back to the office and check the electronic reports on the other six suspects.

First, though, he wanted to stop off at Vauxhall Cross to check up on Alex. Mann's appeal was due to be heard that morning. The chances of him being acquitted were infinitesimally small, but Cooper wouldn't give up hope.

When he arrived at Sharon Williams' office, he was surprised to see Will Horton talking to her.

'Roland,' the chief said. 'Just the man. Have a seat.'

Horton didn't seem that enthused to see him. It could only mean bad news.

'There's no way to sugar coat this, so I won't even try. Alex was transferred to Penal Colony Thirteen late last night.'

Sharon's hand went to her mouth to stifle a cry.

'What?!' Cooper exclaimed. 'I thought he had an appeal this morning.'

'Cancelled, according to Dominic Sloane. He turned up for the case and was given the bad news.'

Cooper was stunned. It was bad enough when the threat of the Widow Maker was hanging over Alex, but for it to manifest into reality…

'There must be something we can do,' Cooper said, though he struggled to think of what that might be. Storm the prison, perhaps?

'What did the PM say?' Sharon asked.

'I haven't spoken to him yet,' Horton replied. 'He's been made aware of the new development, but I haven't been summoned to discuss it.'

'But what do you think he'll do?' she pressed.

Horton looked uncomfortable. 'Not much. Little of any value, at least. There'll be strong condemnation, obviously, but beyond that…'

'No rescue mission?' Cooper ventured.

'Definitely not. Out of the question.'

'Then the idea I floated a few days ago. Kidnap a close friend of Sokolov and offer a trade. Back then, timing was an issue. We couldn't have pulled it off before Alex was transferred. Now, the situation's changed.'

'Timing is still the issue,' Horton said. 'You know the Widow Maker's reputation. Alex will do well to last a week.' He sighed. 'I'll raise it as an option when I speak to the PM, but don't get your hopes up. If we start down that road, things could escalate quickly. I'm not sure Ward is prepared to take that risk.'

'Then what about the newspapers?' Cooper asked. 'Tip them off that Alex is being held. Public pressure will force the PM to do something.'

'It will force whoever leaks that information to lose their job, that's all it'll do,' Horton countered. 'You know that.'

Cooper knew only too well, but he'd been thinking about it a lot recently. Ever since he'd planted the idea in Debra's head, to be exact.

A thought struck him. Why wasn't it all over the papers already? Had Debra misunderstood, thinking *he* was going to leak the news?

It didn't matter now. Cooper had discovered a way to get it out in the open without incriminating himself.

'Maybe the PM could request that he be transferred somewhere else, somewhere less dangerous, while they discuss a diplomatic solution?' Sharon suggested.

'I'm sure that's already on the agenda,' Horton said. He looked at his watch. 'I have to go. Briefing with FoSec. I'll keep you updated.'

The chief left, and Cooper slumped into the chair at his desk.

'Poor Alex,' Sharon said.

Cooper thought she looked genuinely upset, another reason for believing that she wasn't the person who'd put Mann in his current predicament.

One thing was for certain: whoever had done it was going to pay dearly.

Chapter 18

'Check.'

Vladimir Kuzmin eyed the board, his face a mask of concentration. Eventually he moved a bishop to block Mann's move. Mann countered by taking the queen.

'Checkmate.'

Kuzmin shook his head in disbelief. It was the third game in a row that Mann had won.

'I thought I was the best chess player in this place,' the Russian sighed.

'In three days, you may well be.'

Four days had passed since Gregor had given Mann his deadline—dead being the operative word. The fight would take place sometime on Saturday, and the whole place was abuzz with anticipation. Bets were being taken, though not on the winner. No one was foolish enough to bet against Gregor. Instead, they were staking their cigarette rations on how long Mann would last. It was even money that the contest would be over within two minutes.

'It's a shame,' Kuzmin said as he reset the board for a new game. 'I like having you around.'

'I like being around,' Mann said. 'Not here, obviously, but I kinda got attached to living.'

Kuzmin looked at Gregor, who appeared to be bench-pressing the equivalent of a small car, then back at Mann. 'It's hard to see you winning, if I'm honest.'

Mann helped put the chess pieces back in their original places. 'Thanks for the vote of confidence.'

'I mean no disrespect, but you are clearly outmatched.'

Mann was glad to hear it. It meant everyone else would probably be thinking the same thing: he had no chance against the bear. He wasn't going to correct them. As long as Gregor thought it was a foregone conclusion, Mann would hold an advantage. That was why he averted his eyes whenever Gregor looked at him, bowing his head and walking away whenever possible.

Not that it was going to be a walk in the park. Gregor would be a formidable opponent, but he wasn't invincible. For one, Mann would have the speed advantage. Gregor's muscles made him powerful, but slow. If Mann could avoid falling to Gregor's signature move, he stood a chance of winning. At least he was healing better than expected. He could see clearly out of his bruised eye, and the ache in his ribs was no more. Three more days and he'd be back to his best.

A shrill bell rang three times, a signal for the entire hall to fall silent. Chatter immediately ceased, the men in the gym area frozen in mid-move.

'Belsky!'

Gregor looked up to the first floor at the guard who had called his name.

'Visitor.'

Gregor walked to the turnstile and swiped his wristband. He pushed through and walked to a door that opened as he approached.

'I thought you said visitors were only allowed once every three months,' Mann said to Kuzmin. 'Gregor had one a couple of days ago.'

The Russian leaned in. 'I told you, he's mafia. If they request a visit, you don't say no. Not unless you want to go home and find your family in pieces on the floor.' He turned the board around so that Mann had white. 'Your move.'

They were half a dozen moves into the game when Gregor reappeared. He looked smug, like he'd won the lottery.

'What's he so happy about?' Mann asked Kuzmin. 'Did he manage to engineer a conjugal visit?'

'Not even Gregor could arrange that. Someone gave him good news, though. Perhaps his legal team came up with something.'

Gregor suddenly stopped walking and looked around. His eyes settled on Mann.

'Here comes trouble,' Kuzmin said, as Gregor approached the table.

The giant's smile morphed into a malicious grin as he stood over Mann. 'Change of plan. We go in an hour.'

Mann wasn't expecting that. It didn't bother him, now that he could see properly, but he didn't want to appear confident. He looked at Kuzmin for a translation. When it came, Mann tried to appear shocked. 'Why?' he squeaked. 'You said I could have a week to recover.'

Gregor didn't wait for Kuzmin. 'No week,' he said in heavily accented English. 'Today.'

He walked away before Mann could protest further.

Kuzmin started putting the chess pieces back in a tattered box. 'Any last words?' he asked Mann. 'A message for your wife, perhaps?'

Mann looked around. 'Who takes the bets?' he asked.

'For the fight? A number of people. Max over there, the one with the black hair. Also Alexis, with the dagger tattoo on his arm.'

'And what are the odds of me winning?'

Kuzmin laughed, but abruptly stopped when he saw that Mann wasn't sharing the joke. 'You're serious? You think you can beat him?'

'Stranger things have happened. Besides, what else am I going to do with my tobacco ration?'

He'd learned that every Friday, the prisoners received a small pouch of rolling tobacco. It was a precious commodity, highly valued among the inmates, who used it as currency to buy things like proper toothpaste rather than the grainy prison-issue version. Most of the prisoners smoked, but not Mann.

'You could bequeath it to me,' Kuzmin said.

'Oh, ye of little faith. Just bet three pouches that I beat Gregor.'

Kuzmin shook his head in disbelief, then got to his feet.

Mann grabbed his shirt and pulled him back down. 'Not yet. Wait until the fight is just about to start. If Gregor gets wind that I think I can win, he'll be on his guard. I want him to think it's going to be a walkover.'

Kuzmin leaned in. 'And how exactly do you plan on beating him?'

'Let's just say I have something up my sleeve.'

Chapter 19

Cooper pored over the reports from the surveillance team, hoping to find some small detail that might point to the person who had sold Alex Mann to the Russians. So far, there'd been nothing. No brushes, no phone calls, emails, not a single thing to indicate that any of the seven suspects were involved.

Frustrated, he threw the latest report onto his desk and checked his watch. It was just after eight in the morning, and he had a busy day ahead. The polygraph had been set up the night before in an interrogation cell in the basement, and each suspect had been invited along to take part. Cooper planned to be there for the first of them, which was Sarah Mulholland.

Before that, though, he wanted to speak to Aaron Duffield.

He found the head of the surveillance team in his office. Duffield was taking off his jacket.

'Just got in?' Cooper asked.

'Yeah. I rode along with the Whisky team this morning. They're watching Mark Ballam. Nothing to report. He left his house and drove to Whitehall. He'll probably be there for the rest of the day. We're paying people to sit in a van for the next nine hours when they could be working active cases.'

Duffield's annoyance at having his people work a pointless training exercise was obvious. Cooper hoped he could smooth things over. To do that, he would have to go off reservation and let him in on the secret. It didn't matter now. Within the next few hours, the media would know all about Alex Mann's arrest in Moscow, and Duffield would put two and two together.

Cooper also needed Duffield to do something outside the scope of the exercise, and he could only request that by opening up.

'I'm gonna tell you something, but it goes no further, you got me?'

Duffield sat and showed a look of curiosity. 'I'm listening.'

Cooper paused just long enough to picture his career and pension disappearing. 'We lost an agent last week. His name is Alex Mann. The Russians picked him up and gave him a show trial, then sentenced him to life in prison. He was using a legend, but the FSB knew his real name. Someone here gave him up.'

'So the exercise story is bullshit,' Duffield said. 'You've got me looking for a real mole.'

'That's right. I wish I could have told you sooner, but it came from the very top.'

'So why are you telling me now?'

'Because I need something that would have raised alarm bells if I stuck to the script.'

Duffield folded his arms. 'What do you need?'

'Surveillance on the Russian Embassy. We've had no hits so far, and I was thinking that maybe the mole didn't do the work themselves, but got a friend, a cut out, to pass info to the Russians. If we can post someone near their embassy to record everyone going in and out, we might be able to tie one of the visitors to one of our suspects. There's also the chance that once we do the polygraphs, the mole will get nervous and maybe go to the embassy looking for safe haven.'

Duffield considered the suggestion, then pointed to the chair on the opposite side of the desk. 'Bring that around,' he said as he moved his own seat sideways.

Cooper moved the chair so that he could see Duffield's computer screen.

Duffield's fingers danced across the keyboard. 'We've already got a team in place. They've been stationed across from the embassy for the last three years, recording everyone who goes in or out. I've given you access to the surveillance records. It'll appear as a new tab on the software you're already using.'

Duffield opened the record for the previous day. It showed a list of names and the times they entered and left the premises. A tab to the right of the screen said *Unknowns (7)*.

'What are those?' Cooper asked, pointing at the link.

'Most visitors to the embassy are known to us. If they're non-residents, we use facial recognition to match them to passport data collected on entry. We also match passports and driving licences for British citizens. The unknowns are people who haven't got either and who we haven't yet identified. We have pictures, though, and each week we try to match them in case someone makes their way into the

141

system. Sometimes it's impossible, though. They might be wearing large sunglasses, or they've grown a beard. You'd be surprised how easy it is to fool FR.'

'Or a deliberate disguise?'

Duffield nodded. 'Could be.'

'How far back does it go?'

'Three years,' Duffield said, 'give or take.'

'And can it be filtered by gender, date, things like that?'

'Sure.' Duffield ran a quick search for males within the last three months. 'There you go. Over a thousand hits. You can filter it further, but I'll let you play around with that.'

Cooper thanked him and stood. 'Remember, not a word to anyone.' As he left the office, he looked at his watch. It was almost time for Sarah Mulholland's polygraph.

He took the lift down to the basement. A technician was making last-minute adjustments to the equipment when Cooper arrived.

'All set, Grace?'

The middle-aged woman looked up. 'Couple of minutes, I'll be done. Just wanted to check the calibration.'

Cooper went to fetch a coffee, and by the time he returned the technician was sitting to the side of the machine, looking at her phone.

It was ten minutes before Sarah Mulholland was escorted to the room, and she didn't look pleased. FoSec had promised to smooth the way by explaining the reason for the test—to eliminate his staff from the enquiry—but it didn't seem to have worked. Either she was pissed at being considered a suspect, or she had something to hide.

Cooper hoped it was the latter.

'Thanks for coming,' he said, holding out his hand.

Sarah ignored it. 'This is most inconvenient. I've had to postpone three meetings this morning for this…this nonsense.'

She was five-eleven, according to her file, but with the heels she matched Cooper's six-one. Her black hair was tied in a ponytail. Cooper saw that she was staring at his facial scar, as many people did, and he rubbed it subconsciously.

'Can we do this?' Sarah asked. 'I really need to get going.'

'Sure.' Cooper indicated the door, and Sarah entered the room. She took a seat in the only empty chair.

'Please remove your shoes and socks.'

Sarah harrumphed as she did his bidding. 'Is this really necessary?'

'I'm afraid so,' Cooper told her.

When he'd done his own training, he'd learned that one way to beat the lie detector was to place a sharp object like a tack inside a shoe. Pressing down on it while answering the control questions gave a false reading, so it was difficult to tell when the subject was telling the truth.

Once her feet were bare and it was clear she wasn't trying to manipulate the machine, Cooper nodded to Grace, who placed sensors on Sarah's body.

'I'll leave you to it,' Cooper said. He left the room and stood on the other side of the two-way mirror.

Grace looked at the machine, made a small adjustment to a dial, then began asking questions from a sheet Cooper had given her. The control questions had already been inserted, and in the spaces in between Cooper had entered the ones he wanted Grace to ask.

'Are you ready?' Grace asked.

'Just get on with it.'

Grace bristled, but kept her cool. 'Is your name Sarah Elizabeth Mulholland?'

'Yes.'

'Do you work as an aide for Foreign Secretary Geoffrey Taggart?'

'You know I do.'

'Have you ever passed secret information to the Russians?'

'Of course not!'

Cooper noted that she seemed defensive, a sure sign that she was lying.

'Do you drive a green Volvo?' Grace asked.

'No, I have a white Mercedes.'

'Why did you betray Alex Mann?'

'I didn't betray anyone,' Sarah insisted.

'Do you live in Twickenham?'

'Yes.'

'How long have you lived there?'

'Most of my life,' Sarah said. 'It was my parents' house. I inherited it.'

'What is the name of your contact in the FSB?'

'I don't *have* a contact in the FSB.'

Grace continued to fire questions at Sarah, some control questions, others designed to elicit a passionate response. The session lasted fifteen minutes, and once Grace indicated that the test was complete, Sarah reached for her socks.

'Well? Am I guilty?'

Grace started removing the sensors from Sarah's body. 'It's not my place to say. I just perform the test. The results will be analysed and someone will be in touch.'

Sarah mumbled under her breath, then wedged her shoes on and walked out the door. Her escort took her back upstairs.

'What do you think?' Cooper asked as he walked in on Grace, who was preparing the machine for the next subject.

'I'd say she's a prize bitch, but she was telling the truth.'

Cooper ran his fingers through his hair in frustration. He so wanted his hunch to be correct. It wasn't over, though. Perhaps Sarah had been taught how to defeat a lie detector, but there were other ways to trip her up.

'If you get anything from the others, please let me know.'

Cooper took the lift back up to his floor and walked to his cramped office. He unlocked his computer, then opened the surveillance software. As promised, there was a new tab for the permanent embassy placement.

Let's see what we've got.

He opened a search window and typed in the name Sarah Mulholland. When he hit Enter, it immediately came back with the result.

No Match Found.

He tried the same for the other six people on the list, but in each case there were no matches.

Of course there are no matches; they're unlikely to brazenly walk into the Russian Embassy.

Cooper thought back to his conversation with Duffield, and he filtered the results to show unknowns only. It was a stretch to think the mole had actually gone to the embassy, but if they did, they were probably wearing a disguise of some sort.

He set the date range to the last six weeks, then paused. The reports from Sloane said the FSB knew about the microfilm capsule Mann had swallowed, so they must have been watching him for some time. He removed the date parameters and ran the search.

1,217 Matches.

Cooper took his jacket off and hung it on the back of his chair, knowing he was going to be there for a while.

Chapter 20

The entire hall was jumping.

Mann stood in the middle of a human circle fifty people deep, with more standing on the nearby tables. All of them baying for blood.

His blood.

There were men shouting the odds, encouraging their fellow inmates to wager their precious tobacco rations. Guards stood on the upper floors, equally eager to see Mann become Gregor's latest victim.

A huge roar erupted as Gregor made his way to the arena, the crowd parting to allow his enormous frame free passage.

Mann looked over at Kuzmin and nodded. The little Russian shook his head in dismay and scrambled away in search of a bookie who would take the foolish bet.

Gregor turned to face the crowd, arms aloft, whipping them into a frenzy.

Mann simply stood, waiting for the fight to begin. He'd limbered up fifteen minutes earlier, stretching his muscles and tendons in preparation for the confrontation.

Gregor turned and faced Mann, adopting a body builder pose that showed off rippling muscles on every part of his upper body. Gregor's biceps were enormous, unnaturally so. His forearms, too, were freakishly large. It was little wonder Gregor's bear hug was so powerful.

And potentially fatal, Mann reminded himself.

Not that he was overly concerned. He'd fought bigger men in training, and it was technique that won the day, not strength. If he could carry out the moves—and he'd gone over them in his head time and again—he was confident he could emerge the victor.

'You die now,' Gregor growled as he stomped towards the centre of the makeshift ring.

Mann feigned fear as the big man approached, acting as if frozen with fear, but the moment Gregor pulled his right arm back to unleash a piledriver, Mann leaped to his right and drove his fist into Gregor's rib cage. Gregor's punch missed by a mile, and the ferocity of the swing and failure to connect almost spun him off his feet. He regained his balance and turned to face Mann once more, his confidence now replaced with anger.

It was just what Mann wanted to see. An angry opponent was too blinded by rage to think about technique, something Mann would use to his advantage.

He let Gregor come again. This time the giant reached out to grab Mann's head in his meaty claws, but Mann ducked and spun to the side, delivering an elbow to the other side of Gregor's rib cage. The front of Gregor's body was protected by a mound of muscle, but there wasn't much covering the ribs, and the big man felt it. He howled, but Mann didn't know whether it was in anger or pain.

The vociferous crowd was in full flow, shouting words of encouragement to Gregor. Most of them wanted the fight over so that they could collect their winnings. Cries of *finish him* and *kill the Englishman* reached Mann's ears, but he had no intention of dying.

While Gregor was deciding on his next move, Mann made one of his own. He feigned a low kick at Gregor's waist, but when the big man put an arm down to block it, Mann adjusted his stance and his foot connected with Gregor's head.

The noise of the crowd was starting to dim as they sensed that Gregor wasn't going to have it all his own way. This wasn't proving to be the easy kill many had anticipated, and most had wagered a large amount on the outcome.

Gregor shook his head to clear it, but before he could set himself for another charge, Mann leaped forward and landed a telling blow on Gregor's nose.

What happened next was not what Mann expected. Instead of reeling from the punch, Gregor didn't even blink. He grabbed Mann in mid-jump and pulled him in to his chest.

Mann had been caught in bear hugs before, but none as powerful as this one. The crowd whooped and cheered as Gregor got the upper hand, and a chant of *Kill! Kill! Kill!* rang out. Mann barely heard it as blood rushed to his ears and his face turned crimson in seconds. Panic threatened to overcome him, but Mann forced it aside and ordered himself to think.

Gregor had grabbed him just above the elbows, which meant Mann could still use his lower arms. He formed fists with his bent thumbs sticking out the sides, and jabbed Gregor in the ribs. It seemed to have no effect. Gregor's hot, fetid breath filled Mann's nostrils, making him want to retch, but air wasn't going in or out. He tried striking the ribs again, but Gregor simply grinned as he squeezed tighter.

Mann was losing it, but a lesson from his training jumped into his head. *If you find the moves haven't worked, resort to carnage. Bite, gouge, tear, break, anything to regain the upper hand.*

Mann reached for the fountain pen that was tucked into his sock. He tried bringing his legs up to his backside so that he could grab it, but with Gregor's arms wrapped so tightly around him, Mann didn't have the strength. As his vision blurred, he exercised his only remaining option. He forced his head forward and sank his teeth into Gregor's chin, clamping down with all his strength before yanking his head to the side.

Gregor howled in pain and released his grip, his hands going to his bloody jaw as an *Ooooh* erupted from the crowd.

Mann collapsed to the floor and spat out a lump of hairy gristle before sucking in lungfuls of air. His chest heaved as he gathered his breath, but the respite was short-lived. Gregor grabbed Mann by the hair and jerked him to his feet before encircling his arms around him once more, lifting Mann clear of the ground. This time, he was facing away from the Russian, so he couldn't repeat his move.

'Gregor! Gregor! Gregor!'

Mann knew he had seconds to extricate himself before he would start to black out. He got his hand around one of Gregor's enormous fingers and pulled it backwards. It took all of his strength, but he felt the grip on his chest weaken. He kept bending, bending, until the finger inevitably snapped. Gregor let go, but Mann didn't. He kept hold of Gregor's outstretched arm, got his shoulder underneath the bear's elbow, and pulled the hand sharply downwards. The sound of Gregor's arm breaking could be heard over the roar of the other inmates. Mann swivelled and lashed out at Gregor's groin with his foot, the toe of his boot making a sweet connection. As Gregor sank to his knees, Mann brought his knee up into Gregor's face, crushing the giant's nose into a bloody pulp. Gregor collapsed onto his back, and Mann went in for the kill. He could let Gregor live, but he'd always be looking over his shoulder if he did so. Better to remove the threat while he had the chance. He wrapped his legs around Gregor's throat and began to squeeze, all the time keeping out of reach of the Russian's good arm.

'Wait!' Gregor wheezed in Russian. 'Wait!'

'Not a chance.' Mann tightened his grip, cutting off Gregor's airway.

Gregor slapped the cold stone floor with a mighty palm. 'I…give you…out,' he managed in English.

'Give me out? What the hell's that supposed to mean?' Then it occurred to him. Mann leaned in and whispered in Russian. 'You mean get me out of here?'

Gregor squeezed his eyes shut as he fought to remain conscious. He managed to move his head up and down a fraction of an inch.

'You better not be bullshitting me.'

'It's…the truth.'

Mann trusted few people, and Gregor was right at the bottom of the list. 'Sorry, but I don't believe you.' He clamped his thighs together with all his might.

'Tonight,' Gregor gurgled as his face flushed red.

Mann eased off a little. 'How?' he asked quietly.

'My friends…come for me…tonight.'

It suddenly made sense. Why else would Gregor bring the fight forward? He wanted one last kill before he was rescued by his mafia boss.

'How do I know I can trust you?' Mann asked.

'You have…my word. If you spare…my life…I owe you…'

Mann had nothing to lose. If he killed Gregor and the rescue attempt was real, Gregor's friends would want retribution. If it was all a lie, then he and Gregor would have another coming together.

Mann released Gregor and kicked him away. The crowd howled in disappointment as Mann got to his feet. He held out a hand and helped Gregor from the floor.

'You better keep your word,' Mann said in his ear. 'I'm in cell 382. What time is it going to happen?'

'Two o'clock,' Gregor heaved. 'When your door opens, run down here. We all leave together.'

'How many?' Mann asked.

An inmate came over to see if Gregor was okay, but the big man pushed him away. 'As many as we can. The more we get out, the thinner the police will be spread.'

Mann looked at the huge arm hanging limp at Gregor's side. 'You better get that fixed.'

Gregor glanced down, nodded to Mann, then walked to the turnstile where a couple of guards were waiting.

'How did you do that?'

Mann turned to see Kuzmin standing next to him. 'Just luck, I guess.'

'Rubbish. You knew you could beat him.'

Mann smiled. 'How much did we make?'

Kuzmin didn't look happy. 'He won't pay. Said it was a draw.'

'Did he now? Then let's go and have a word.'

Several prisoners clapped Mann on the back as he passed, hailing the new Alpha, but he ignored their praise and made for the bookie who had taken Kuzmin's bet. He was bald, with tattoos down one side of his face.

'Why didn't you pay him?' Mann asked the bookie in Russian.

The prisoner seemed surprised to hear his mother tongue from the foreigner, but he soon regained his stern look. 'You didn't win. Gregor is still alive.'

'I beat him,' Mann said calmly. 'Sometimes I let them live, sometimes I don't. Depends on the mood I'm in.'

'Doesn't matter. The bet was for you to kill him.'

Mann turned to Kuzmin. 'Go tell the guards I want this one on selection. I'll take him tomorrow.' To the bookie he said, 'Let's see how I feel after a night in the cell.'

Kuzmin made to leave, but the bookie stopped him. 'No need for that,' he said, suddenly all warmth and charm. 'I'm sure we can sort this out.'

'We can indeed,' Mann smiled. 'You pay him, or we go. The choice is yours.'

While the bookie tried to decide, Mann asked Kuzmin how many ounces he was due.

'Thirty.'

'I haven't got that many,' the bookie spluttered.

'Then I suggest you find it, and quickly.'

'I only have twenty, I swear.'

'Give that to my friend here and go and find the rest. Beg, borrow, steal, I don't care. You have two hours. If he hasn't been paid in full by dinner time, I won't be happy.'

The bookie reluctantly handed over his stash of tobacco to a gleeful Kuzmin, then skulked away with his chin on his chest.

Kuzmin cradled his winnings against his chest like it was a newborn child. 'So you speak Russian.'

'A little,' Mann said.

'Nonsense. You speak it like a Muscovite. Why the pretence?'

'I planned to use it to my advantage in here, but it doesn't matter any more.'

'Why not?' Kuzmin asked.

Mann considered telling him about the escape plan, but decided to leave it until later. Much later.

Chapter 21

Gregor's arm ached, but he'd refused any pain relief from the prison doctor. For one, he wanted a clear head for the remainder of the night. The discomfort also served as a reminder of his defeat to the English spy.

His embarrassing defeat.

His humiliation.

He'd been tempted to get a few of his followers to ambush the Englishman in the shower and show him what prison justice felt like, but that would have brought him no satisfaction.

He wanted to kill Mann himself.

With his bare hands.

Slowly.

To do that, he would have to follow through on his promise and help the man escape. The spy had proven himself to be a formidable opponent, and Gregor knew there was little chance of beating him in his current condition.

He would have to be patient. Once on the outside, he would seek proper medical attention for his injuries, then give himself time to heal. Six weeks should be enough.

Perhaps eight. In that time, he would keep Mann locked in a cellar, chained to a wall or radiator. He would feed him scraps. And when the time came, he would rip Mann apart. His bear hug move would be too quick. Instead, he would make Mann's death last days, not minutes. He didn't yet know how he'd do it, but he would have plenty of time to think about how to exact his revenge.

* * *

Alex Mann didn't bother trying to sleep. He knew he wouldn't be able to, and he wanted to be wide awake when Gregor's mafia friends struck.

After returning from the infirmary sporting a cast on his arm, a swollen nose, and a bandage over the wound to his jaw, Gregor had taken Mann to one side and explained the plan.

'You'll know when the attack starts. When you hear the signal, be ready to leave your cell. The doors will open automatically and when they do, you run down here and wait by the door to the shower room. Everyone else will be guided to the main entrance.'

'Then what?' Mann asked.

'Then we wait for the explosion,' Gregor grinned, revealing two missing teeth. 'They will breach the outer wall first, then blow a hole in this wall directly below that window.'

Mann looked to where the Russian was indicating. High on the wall, thirty feet off the ground, was a barred window. It was covered in grime and exuded the faintest hint of natural light.

'As soon as you hear the explosion, follow me. Transport will be waiting for us. While the police and army concentrate on rounding up those on foot, we'll be on our way to St Petersburg.'

Mann didn't like the idea of getting in a vehicle with Gregor and his mafia friends. He'd humiliated Gregor in front of the other inmates and broken his arm, so there was a good chance the Russian had planned revenge. The alternative, though, was to make his way from the prison on foot, and the area would be swarming with police and troops within minutes. He'd either be recaptured, or worse, shot.

Mann lost track of time. Prisoners weren't allowed to wear watches, and there was no need for clocks in the cells. He began to feel sleepy, so he stood and strode back and forth in his bare feet, not wanting to wake his bunk mate.

Pyotr Balakin was aptly named. His surname meant someone who was very talkative, and Balakin never stopped chattering. If babbling on about anything and everything was an Olympic discipline, Balakin was a shoo-in for gold every time. The last thing Mann wanted was a late-night conversation.

Mann stopped in mid-stride when he heard a bang, but it sounded like it was just a guard entering or leaving the secure area. Once he was sure it was nothing more, Mann continued pacing.

A few moments later another sound reached his ears, but this wasn't the normal nocturnal clunks and slamming doors.

It was automatic rifle fire, a mixture of chattering AK-47s and some other variety that sounded to Mann like a chain gun from the movie Predator, a long, harsh *BRRRRR!*

Seconds later, a klaxon burst into life, the noise reverberating around the tiny cell. Mann clasped his hands to his ears to soften the impact, but his head still vibrated. Remembering Gregor's words, Mann leaned against the door, but it didn't swing open as expected. He banged it with his shoulder, but still it remained stubbornly locked.

The bastard lied to me!

Mann tried again and again, but there was no way he was leaving the cell.

He began cursing Gregor when the klaxon stopped as suddenly as it had started. A series of explosions rang out before the firing started again, much closer now. Mann noticed that it wasn't answered by the guards' AKs this time.

The gunfire petered out, and silence descended. The only sound Mann heard was the lock click. He pushed again, and the metal door swung open. A few inmates were already out and running, and by the faint glow of emergency lighting, Mann caught sight of Gregor's giant frame on the floor above. He was racing along the gantry towards the stairs.

Mann ran in the same direction. When he reached the stairs, he saw that Gregor was already on the level below. Mann followed him down and through the turnstiles, which had been deactivated. It appeared that the rescue party had cut power to the entire facility.

'How long before they blow it?' Mann asked breathlessly as he looked up at the prisoners fleeing their cells. He was hoping to see Kuzmin, but there was no sign of the old man. He'd wanted to give him advance notice of the attack, but decided against it. There was no telling how Gregor would react if Mann brought someone else along for the ride. He'd already convinced himself that tagging along with the bear was risky, so he'd decided against exposing Kuzmin to danger. Better to let the old man make up his own mind. He could either try to flee, or remain in his cell and see out his sentence. Mann hoped he chose the latter. Kuzmin had just a little over two years left to serve, and then he would be a free man. If he had any sense, he'd stay in his bunk and wait it out.

'Shouldn't be long,' Gregor said. 'Come.'

The bear led the way to a spot ten yards to the side of the window, where three of his closest friends in the prison were gathered.

'Is it safe here?' Mann asked, worried.

Gregor only shrugged.

'Well, what type of explosive are they using?'

'RPGs,' Gregor said.

Mann took a few steps backwards. A shaped charge would have made a hole in the exact spot, but anything could throw off the aim of someone firing an RPG. It felt like the plan had been cobbled together at the last minute— or by amateurs.

Mann turned to see two more of Gregor's associates urging the other prisoners to make their way through the building to the front gate. Part of the strategy was to give the authorities plenty of targets, leaving Gregor and his cohorts to sneak away in their convoy of vehicles.

They would only be able to do that if they got out in the next couple of minutes.

Sloane had told Mann that an army barracks was located just a few miles down the road, so they wouldn't have long before reinforcements arrived. Mann hoped to be well away from the area by the time the troops got there.

Gregor was looking up at the clock and turning the air blue with expletives, spitting one out every few seconds. He continued his rant until three loud blasts in rapid succession reached their ears and the floor shook.

'Back!' Gregor shouted, and Mann was happy to oblige. With the outer wall demolished, it would be seconds before the hall was breached. Mann retreated another ten steps, ready to sprint for the hole that was about to appear.

Instead of another explosion, gunfire erupted outside. Most of it was the familiar staccato chatter of the AK-47 favoured by the local police and armed forces. It sounded like the rescue attempt was stalling. The army must have arrived earlier than expected, and Mann envisaged Gregor's friends being cut down before they could execute their plan.

That vision was cut violently short by a tremendous detonation that lifted Mann off his feet. He woke in a cloud of powderised concrete, and as the air cleared he could see torch lights illuminating the inside of the dark hall.

'Quick!' Gregor said, using his good arm to pick Mann up off the floor. The bear dragged Mann over rubble, into the night.

The source of the gunfire soon became clear as Mann stepped over dead bodies dressed in army fatigues. A dozen corpses littered the ground, while four men dressed entirely in black stood over them. One of them whipped off a black balaclava as he strode over to Gregor.

'What happened to you?'

Gregor raised his injured arm. 'Accident,' he simply said.

The soldier looked beyond Gregor, and his mouth screwed up in frustration. 'You said six men. There are seven.'

'I'll explain later,' Gregor snapped. 'Let's go.'

'But we only have room for six,' the rescuer insisted.

Gregor looked like he was about to argue, then swore and turned to the other escapees.

'Anyone have claustrophobia?' he asked.

One man, his shaven head a mass of prison tattoos, tentatively raised his hand.

Gregor reached down and took a pistol from the side holster of the nearest dead body. He grimaced as he used his injured hand to ensure there was a round in the chamber, then flicked off the safety and shot the painted man in the face. The prisoner's head snapped back, and he wavered for a second before collapsing to the ground in a heap.

'Now we are six,' Gregor said. He took a spare magazine from the dead guard's belt pouch and strode away from the building.

Mann, stunned at what he'd just seen, followed. Gregor had just dispelled any doubts about how ruthless he could be.

They passed through a large gap in the outer wall and saw that three cars awaited them, black SUVs with tinted windows, like props straight out of a Hollywood movie. The prisoners began to pile in while the attacking force regrouped for the exfiltration. Mann saw two men carrying an injured colleague, but he seemed to be the only one of the rescue party to have been hurt in the skirmish.

Mann climbed into the back seat, sandwiched between one of the men in black and Gregor. Once everyone was on board, the bear slapped the driver on the back and the vehicle shot forward.

Traffic was almost non-existent at such an early hour, and the three cars were soon doing eighty.

'You said we're heading to St Petersburg,' Mann said to Gregor. 'What's there?'

'A safe house,' the bear replied.

'There's nowhere closer we can go? St Petersburg is about eight hours away.'

'Ten, if we stay in this,' Gregor said, 'but we're not.'

'What do you mean?'

'You'll see.'

Ten minutes later, Mann discovered what Gregor meant. They pulled off the road and into a forest, where a truck and a minibus were waiting. The soldiers discarded their black clothing and weapons, placing them in black plastic bags. Mann noticed that they were wearing latex gloves, which they took off and binned. They all washed their hands and faces—Mann assumed to get rid of any residue from the gunfight—then dressed in regular clothing.

Gregor walked towards the truck. It was a three-tonne delivery vehicle, the writing on the side from a grocery wholesaler. Boxes of vegetables and tinned goods lay on the ground around it.

'We're in here.'

* * *

Gregor approached the truck driver, who handed him a phone. There was one entry in the contacts list, and Gregor selected it.

'It's me,' he said when the call was answered.

'Good to hear your voice,' Gregor's boss said. 'I trust everything went as planned?'

'Almost,' Gregor said. 'There was a last-minute change of personnel. Instead of Borovich, I brought someone else along.'

The voice sounded surprised. 'Why?'

Gregor looked around to ensure he couldn't be overheard. There was no one near him, but he lowered his voice anyway. 'We fought, but he got the better of me. He broke my arm and took a bite out of my face. He almost killed me.'

'And after he did all that, you helped him escape?'

Gregor could almost feel the incredulity. 'Yes, but for good reasons. If I hadn't agreed to it, I would be dead by now.'

'You could have lied,' the voice said.

'I could have, but I want my revenge. He embarrassed me, and he has to pay.'

There was no answer for a moment, and Gregor checked the screen to ensure he still had a connection. He put the phone back to his ear just as the voice spoke again.

'Who is this man that can get the better of Gregor Belsky?'

'An English spy. I was told he was captured a few days ago.'

'A spy?'

'That's right. I'm going to take him to the safe house and make his last days on this planet the most mis—'

'—not so hasty,' the other man said. 'What does Russia do with spies?'

'Kills them,' Gregor answered.

'No, we swap them. We give them their spy in exchange for one of ours. That's how it works.'

'Then why was he sent to The Widow Maker?' Gregor asked. 'That's a death sentence.'

'Perhaps there was no deal to be done. Perhaps Sokolov asked for someone the English were not prepared to hand over. I don't know. But the English will want their man back. All we have to do is find out how much they're willing to pay.'

'But I—'

'—No buts, Gregor. Keep him alive. He's too valuable to waste on petty revenge. Once he's back in England, perhaps you can go and pay him a visit.'

Gregor didn't want to wait that long, but he had to balance his impatience with the need to keep his boss happy. 'As you wish. I shall deliver him unharmed.'

'Thank you, Gregor. I'll ensure you get a large slice of any ransom we collect.'

'And if the English won't pay?' Gregor asked.

'Then he's all yours.'

The conversation couldn't have ended on a more pleasing note, and Gregor suppressed a smile as he strode back to Mann.

* * *

'Time to get moving,' Gregor said.

They climbed in the rear of the delivery truck, and Mann saw that most of the cargo was pushed up against one side of the interior. The driver motioned for them to squeeze past the boxes to the back of the compartment, where a wooden bench had been fixed behind the driver's cabin. The six prisoners sat down, Mann taking his place in the middle next to Gregor. He would have preferred to be sitting as far away from the bear's stench as possible, but he needed information.

Mainly, how to get out of Russia.

The driver placed a large sheet of plywood in front of the prisoners, enclosing them in yet another makeshift cell. He nailed it in place, leaving the six men in complete darkness. Mann's knees just about touched the new wall. Now he knew why Gregor wanted to eliminate the man with claustrophobia. Mann didn't suffer from it, but the thought of spending half a day in such cramped conditions was enough to raise his heartbeat well above normal.

Within moments, the confined space began to warm up, amplifying the stink emanating from Gregor. Mann wondered if the lack of personal hygiene was just a prison affectation, or if Gregor always smelled like a wet dog.

Mann heard boxes being shuffled around. He suspected the driver was replacing the ones he'd taken out to give them access to their hiding place. That should be enough to pass a rudimentary inspection if they came across a roadblock, but if a cop wanted the entire van emptied, they would soon be discovered.

Mann didn't dwell on it. It was pointless worrying about things he couldn't control, and this was as good a plan as any. Eyewitnesses or survivors would surely mention the three black SUVs, and that's what the police would be looking for.

'What are you going to do with the vehicles we just rode in?' Mann asked Gregor.

'They'll be destroyed. The VIN numbers have already been filed off and the plates will be removed before they are set alight. There's no way they can be traced back to anyone.'

'Not even insurance records?' Mann asked. 'I imagine it would be easy for the FSB to see who had insured three vehicles of that make and model. Can't be many people in Russia who could afford that.'

The bear chuckled. 'Then the people we stole them from are going to have a fun few days.'

At least that potential problem had been covered. It appeared that Gregor's men had bought them some time, which was what Mann desperately needed. If he could get to St Petersburg safely, he'd be able to contact home and organise an exfil. The sooner, the better.

It occurred to Mann that he hadn't asked who Gregor worked for. Up until now there'd been no reason to, but if the crime boss was into people smuggling, they might be able to help Mann out of the country.

'So who exactly do I need to thank for getting us out?' he asked Gregor.

As his eyes adjusted to the darkness, Mann saw the bear look at him strangely. 'Me.'

'No, I mean, who organised the escape? Who's your boss?'

'Ah. That'll be Nikolai.'

Mann knew most of the crime families in Moscow and the surrounding cities, and only one of them was named Nikolai.

'Nikolai Levchenko?'

Gregor nodded.

Mann gulped.

Nikolai Levchenko, also known as The White One, was by all accounts an evil bastard. Some say his malice stemmed from a traumatic upbringing caused by his albino condition. Relentlessly taunted as a child, he'd learned that ignoring the insults encouraged the bullies. The only thing that stopped them was physical violence, and on that score Levchenko was a natural. He was feared by many, including those in his employ.

It made sense that Levchenko would be behind the rescue mission; few others would be crazy enough to attempt it.

The more Mann thought about it, the less he liked his chances. The other prisoners—those that were recaptured and not shot—would be interviewed and the authorities would soon learn that he and Gregor hadn't run like everyone else, but had stayed in the congregation area. That fact alone would point the FSB to Levchenko. Despite wanting to use Levchenko's smuggling operation to get home, Mann thought it best to be as far from the albino as possible when the secret police came calling.

'Are we planning to stop anywhere along the way?' Mann asked Gregor.

'No.' The bear drank water from a plastic bottle, then handed it to Mann. 'If you need the toilet, go in there.'

'What if I need a shit?'

'Pray you don't,' Gregor told him.

That put paid to Mann's plan to slip away during the next toilet break. He would have to think of something, though. Even if they got to St Petersburg safely, Mann would face the double threat of the FSB and Levchenko.

Thankfully, he had a few hours to come up with finding a way off the truck.

Chapter 22

Roland Cooper rubbed his watery eyes and yawned. Boring, repetitive tasks always had this effect on him.

He checked the counter.

File number 347.

As Sarah Mulholland was his chief suspect, he'd set the filter to females and spent the entire previous day clicking from one file to the next, hoping to see someone who matched Sarah's stature. He'd had no joy then, and a hundred files into today he was sure it was a waste of his time.

There was not much else he could do, though. Duffield's teams were all over the suspects, and if something came up, Cooper would soon hear about it. For now, it was either this or twiddle his thumbs.

Click. No. Click. No. Click. No. Click…

Cooper hesitated, then went back to the previous file. There was definitely something familiar about the woman on the screen. He tried to think of people he knew who were short and had long black hair, and only one sprang to mind.

Sharon Williams.

Only, it wasn't her. Cooper was certain of it. The height appeared correct, but the shape of the body was all wrong. It's easy enough to disguise a figure by making it appear larger, but not thinner. The woman in the picture was at least two sizes smaller than Williams.

Frustrated, he printed off the picture and stared at it. Whoever it was, she was wearing a long tan overcoat that reached her ankles, plus a wide-brimmed hat and huge, round sunglasses that covered most of her face. Jet black hair cascaded over her shoulders. Recognition remained tantalisingly out of reach.

Cooper put the photo on his desk and went for a coffee. He knew that staring at a problem often pushed it out of reach. Better to let the name come in its own time.

He was returning from the canteen with his drink when his phone rang.

'Cooper,' he said, when he saw that it was the chief.

'There's been a development. My office, five minutes ago.'

Cooper placed his coffee on a windowsill, jogged back to his cramped office and locked the door, then ran out of the building and across Vauxhall Bridge. He was pretty sure he knew what it was about.

Two days earlier, he'd written an email addressed to Horton and several news outlets. It detailed the plight of Alex Mann and the PM's decision to leave him to his fate. The Gmail address he'd sent it from had been created that morning and Cooper had set a delay so that the message arrived in Horton's inbox while he was hosting a meeting with Cooper and FoSec for updates on the mole hunt. That way, Cooper couldn't be suspected of sending it. He'd done some tests and checked the message headers to see if the time he'd created the message could be detected, but he hadn't seen anything to make him nervous. After scheduling it on an untraceable mobile phone while riding the tube in a disguise, he'd destroyed the device.

Could the boffins at GCHQ have seen through his ruse?

Something told him he was about to find out.

Ten minutes after Horton's call, Cooper was knocking on the chief's door.

'Come.'

Cooper raced inside and saw that Sharon Williams was already there. She looked nervous. 'What is it?' he asked the chief, his excuses already prepared.

'The Widow Maker was attacked last night.'

Cooper was relieved that he wasn't the topic of conversation, but this news was equally unnerving. 'Attacked? Who by?'

'Unknown at the moment. The Russians seem to want this kept under wraps, but several videos were posted on social media. None of the actual event, just the aftermath. Police, army, FSB, you name it. Plus, there's a huge hole where the outer wall used to be, and an inner wall was breached, too.'

'A breakout?' Cooper asked.

'More likely they were broken out,' Sharon said. 'The walls were blown inwards, suggesting someone did it from the outside.' She paused for a moment. 'There were lots of body bags, too.'

Cooper knew why she'd hesitated, but the question had to be asked. 'What about Alex?'

'We simply don't know,' Horton told him. 'As I said, they're keeping a lid on it for now. Details are sketchy at best, and most of what we've got so far is supposition. I've asked Moscow Station to dig as deep as they can.'

'Russian officials are unlikely to open up to embassy staff,' Cooper said. 'Why not get the PM to make contact? FoSec at the very least.'

'That's being actioned as we speak,' Horton assured him, 'but you know Sokolov. He's not going to openly admit that his most secure prison has been compromised.'

Cooper had to admit that the chief was right. It could take days, perhaps weeks before they had any concrete news on Mann's status. He was either still incarcerated, dead, or free. Cooper prayed it was the latter. If it was, there were questions to address.

'I'm just thinking out loud here,' Cooper said, 'because we don't know the facts yet, but let's say Alex managed to escape. Who would want to free him? And, where is he now?'

'The only people who would want to free him are us,' Horton said, 'and we had nothing to do with this. If anything, the breakout was to free someone else and Alex just happened to get caught up in it.'

Cooper thought that a reasonable hypothesis. 'So if we could figure out who had the money and resources to pull this off, we might have an idea where Alex is.'

'Assuming he got out,' Sharon said.

'Assuming he got out,' Cooper agreed.

'I'll get Sloane to look into it,' Horton said. 'Prison records might be in the public domain. If not, he can ask around, spend a little money if necessary.'

'I also have one other suggestion,' Cooper said.

Horton looked like he didn't want to hear it, but he gestured for Cooper to spit it out.

'I go and provide Alex with assistance.' Horton looked like he was about to object, but Cooper steamrollered on. 'If he did get out, then he'll need to contact someone. The FSB have the names of everyone at the embassy and they'll be under tight surveillance. We need a fresh face to help get Alex out.'

'It makes sense,' Sharon said. 'If Alex calls, none of the personnel currently in place can help him without compromising him. If we can come up with some kind of code, something that only Alex will understand, we can guide him to a location where Roland can meet him.'

Horton chewed the idea over for a moment, lips pursed. 'I'll suggest it to the PM when I meet him at nine,' he said, 'but don't get your hopes up. We've already lost one man, I'm not sure he's ready to risk a second.'

The chief nodded towards the door, signalling an end to the meeting.

They left, but Cooper told Sharon he'd catch up with her. He returned to Horton's office and closed the door.

'Do you think it was wise having Sharon here? If she's the mole, we might be handing Alex right back to them.'

Horton stood and put on his jacket. 'It was Sharon who alerted me to the prison break,' he said. 'I could hardly cut her out of the loop once she'd done that. Besides, if she was playing us, one, she would have kept it under wraps, and two, the surveillance would have picked up the conversation with whoever told her.'

That was fair enough.

'How's it coming, by the way?'

Cooper considered telling Horton about the mystery woman who had piqued his curiosity, but he decided to hold back until he had something concrete. It could turn out to be a waitress he'd encountered, or a woman he'd seen in a bar. No point getting the chief's hopes up.

'Slowly,' Cooper said, 'but I'll find them.'

'I'm sure you will,' Horton said as he headed to the door. 'In the meantime, pack a bag, just in case.'

Chapter 23

As Maksim Kuznetsov entered Dmitri Gudkov's office, he found the head of the FSB on the phone.

'…yes…of course…I understand…'

Gudkov took the phone away from his ear, looked at it, then replaced it in the cradle.

'Igor isn't happy,' he said to Kuznetsov.

Sokolov rarely is, the FSB's second-in-command thought. 'I just spoke with the commander in the field. Thirty-seven guards were killed, three seriously injured. It will take at least three weeks to rebuild the walls and—'

'—I don't care about any of that,' Gudkov barked. 'How many escaped?'

It was unusual to see Gudkov in such a state. The president must be really busting his balls.

'Eleven,' Kuznetsov said. He reached into his pocket and took out a notepad. 'Gregor Belsky, Yerik Asimov, Yevgeny Salo—'

'Belsky!' Gudkov slammed his hand on the table. 'I bet the albino motherfucker he works for had something to do with this!'

Kuznetsov had already had the same thought. 'I've sent a team to watch him,' he said. 'If Belsky turns up there, we'll know about it. There's another problem…'

Gudkov's eyes narrowed. 'Go on.'

'The Englishman, Alex Mann. He's still unaccounted for.'

Gudkov looked fit to burst. 'How is he even still alive? Igor wanted to make an example of him, to show the West what happens when they meddle in our affairs.'

'I don't know all the details, just that there was a fight between Belsky and Mann, and Belsky came off worse.'

Gudkov pumped his fists in frustration as he glared at Kuznetsov. 'It appears we underestimated Mann,' he said.

The inference was clear. It was Kuznetsov who had underestimated Mann, and if things turned sour, it was his head on the block.

'We'll find him,' Kuznetsov promised. 'We'll find all of them. We've already set up roadblocks in a fifty-mile radius and the local army units are going house to house. There's nowhere for them to go.'

'I hope you're right,' Gudkov said. 'If you have aspirations of taking over when I retire, know that this kind of thing will reflect badly. Resolve it before it becomes too big a stain to remove.'

Gudkov flicked a hand towards the door, and Kuznetsov took the hint. He left the general's office and walked back to his own, knowing that he couldn't afford to leave this in the hands of others. Delegation had its advantages, but not when one's career was on the line.

He picked up the phone and buzzed his assistant. 'I want a plane ready to go in thirty minutes.'

'Certainly, sir. Where to?'

'Yaroslavl.'

* * *

When the plane landed at the airport just outside Yaroslavl, Kuznetsov waited for the pilot to lower the stairs and stepped out onto the tarmac. A car was waiting, and he instructed the driver to take him to the Widow Maker.

He'd spent the short flight on the phone, issuing instructions to the commander on the ground. The first thing he wanted was the area around the prison properly secured. He'd been informed that videos were already circulating on social media, and he demanded that the public be kept well back from the scene. Kuznetsov had also informed Roskomnadzor, the Federal Service for Supervision in the Sphere of Telecom, Information Technologies and Mass Communications, to block all videos of the prison break from appearing on the Internet. In most countries, such action would require a court order; in Sokolov's Russia, all it took was a phone call. Next, the news outlets had been told that a gas explosion had caused damage to the prison and that there had been some casualties. Further details, he'd informed them, would be released at the appropriate time.

With damage limitation out of the way, Kuznetsov could concentrate on finding Gregor Belsky and Alex Mann.

His official car was waved through a barrier manned by two soldiers. Half a kilometre later, the driver pulled up outside a large military tent. A uniformed soldier wearing the FSB insignia opened the rear door and Kuznetsov stepped out.

'Where's Major Babin?'

'Inside, sir.'

Kuznetsov strode into the tent and found the commander leaning over a map and surrounded by junior ranks. They all leapt to attention as Kuznetsov walked towards them. He flicked off a return salute and dismissed the subordinates with a wave of his gloved hand.

'What's the latest?' Kuznetsov asked.

'We've just found the vehicles some of them escaped in,' the major said. 'A local was awoken by the sound of explosions and saw three black SUVs speeding from the area.'

It was the first piece of good news Kuznetsov had heard in a while. 'Show me where they're heading and seal off all the roads in that area. Instruct all local police to be on the lookout for them.'

Babin swallowed. 'No. What I meant was, we found the vehicles. Burned out. In the woods.'

Kuznetsov's euphoria was short-lived. 'Where?'

Babin pointed to a location on the map.

'Do you have men there?' Kuznetsov asked.

'A dozen, but there are no clues. No tracks leading out of the woods, and the vehicles are so damaged that it'll be impossible to get any DNA from them.'

'So you don't even know which type of vehicle they switched to?'

'Nor the number of them,' Babin confirmed. 'It could be three more cars, two buses, anything.'

Whoever had planned this had done a thorough job, Kuznetsov thought. They'd dumped the vehicles near a major intersection, which meant they could be travelling in one of four directions. Well, three if they were smart enough not to double back to the prison. Most likely they would stay on the highway all the way to Moscow, where the albino was based.

'Double the roadblocks here, here and here,' Kuznetsov said, indicating points on the map.

'Yes, sir.' Babin picked up a slip of paper. 'We've recaptured and accounted for over a thousand prisoners,' the Major said. 'Twenty-seven are dead after resisting arrest, and six are still unaccounted for.'

'What are the names of the six?'

Babin produced another sheet of paper and handed it over.

There was one name Kuznetsov didn't want to see, but there it was, staring him in the face, almost mocking him.

Alex Mann.

Gregor Belsky was also on the list, and Kuznetsov couldn't shake the feeling that they were still together.

'On the phone you told me there was a fight between Mann and Belsky. Have you discovered anything more?'

'I interviewed a few of the prisoners,' Babin said. 'A fight between them was scheduled for this Saturday, but Belsky had a visitor yesterday afternoon and suddenly he brought it forward.'

That sounded suspicious. Perhaps Belsky had been told about the escape attempt, and didn't want to miss out on a little fun before he left. Only it hadn't turned out as he'd planned. 'Why schedule a fight?' Kuznetsov asked. That seemed strange, too. From what he knew about prisons, violence was often swift and spontaneous, not premeditated.

'Apparently it gives the prisoners time to get their wagers in place. Also the guards. It seems a lot can be made on the outcome of these events.'

Kuznetsov didn't care about such trivial matters. 'How did Mann survive against Belsky?'

'He landed a few blows, but then Belsky got him in a bear hug. Mann bit his face, if you can believe that. Then Belsky grabbed him again, but Mann broke his arm. He had Belsky in a choke hold and it was almost over, but then Mann let him go.'

'Just like that?'

'A couple of prisoners said Mann was talking to Belsky while he was choking him, then he just kicked him away and walked off.'

'Let me get this straight. Mann has a chance to kill Belsky, but he doesn't do it?'

'That's what they all say,' Babin agreed.

It was getting stranger by the second. 'What did they say to each other? Did anyone hear the conversation?'

Babin shook his head. 'No one knows.'

Kuznetsov had a pretty good idea. Belsky plans to kill Mann before the escape, only Mann gets the better of him. As he's beaten, Belsky makes a deal: let me live, and I'll take you with me.

'Did you instruct the roadblocks to record every vehicle that goes through?'

'As per your orders, Colonel.'

'I want to see the logs. Now.'

'But they're all handwritten,' Babin moaned. 'It'll take hours to collect them all and—'

'Get your men to call them in and have a team here collate them all. I want this done in the next half hour. I want vehicle make, licence plate and direction of travel for each of them.'

179

Kuznetsov stormed off before the major could protest further. It angered him that Babin wasn't feeling as much pressure as he was, but then Babin wasn't about to lose his only chance at the top job. That was certainly the fate Kuznetsov faced if he didn't find the six missing prisoners, Mann in particular.

Kuznetsov stood outside the tent and looked around. A perimeter had been set five hundred yards from the prison walls to deter the curious. One or two gathered to see what was going on, but when an FSB sergeant walked up and took their photograph on his phone, they quickly made themselves scarce.

Kuznetsov walked around the back of the building, where a giant black screen had been erected to cover up the gaping hole in the outer wall. It wasn't there to provide protection from the elements, but to stop people taking photographs of the damage and sharing them online.

Where are you? he wondered. *Where are you heading?*

The albino, Nikolai Levchenko, was the key, Kuznetsov was sure of it. He was rich and brazen enough to pull this off, and Gregor Belsky was one of his top men.

He tried to put himself in Levchenko's position. After getting them out, what would he do? Obviously, swap vehicles, he knew that now. They wouldn't drive into the forest, burn their cars and walk the rest of the way. But where would they go? Levchenko wouldn't be foolish enough to place Belsky with someone he didn't know or trust, so it had to be somewhere the albino could guarantee secrecy.

He took out his phone and called his adjutant in Moscow. 'I want a complete list of every property owned or controlled by Nikolai Levchenko...yes, that Nikolai Levchenko.

Anything in his name, his family's name, or owned or rented by his businesses...yes. Send the results to my phone as soon as it's done.' As an afterthought, he added, 'And have a hundred men on standby.'

There was a substantial file on Levchenko, so it shouldn't take long to get the information he'd requested. Once he received the results, he would prioritise them and send a dozen men to the top eight most likely locations on the list simultaneously.

Kuznetsov was walking back to the command tent when his phone pinged. It was the office. He looked at the file he'd been sent and it contained more entries than he'd expected. Fifty-four properties in all.

Six men were still missing. Would they stick together, or go their separate ways? What would Levchenko do? If they split up and one was recaptured, it was likely he'd talk. The albino wouldn't want that. No, they'd remain together. Kuznetsov needed to find which property was large enough to accommodate so many people comfortably. He was able to discount a couple of two-bedroom apartments in the centre of Moscow, but the list was still considerable, too big to easily view on his tiny screen.

When he reached the tent, he told Babin to make a terminal free. A young analyst was instantly ejected from his seat, and Kuznetsov sat at the empty terminal and entered his FSB credentials. A moment later he had the spreadsheet open.

'I have the vehicle details you requested, Colonel.'

Kuznetsov turned to see Babin with a sheet of paper in his hand. 'Does it contain the names of the registered owners, and have you checked to see if any of them have been reported stolen?'

Babin looked pained, started to speak, then turned and got on the phone.

Kuznetsov returned to his own task. He highlighted the two apartments he'd rejected in red, then sorted the buildings by type. The albino wouldn't want six fugitives mingling with his legitimate staff, so all businesses were crossed off. That left thirty-five addresses, all residential. Most were rental properties, but four were used solely by Levchenko. Kuznetsov marked these in green, then looked for others that might fit the bill.

'Where are you going, Belsky?' Kuznetsov mumbled to himself.

'Not to Moscow,' the analyst who'd lost his seat said.

Kuznetsov rounded on him. 'What did you say?'

'I'm sorry, Colonel, I…'

'You said not to Moscow. Why not?'

The young man regarded him as if the answer was obvious, but that pointing it out would be fatal. 'I just thought…'

'You thought *what*?' Kuznetsov barked.

'I just thought…too many people know Belsky. He'd be easy to spot there, either by police or a rival.'

Kuznetsov thought about it for a moment, and decided the kid might be on to something. 'So where do *you* think he'll go?'

The analyst gulped. 'I don't know. Somewhere quiet, where he can ride out the storm, then make his way out of the country, maybe.'

The boy made a lot of sense. There was no way Belsky could just reintegrate himself into society. He'd be on the run forever, so the wise move would be to flee Russia and start again elsewhere. That meant a way out of the country, and as the commercial airlines were too risky, it meant overland or by boat.

He turned back to the spreadsheet and ordered the list by city. Only two of Levchenko's properties were outside Moscow. One was in St Petersburg, the other in Nizhny Novgorod. It was just over a hundred kilometres from St Petersburg to the Finnish border, a little farther to Estonia, and a boat could take him through the Gulf of Finland to a host of nearby countries. From Nizhny Novgorod, it was at least seven hundred kilometres to the nearest neighbour.

They're heading north!

'What's your name?' Kuznetsov asked the analyst.

'Gurin, sir. Fyodor Gurin.'

Kuznetsov rose and instructed Major Babin to send the list of vehicles to his phone when it was complete, then put a hand on the analyst's shoulder. 'Come with me, Fyodor Gurin.'

Chapter 24

Nikolai Levchenko sat in his armchair and sipped his whisky, a smooth 30-year-old Macallan, then placed his glass carefully on the coaster on his side table.

'Any problems?' he asked Andrei, his trusted lieutenant.

'None so far,' Andrei said. He was standing in front of Levchenko, his hands behind his back. 'As you predicted, they had roadblocks set up almost immediately. The driver reported one fifty kilometres from the prison, but he breezed through with just a cursory inspection.'

'And the others?'

'They were stopped and questioned, but their story held up.'

Levchenko had expected as much. Local police would be expecting to see soldiers and men in prison garb, not a delivery truck and a minibus full of men on their way to a stag party. He'd sent the soldiers south, to a hotel in Dobrograd. Their booking had been made weeks earlier, and they would party for two days before driving back to Moscow.

'And the one who was injured in the attack?' Levchenko asked.

'Disposed of, as you ordered. The body will never be found.'

Levchenko was pleased that his instructions had been carried out. One of the advantages of using mercenaries was that they were expendable. If the police had seen the gunshot wound, the entire plan would unravel.

Levchenko took another sip of his drink, savouring the mellow burn as it cruised down his throat. 'What of the other matter?' he asked Andrei.

'We found Yuri a couple of hours ago. He was hiding out in a drug den.'

'And was he full of remorse?'

'Of course, Nikki. He swore that it was a mistake and that it would never happen again.'

'Make sure it doesn't,' Levchenko said.

He would have liked nothing more than to deal with Yuri personally, but these days he had to remain at arms' length from his illegal activities. The FSB were always looking for a chance to take him down, which was why he would have to leave it to others to dismember the snitch.

Ivan Barkov burst through the door. 'We have a problem,' he said to Levchenko.

When his intelligence officer spoke in such terms, Levchenko always listened. Ivan had sources in both the police and the intelligence agencies, and the information they passed on meant Levchenko was always one step ahead of the law. Well, almost always. Five months earlier, news of a police raid hadn't filtered through in time. The man responsible for warning Levchenko had been off work ill that day, but thankfully Gregor had put his own life on the line to allow Levchenko to escape from the nightclub. If he'd been on the premises when the haul of cocaine had been discovered, he'd have joined Gregor in the Widow Maker.

'Is it Belsky?' the albino asked.

'Yes,' Ivan said. 'News from my man in the FSB. Colonel Kuznetsov was at the prison an hour ago, and he just filed a flight plan to Pulkovo Airport.'

'He's going to St Petersburg? What did he find?'

'We don't know, but he ordered a dozen men from Alpha Group to meet him there.'

Alpha Group was the FSB's very own special forces team, designed for counter-terrorism operations. They were only deployed against the toughest of targets.

Gregor Belsky fit that description, but his old lieutenant wasn't the only one that Levchenko was concerned about.

Gregor had called him and relayed a message that made Levchenko's heart skip a couple of beats: he had a British spy, Alex Mann, and he was taking him to the safe house on the outskirts of St Petersburg. Levchenko had immediately seen an opportunity. The British would want their man back, and he could always use another twenty million dollars. There was a deal to be done, but not while Maksim Kuznetsov was applying heat. The FSB's deputy director was a constant pain in Levchenko's arse, always looking for a chance to put him away.

Levchenko ran his hand over his head. His hair was cut so close to the skin that it felt like peach fuzz.

Where to send them? he thought. In order to know that, he had to work out how Kuznetsov had known to target his place in St Petersburg. What had given it away? It wasn't a leak, Levchenko knew that for sure. Only himself, Andrei, Ivan and the driver knew the final destination. If the driver had talked, Kuznetsov wouldn't have let the attack on the prison go ahead; he would have had men stationed to repel the invaders. At the very least, he would have had the truck picked up by now. No, Kuznetsov had worked it out by himself, somehow.

Levchenko liked to think of himself as a smart guy. Not because he knew everything, but because he wasn't afraid to ask his confidants for their input. His rivals would never do such a thing, thinking it a weakness to seek the counsel of their underlings. That was why he'd seen their empires crumble and fall over the years.

'Andrei, how could Kuznetsov possibly know to target my house in—'

As Levchenko spoke the words, it struck him.

My house.

'I'm sorry, Nikki. What was the question?'

'Never mind,' Levchenko told him. He stood and walked to the window, where heavy net curtains blocked out most of the sun's rays. His albinism affected his eyesight, cursing him with photophobia. His sensitivity to light meant that wherever he went, the lighting had to be subdued. If he ventured outside, he was always wearing sunglasses, whatever the weather.

Levchenko knew he'd slipped up by thinking he could put Gregor Belsky up in one of his own properties without Kuznetsov finding out. He couldn't afford to make such a stupid mistake again.

'I need to hide six men for the next few weeks. It must be isolated, a place we can defend, but not somewhere that has any ties to me. Suggestions?'

In the dim glow from a table lamp, Levchenko could see Andrei and Ivan chewing over the problem.

'What about your new dacha?' Ivan said.

Andrei shot him a look. 'Not connected with Nikki, idiot!'

'I know Nikki owns it, but it's still under construction. Work is delayed because of the issue with the permits, so there's no one on site. The roof is on, there's a generator, running water…'

Levchenko looked at Andrei. 'He could have a point. Kuznetsov is unlikely to consider it, and there's only one road in and out. We could set up an early warning system in the surrounding forest if they decide to come in that way, and have a team to provide security.'

'We'll need an exfil plan in case they turn up heavy handed,' Andrei suggested.

'Draw one up,' Levchenko said. 'And call the driver. Tell him there's been a change of plan.'

Chapter 25

Henry Ward slammed the palm of his hand on the desk, startling everyone at the table.

'How can the most sophisticated electronic surveillance agency in the world not know who sent a goddamn email!'

Horton watched the prime minister catch his breath after the unexpected outburst. He'd never seen Ward act so passionately, but then he'd never been under so much pressure. The newspapers had run with the story of a British spy being jailed in Russia, and the PM's refusal to do a deal to release him. That had resulted in a huge slide in the polls. No government wanted that just months before a general election.

'That's the problem with anonymous email accounts,' Horton said. 'Anyone can create them. We've been on to Google for information about the person who set it up, but we're not hopeful. At best we'll get an IP address, but if they're smart, they won't have done it from work or home.'

Ward wasn't mollified by the explanation. 'I want whoever did this found and dealt with. Severely. The full works.'

Horton could only agree. The media had gone into a frenzy over the incident, with reporters camped outside Vauxhall Cross hoping for a sound bite or two, but they were wasting their time. No one was going to talk to them beyond the standard, 'We never comment on national security matters'. It was the PM's stance, too, but it wasn't helping his cause. Instead of facts, the papers and news channels were rife with speculation. Who had the Russians asked for in exchange for the British spy? The anonymous email hadn't specified, only that the PM wasn't going to deal. Even the government-supporting nationalist newspapers had found that troubling.

'We could still come out of this with our reputation intact,' FoSec said, hoping to bring the PM down a couple of notches.

'How could we possibly spin this to our advantage?' Ward scoffed.

'We get Alex home.'

Ward glared at Geoffrey Taggart. 'And then?'

'Then we say it was all a ruse. Well, not so much a ruse, more a calculated gamble that paid off. Not officially, of course. We'll stand behind our reticence about such things, but word can get to certain friendly journalists that we were always confident of getting him back, but on our terms.'

'That only works if Alex gets out of Russia,' Horton added, 'which is why I'd like to send my people in to make sure he does.'

Ward looked at him as if he was deranged. 'You've already lost one man there, and now you want to send more to help someone who's probably got the entire FSB on his tail? Can you imagine the stink if they get caught, too?'

'I can imagine what the press will say if we just sit back and do nothing,' FoSec said, coming to Horton's defence. 'If Alex is recaptured and it gets out that we had a chance to help him and passed it up, they'll crucify you.'

'And until we find out who was behind the initial leak, there's every chance they'll go to the press again.' Horton didn't like blackmailing anyone, let alone the prime minister, but it seemed the only way to get the man on board with his plan. By denying his team the chance to bring Alex home, Ward was effectively sealing his fate.

'If I send more people in, it could spark an international incident the likes of which we've never seen.'

'With all due respect, Prime Minister, Sokolov has no room to complain. How many assassinations has he carried out on British soil?'

Ward considered the argument for a moment, then sighed. 'Who do you plan to send?'

'The Increment,' Horton said. Also known as E squadron, the Increment was a specialist SAS unit attached to MI6.

Ward shook his head theatrically. 'No, no, no. I hesitate to send civilians in, but not the military.'

'But they wouldn't be dressed for combat,' Horton countered. 'As far as the Russians know, they're British citizens.'

'No!' Ward said once more, his voice rising. 'You can send in another spy, but that's as far as I'm prepared to stretch.'

It's overseas operative, you asshole! Horton hated politicians more than ever. Why give you the tools to do the job, then prevent you from using them?

'Where is Mann, anyway?' the PM asked.

'As yet we don't know,' Horton admitted. 'The FSB are saying nothing, but there's lots of activity. We're trying to keep track of it in the hope it'll give us a clue as to his whereabouts.'

'So even if you send someone else, they'll be looking for a screw in a bolt factory. It doesn't seem like the best use of resources.'

Horton could see the conversation going round in circles all day unless he put a stop to it. 'We'll only deploy once we have confirmation that Alex is alive and well. Until then, we'll stay clear of trouble.'

That seemed to pacify Ward. 'Very well. One man, and he's to get Mann out, not start a war.'

'Thank you,' Horton said, relieved to have got something out of the negotiations.

'And I want to make myself absolutely clear. No soldiers. Not serving members, ex-members, or soldiers who are currently on leave. No military, period.'

'Understood.'

Horton rose, and Taggart followed him out of the PM's office.

'That went well,' FoSec said sarcastically.

'At least we got that small concession. It's better than abandoning Alex, but not by much.'

'The question is, do you have anyone who is willing to go and get him out?'

Horton stopped walking and looked at Taggart. 'You mean, do I know anyone who's eager to risk their life to go to a hostile country and look for a man who probably has hundreds of thousands of law enforcement and state security personnel looking for him?'

'Yeah, that.'

Horton smiled. 'I have just the man.'

Chapter 26

Mann jerked awake as a sound like a dentist's drill filled the tiny space. He noticed that the truck had stopped, the engine turned off. Moments later, bright light assaulted his eyes, and he squeezed them shut.

'Change of plan,' he heard the driver say.

Mann squinted and saw Gregor get up and squeeze past the pile of groceries. Mann followed, his legs like jelly after sitting in the same position for hours. Outside, he saw the sun low on the horizon, suggesting it was early evening. They were once again in a wooded area, and Gregor had wandered off with a phone to his ear. The other prisoners had taken the chance to stretch their legs and relieve themselves. Mann had the same idea. He strode over to a bush and squatted down behind it.

The change of plan concerned him. It suggested not everything was going as smoothly as Levchenko had anticipated. Did the FSB know about the van? Was the safe house compromised?

Mann finished up and returned to the truck, where Gregor was chatting to the other prisoners. A couple of them were smoking, and Gregor seemed in good spirits.

'What's the news?' Mann asked as he approached the group.

The others fanned out, which wasn't a good sign. It looked like they were preparing for an assault. Mann pulled up short. 'What is it?'

'We're changing direction,' Gregor said. 'New destination.'

'Is that all?'

'We're just waiting for new transport, too.'

'So where are we now?' Mann asked, using his peripheral vision to watch for signs of an attack.

'Five hours from where we need to be,' Gregor replied.

'If you just tell me where we are, I can make my own way from here.'

Gregor folded his arms across his huge chest, despite one of them being in a cast. 'I don't think so.'

'Why not? I don't know where you're going, so I can't tell the police anything if they capture me.'

'My boss has plans for you,' Gregor smiled. 'He wants to ensure you get home safely.'

Mann couldn't detect the slightest hint of sincerity. 'Thank him for the generous offer, but I'm fine on my own.' He turned and started walking towards the trees, but two men stepped in front of him, and Mann heard the ominous sound of a pistol being cocked.

'It's not wise to disappoint Nikki,' Gregor said. 'He insisted I make you my guest, and that if you refuse the hospitality he's offering, then I'm to make sure you don't tell the authorities about his involvement.'

The message was clear, leaving Mann no option. There was no way he could take on all five of them, even if Gregor was handicapped by his broken arm. The bear still had the pistol he'd taken from the dead guard at the prison, and he'd already shown that he was willing to use it.

'Then I guess I'll hang around with you guys for a while.'

Mann strolled to the truck and sat on the tail gate. He'd been worried about Gregor's intentions from the moment they'd left the prison, but now the situation was becoming clearer. There weren't many reasons why Nikolai Levchenko would want to keep hold of Mann, but it certainly wasn't a desire to play the genial host. Mafia bosses were not altruists, they were businessmen. They made money. To the albino, Mann was an asset, something to be traded.

But who was he willing to trade with? Did Levchenko plan to ransom him to Britain, or would the Russians pay a higher price?

Either way, the outlook was bleak. His own prime minister had refused a deal once, and if the price was too steep, he might do so again. That would leave Mann back where he started, in the hands of Kuznetsov and the FSB.

He wasn't going to let that happen. He'd bide his time, allow Gregor to become complacent, then strike. It wouldn't be easy with just a fountain pen as a weapon, but if he could get his hands on the pistol, he'd have a good chance of escaping.

His stomach rumbled, so Mann searched the boxes for something to eat. He settled on a tin of peaches, only because it had a ring pull lid. The others saw him tucking in and climbed into the truck to join the feast.

'So, is there a shower at this place we're going to?' Mann asked Gregor, choosing his words carefully. If he'd said *this place you're taking me to*, it would have sounded like he wasn't happy with the arrangement. This way, he came across as a willing participant.

'Don't count on it,' the Russian answered. 'Nikki prefers a bath.'

Mann suspected as much. Few of the Russians he knew liked to shower, preferring to lounge in hot water. It wasn't something Mann had taken to. His and Debra's home had two shower rooms, no tub.

The thought of home brought a vision of Debra. She must be going through hell, not knowing his situation.

He wondered if Cooper had told her that he'd escaped from prison. But then, he couldn't be sure that Cooper even knew about the breakout. Sokolov wasn't exactly the most transparent leader on the planet. He could have covered it up, hoping to round up all the prisoners and pretend it never happened. If that was the case, MI6 wouldn't be working on an exfil strategy; he'd have to figure one out on his own.

The first thing he'd have to do was to contact friendlies, but that presented its own problems. The Russians would be monitoring all lines to the embassy, and possibly all calls to England. If he was going to speak to someone and give them his location, it would have to be in code. Not an alphanumeric algorithm that the Russians could crack, but something that only his people back home would know. That meant talking to Roland Cooper. He was the only one Mann could call a friend; the rest were acquaintances, colleagues. The people he worked with didn't know him as intimately as Cooper did.

Having decided whom to call, all Mann needed to do was work out how to communicate his location without eavesdroppers knowing where he was. The best way to do that would be with co-ordinates, but that would mean coming up with a code for each digit, and there were nine in the longitude and nine in the latitude. To pass that information on cryptically would take forever, and the longer Mann was on a phone, the more likely the FSB would pinpoint his location. He needed to pass the information to Cooper in as few words as possible.

The exact number leaped into his head.

'What are you smiling at?' Gregor asked.

Mann swallowed a mouthful of peach. 'Just picturing a nice hot bath.'

* * *

Mann might have lied about dreaming of a long soak, but it would have been nice to at least see a tub. As it was, the dacha was nothing more than a building site. The house was just a shell with a roof, and that was where the luxuries ended. The windows and doors were thick plastic sheets designed to keep the rain out but not the cold. Inside, the floors were bare concrete covered in a fine layer of dust, and only one of the interior walls in the hallway had been plastered. The rest were just brick.

'I think Nikki should sack his interior designer,' Mann said to Gregor as the six men entered the house. They'd been picked up by another truck, but Gregor said there was no need to be cocooned again. They were far enough from the prison that they were unlikely to come across any police roadblocks. Instead, they simply sat in the back for the next three hours, and Mann listened to their plans for the future. They all had the same one, it seemed: girls, drugs and vodka, all in copious amounts. All Mann wanted was his wife, a bottle of wine and clean sheets.

'Would you prefer to be back in the prison?'

Mann shook his head.

'Then shut up,' Gregor said, making his way to the kitchen.

Mann followed, vowing never to practice humour in the bear's company again.

There were no furnishings apart from a large metal sink. Gregor walked over to it and tried the tap. Water spluttered before a clear, steady stream emerged. He turned it off and walked to a pile of boxes in the corner of the room, opening the first and pulling out some instant coffee.

'*Sacha!*'

One of the prisoners came running in. He was squat and top-heavy, like a bulldog.

'There's a builder's hut around the side of the house,' Gregor said. 'See if they have any kitchen utensils. A kettle, pots and pans, cutlery, anything. Take Yerik with you.'

Sacha disappeared, and Gregor went to what would eventually be the back door. For now, it was just another sheet of plastic taped to the frame. Gregor removed the tape from one side and stepped into the cold, with Mann just behind him.

There wasn't much to see. A generator sat against the rear wall, with two cans of fuel next to it. Gregor lifted them both and they appeared full. The bear then pressed a button and the generator chugged into life. It made a racket, but Gregor didn't seem fazed. Looking around, Mann could understand why. There was nothing for miles. Trees began about half a kilometre away and encircled the building. Where the nearest neighbour was, Mann had no idea. They couldn't have been close, though.

Gregor walked back inside, waiting for Mann to join him. He taped the sheet back in place, then led Mann through to what would one day be the living room. It was empty apart from six mattresses on the floor—one of them loaded with a pile of blankets—and a couple of electric heaters. Extension leads snaked through from an adjoining room, and Gregor plugged a heater into one of them. He stood in front of it as three bars slowly transitioned from grey to red.

'How long are we gonna be here?' Konstantin asked. He had a shaven head that was covered in tattoos. Most looked to have been inked by a child.

'Until we're told we can leave,' Gregor said.

Konstantin slumped onto one of the mattresses, clearly not pleased with the arrangement.

'What about supplies?' Mann asked. 'Food? Drink?'

'Girls,' Mikhail added with a grin. He was a six-footer with a body that was going to fat. Mikhail sported a pencil moustache that made him look like the fast-food version of Errol Flynn.

'No girls,' Gregor growled. 'No girls, no booze, no drugs. We stay focused, just in case the police find out where we are.'

'Then what about weapons?' Konstantin asked. 'How can we defend ourselves if the cops show up?'

'That's being arranged. We'll have weapons and food by seven this evening. For now, there's bread.'

Sacha and Yerik returned, their arms full. 'We got a kettle,' Sacha said, 'and an electric hob.'

Yerik placed a bucket on the floor. Gregor reached in and pulled out a mug, which he threw to Mann.

'Two sugars.'

Chapter 27

At the sound of the approaching vehicle, Mann was first to react. He leapt to his feet and ran to the window as a Mercedes drove towards the house. Gregor appeared next to him a moment later, his pistol drawn. He pushed Mann aside and pulled back some of the plastic sheeting so that he could get a better view. A grin appeared on the bear's face, and he de-cocked the gun and slipped it back into his waistband.

'Dinner has arrived,' Gregor declared. He ran and pulled aside the plastic covering the front door as the Mercedes came to a stop.

'Gregor!' the driver declared as he got out.

'Igor!' Gregor replied. He spread his arms wide and gave the man a bro hug.

The other prisoners emerged, and the driver dragged himself away from Gregor and opened the boot. He handed out box after box, then slammed the boot closed and walked back to Gregor, his eyes on Mann all the time.

'This is him?'

'It is,' Gregor said.

Alan McDermott

Igor turned and spoke quietly to Gregor, then handed him a phone, gave him another hug and got back into the car.

Gregor watched him drive away, then ushered Mann back inside the house.

The others were already rifling through the delivery. Food lay scattered on the floor as the four prisoners fondled their new toys.

'AK-74s,' Mann said. 'Nice. Where's mine?'

Gregor leaned into a box and pulled out something that Mann was now familiar with.

'Handcuffs?' Mann groaned. 'Seriously?'

'Nikki's orders,' Gregor said. He tossed the cuffs to Sacha. 'One on his right wrist, the other on the radiator.'

Faced with a room full of men holding automatic weapons, Mann didn't feel inclined to argue. He picked up the corner of his mattress and dragged it across the room, dumping it next to the radiator, then held out his left wrist.

'The other one,' Sacha said.

The bulldog wasn't as stupid as he looked. Mann held out his favoured arm and Sacha snapped the irons around it. He tugged Mann closer to the radiator and secured the other link to a sturdy pipe. Sacha tugged to make sure Mann wasn't going anywhere, then wandered off to look through the supply of food.

'What's the latest?' Yerik asked Gregor.

'We're getting a security team. They'll be here tomorrow afternoon.'

Konstantin cocked his weapon. 'We don't need security. We can handle the police and anyone else who shows up.'

'Really?' Gregor asked. 'Then why did you just insert your magazine upside down?'

Konstantin frowned and inverted his rifle, checking to see if it was true. His actions brought roars of laughter from the others.

'See?' Gregor said. 'You didn't even know that it's impossible to put it in the wrong way round. What hope have you got of actually firing it and hitting someone?'

Konstantin looked sheepish. He took his new possession and slumped down on his mattress.

Mann didn't join in the merriment; he was too concerned with Gregor's announcement.

When they'd first arrived at the house, Mann's plan had been simple: wait for the others to get drunk and fall asleep, then take Gregor's gun and run. Now that booze had been ruled out and he was chained to the wall, it was time for a rethink. It was going to be difficult enough to get away as things stood, but the added threat of a security team would make his task almost impossible.

He had to make his move before they arrived.

The alternative was to allow Nikolai Levchenko to make his demands and hope Downing Street agreed to the price. Would his government negotiate? That was the million-dollar question—literally—and Mann didn't like the answer.

No, it was tonight or never.

Things got worse a couple of hours later. As the men were settling down for the night, Gregor ordered Sacha and Konstantin to take first watch.

'But it's freezing outside!' Konstantin moaned.

'Then wrap a blanket around you.'

That wasn't enough to pacify Konstantin. 'Why can't we just stay inside and look out the window?'

Mann expected Gregor to explode, but the bear simply gestured to the window. 'Take a look, tell me what you can see.'

Konstantin rose from his bed and walked past Gregor. As he did, Gregor pulled the pistol from his waistband and shot him in the temple. Konstantin fell sideways, dead before he hit the ground.

Gregor stood over him and put his foot over the bullet hole to prevent the flow of blood staining the floor. He looked at the others. 'Anyone else have any objections to guard duty?'

Sacha and Yerik grabbed their rifles, wrapped themselves in grey blankets and headed for the door.

After getting over the initial shock, Mann was grateful for the sudden outburst of violence. It meant one less adversary to worry about. Now there was just Gregor, Mikhail, Sacha, and Yerik to deal with.

In order to take down Gregor and Mikhail, though, Mann would need a gun, and the shots would alert the other two outside. He would have preferred to take them by surprise, but it was what it was. Perhaps they'd think it was Gregor again, which would buy him a few precious seconds.

Mann realised he was getting ahead of himself. Everything was contingent on him getting out of his restraints.

Though he wasn't tired, Mann yawned, gave an exaggerated stretch, pulled his blanket over him and pretended to settle down to sleep.

A second later, Gregor kicked him in the kidneys.

'Wake up. There's work to do.'

Mann turned and rubbed his back. 'What work?'

Gregor pointed at Konstantin's body. 'Bury that. Mikhail, give him a hand.' He tossed Mikhail the keys to the cuffs.

Once freed, Mann got up, wrapped himself in a blanket, and took Konstantin's arms. Mikhail took the legs, and they dragged the body towards the front entrance. Gregor created a gap for them to go through, and they ventured out into the freezing night.

'How the hell are we supposed to bury him?' Mikhail grumbled.

Mann pointed towards the workmen's hut. 'There must be shovels in there.'

As they walked to the hut, Mann considered acting now, while he was free. That notion was swiftly cast aside as Sacha appeared, holding his AK-74 across his chest.

'This is bullshit,' the bulldog complained.

Mikhail agreed. 'It's not what I signed up for.'

Sacha looked around conspiratorially, then moved closer to Mikhail. 'I say we do Gregor and blow this place,' he said. 'It could be one of us next.'

Mann hastily considered the implications, and there were none that had a favourable outcome. If they killed Gregor, they would be severing all ties with Nikolai Levchenko. That meant they would have no further need for a hostage. He had to convince them that it was a bad idea.

'I'm not from Russia,' he told them, 'but even I know of Levchenko's reputation. What do you think he'll do if the man he just rescued from prison is found dead and the other inmates are gone? He'll come for you, that's what he'll do. You, your families, your neighbours. He's not gonna stop until you're all dead, and from what I've heard, he won't kill you straight away. It'll take days, maybe even weeks.' Mann gave them a second to think about it, then added, 'The alternative is to be patient, do as Gregor says. When this is all over, maybe Nikki will offer you jobs. You'll be protected, untouchable.'

The two Russians looked at each other, then Sacha fixed his eyes on Mann. 'Why do you care?'

Because I don't want you to shoot me in the face, dumbass. Mann knew he was dealing with people of limited intelligence, so he kept it as simple as possible. 'I think we should stick together. If the police do show, we'd have a better chance of survival, with or without a security team to back us up. If you go on your own, you'll have the police *and* Nikki on your back. It would be better to have Nikki on your side. I mean, you kill Gregor, then what? You've got no transport, no money, just the clothes you're wearing and a gun. How far will that get you? Nikki will provide shelter, food, everything you need. It's a bit spartan at the moment, but we won't be here forever. Things will improve, I'm sure of it.'

'Until the next time Gregor gets pissed and blows us away,' Mikhail said.

Yerik walked over to the group, his weapon slung over his shoulder. 'What's going on?'

'Nothing,' Mann said before the others could react. 'We were just saying it would be best to do as Gregor says. He'll only want guard duty tonight because we have reinforcements coming tomorrow. Plus, we'll soon be moving on, and maybe Nikki can help get us all out of the country. Isn't that right?' Mann looked at Sacha and Mikhail, hoping they'd taken it all in.

'Yeah,' Sacha said. He didn't look pleased with the arrangement, but at least it gave Mann a reprieve.

'Come on,' Mann said to him. 'Let's find some shovels and get this done. I wanna sleep.'

He walked towards the workmen's hut, and a moment later, Mikhail followed.

* * *

It took over two hours to dig a hole deep enough in the frozen ground to bury Konstantin, and by the time he was done, Mann really was ready to sleep. He lay on his mattress and allowed Gregor to apply the handcuffs once more, then turned and faced the wall.

Rather than close both eyes, though, he kept one open to preserve his night vision. Gregor didn't want any lights on in the house, so the room was pitch black.

It was an hour before Mann heard the first snore. He turned over to face the others, pretending to be asleep, but his eyes were open a fraction. He doubted Gregor or Sacha would be able to see him in enough detail to realise he was awake, but he wasn't taking any chances.

Sacha had swapped with Mikhail, and Gregor had warned him that he was expected to go out again in four hours to relieve Yerik, who had drawn the short straw and got double stag duty. Sacha had hit the sack immediately, and it was his snores that Mann could hear. There was nothing to indicate that Gregor was also asleep, but after watching his motionless body for a few minutes, Mann decided it was time to act.

He slowly reached down to his ankle and took the fountain pen from inside his sock. He unscrewed the top, then inserted the nib into the keyhole of the cuffs, all the while keeping his eyes on the two sleeping forms. The faint scratching sound seemed horrendously loud to Mann, like someone running their fingernails down a chalkboard, but neither of the Russians stirred.

After a couple of minutes of blind fiddling, Mann heard the satisfying click as the lock relented. He gently removed the restraint, placing the loose end silently on the floor.

Gregor was facing away from him, while Mikhail was lying on his back, his mouth open as he continued his nocturnal chorus. Mann could make out the faint outline of Mikhail's AK-74 resting against the wall with the barrel pointing at the ceiling. Gregor's weapons were nowhere in sight, so Mann assumed they must be close to him.

That made up his mind: he would take the bear first. If he prioritised Mikhail and it went noisy, Gregor would be ready to shoot in a heartbeat. This way, he'd have at least ten seconds before Mikhail was in a position to pose a threat.

Mann had thought long and hard about how to kill Gregor, and he'd decided to use the pen. Several swift jabs in the neck, puncturing his carotid artery. Alternatively, he could stab him in the eye. Either way, Gregor would be too caught up in his injury to mount a defence, leaving him to take out Mikhail.

Mann forced himself to calm his breathing. Gregor was ten feet away, under the fireplace. Mikhail lay in the far corner of the room, twelve feet from the bear. Mann slipped his boots on and hastily tied them, then held the pen in an overhand grip.

The way Gregor was lying, his neck offered the best chance of a quick kill. Mann trod carefully towards the bear, silently urging the big man not to wake. He got to within three feet when disaster struck.

Mann's right foot connected with a grey mug that Gregor had used to drink his coffee. The spoon inside tinkled onto the bare concrete and chimed a little dance as the cup skittered across the floor. Gregor spun to face Mann, and his hands immediately went for a weapon.

With the element of surprise shattered, Mann lunged for the bear. He aimed for Gregor's eyes, but an arm encased in plaster blocked the attack. Gregor's leg shot out, catching Mann on the shin, and even with bare feet the Russian's strike brought a wave of pain. Mann fought through it and leaped onto Gregor's back as he reached for his AK-74, stabbing him repeatedly in the shoulder to prevent him picking up the weapon.

It worked. Gregor abandoned the rifle, but whipped his body around, throwing Mann across the floor.

Mann hit the wall hard, and something clattered across his chest. He grabbed the object and realised it was Mikhail's rifle, just as Gregor rose and reached into his waistband for his pistol.

Please be loaded.

The magazine was in place, so Mann flicked off the safety, pulled back on the charging handle and aimed at Gregor's chest. He squeezed the trigger just as something clattered into the side of his head, and the rounds went wide.

Mann had forgotten about Mikhail. He shook his head to clear it as another foot flew towards his face. Mann blocked it with the barrel of the AK, then jabbed the stock into Mikhail's groin. That took him out of the fight long enough for Mann to focus on Gregor, but when he swung the rifle back round the big man was moving. In the darkness, Mann could see the outline of a pistol in his hand, and the barrel was turning his way.

Mann rolled twice, then got to his knee and fired a three-second burst at Gregor just as a bullet flew past his own head, so close he could feel it. Mann fired again, and he heard a grunt as Gregor spun and collapsed.

Mann got to his feet and quickly closed on Gregor, placing his foot on the Russian's gun hand. So far, things hadn't gone as Mann had envisaged, but there was one part of his plan that was immutable: he couldn't take any prisoners. He pointed the rifle at Gregor's head and pulled the trigger, then turned and took Mikhail out of the equation.

There were two left, and Mann manoeuvred himself so that he had a bead on the front entrance. He'd expected to see Sacha and Yerik before now, but they clearly weren't keen on entering the house during a firefight. Now that the shooting had stopped, he expected to see them at any moment.

They didn't disappoint him.

The moment the plastic covering the doorway was brushed aside, Mann fired a sustained burst at it. He heard a body fall and screams of pain, but he couldn't be sure he'd hit both of them. Mann backpedalled to Gregor's body, slung the rifle over his shoulder and picked up the pistol. He quickly checked that there was a round in the chamber, then moved back towards the front door. He heard someone crying out in pain.

Mann pressed himself against the wall and reached over to grab the plastic sheeting. He ripped it free, the sheet fluttering to the ground, but there were no gunshots. Mann crouched and stuck his head around the frame to see Yerik lying on the ground, his shirt bloodstained from two hits in the stomach.

There was no sign of Sacha, but the remaining Russian announced his presence by sending a burst of lead into the frame just above Mann's head. Had he aimed for centre mass, Mann would have been riddled with bullets, but thankfully Sacha had gone for the more difficult head shot.

Mann knew he must have come in the back way rather than both men taking the obvious route into the house. That told him Sacha wasn't to be underestimated.

Before Sacha could adjust his aim, Mann spun, fired three rounds in his direction and ran into a side room. Bullets chased him as he threw himself through the large doorway. The room had another entrance, one that led to the kitchen, but that was where Sacha had come from.

Mann was stuck in an empty room, and he had to cover both entrances as he had no idea which one Sacha was going to come through. The only thing in his favour was the darkness. He transferred the pistol to his left hand and slowly shook the AK-74 from his shoulder, holding it in his right. He pointed one at each doorway and backed up against a wall so that the doorway he'd just come through was along the wall to his right. He crouched down with one leg in front of the other, ready to push away at the first sign of his enemy.

He didn't have to wait long. Sacha burst through the entrance Mann had used, his rifle blazing as he sprayed bullets at chest height. Mann, safely out of the line of fire, squeezed the trigger on his AK.

The firing pin fell on an empty chamber.

Unfazed, he brought the pistol around and got Sacha in his sights just as the Russian's gun ran dry. Mann aimed at the Russian's chest and fired.

His left-handed aim was slightly off. Sacha grunted and spun ninety degrees, hit in the shoulder. Mann fired again, but when he squeezed the trigger all he got was a devastating *click*.

Sacha wasted no time. He flipped his rifle end over end and caught it by the barrel, then swung it like a baseball bat at Mann's head. Mann pushed away from the wall and rolled, avoiding the blow. He abandoned the pistol and switched his grip on the AK-74 so that it was the same as Sacha's. Mann leapt to his feet and swung the gun at Sacha's head, but the Russian's weapon blocked the strike. He swung again, but Sacha ducked the blow and smashed the stock of his gun into Mann's knee. Mann's leg gave way and he collapsed onto one knee, just as Sacha came back for more. The Russian jabbed the rifle at Mann's head, but this time he was able to dodge it. He rolled and swept Sacha's legs from underneath him, and when the stocky body hit the floor, Mann was on him instantly. He sat astride Sacha's big chest and pushed the side of the rifle into the Russian's throat. Mann pressed down with all his weight, ignoring Sacha's attempts to strike out at him. Those efforts became increasingly feeble, and eventually Sacha gave up, his body going limp. Mann didn't relent. If the roles were reversed, he might have played dead, waiting for the moment to counter, so for the next minute he kept pressing the cold steel against Sacha's throat.

When he finally released the pressure, there was no response from the Russian. Mann stood and kicked him in the ribs, but there was no grunt, no cry of pain. In fact, the only sound Mann could hear was that of Yerik, who was still clinging on to life. Mann went through to the living room, found a spare magazine for the AK-74 and switched it for his empty one. He went outside and ended Yerik's misery.

With one hurdle overcome, it was time to move on to the next one. He had to contact home and let them know where he was. He took the phone from Gregor's pocket, relieved to see it hadn't been damaged during the fight. He was also glad to see the bear hadn't bothered with a PIN code to unlock it.

Mann opened the app store and downloaded What3Words. Once it installed, he checked his current location.

///rookery.corroding.voltages

That wasn't very helpful. What he was looking for was a word that only he and Cooper would know, something personal that couldn't be guessed by the average crossword lover.

Mann moved a few paces and checked again.

///forest.mustiness.courtroom

He'd never spent time in a courtroom, nor shared any experiences with Cooper in a forest. Mann was beginning to think this wasn't such a good idea. He moved from room to room, letting the app update. Each time he found the three words were too obscure or had no relevance whatsoever. After doing a circuit of the ground floor he was almost back where he started. The app refreshed once more.

///laundry.introducing.fishbowl

It was the first word that caught his attention. While it wasn't something Cooper would know, he could easily find the answer. For any eavesdroppers, it could be one of a thousand things. The second word would take some thinking about, but the third was something Cooper would pick up on immediately.

Mann spent a couple of minutes thinking about how to phrase it, then dialled Cooper's number from memory.

Chapter 28

Cooper checked his pockets one last time. Passport, phone, wallet, keys. Satisfied that he had everything he needed, he locked the door to his apartment and put his bag in the boot of his car.

It had been more than half a day since Horton had spoken to the prime minister, and as usual things weren't moving swiftly. Cooper knew that was entirely down to the PM. If it had been up to the chief, he'd be in Moscow by now, hitching a ride on a charter plane. As it was, he had booked onto the next available commercial flight, which would be leaving just after six in the morning.

This was where shit started to get real. The FSB would be on high alert for anyone arriving from the UK, and Cooper could expect to pick up a tail the moment he arrived. That didn't worry him. He was trained for this, and though he might be a little ring rusty, he was confident that his tradecraft was up to scratch.

Even if it wasn't, he was going anyway. Alex needed his help, and he wasn't going to let him down.

Cooper drove to Heathrow, and two hours after leaving his flat he was sitting in the airport lounge, waiting to board his flight.

He plugged his new phone into a portable charger. Horton had instructed him to keep his mobile on at all times, just in case they had to update him on any real-time developments. Cooper had thought that risky, especially as Mann had called him on that number in the past. If the FSB had access to Mann's phone contacts and were monitoring all the numbers, his rescue mission would be the shortest in history. It was eventually decided that Cooper would get a new, unregistered phone for contact with the office, and only turn his old phone on for seconds at a time to check for messages from Mann.

Cooper was just about to turn his regular mobile off when it rang. When he saw that the number began with +7—a Russian number—his heart began to beat faster. Was this the Russians pre-emptively warning him not to bother turning up? There was only one way to find out.

'Hello?' he said after swiping to connect the call.

'It's me,' a familiar voice said. 'I need an out.'

Cooper rose from his seat and wandered into an area where he couldn't be overheard. The first thing he had to establish was whether Mann was free, or had been coerced into making the call. 'What's the weather like there?' he asked.

'Better than expected,' Mann replied.

Cooper was satisfied that his friend wasn't under duress. If Mann had described the weather—rainy, windy, cold—it would have been a red flag. 'Where are you?'

'Three words will cover it,' Mann said. 'The first is something her indoors does every Thursday without fail.

The second is by the tribute act we saw in Dublin three years ago. It's your birth month, git, and it precedes Maisie. The third is the incongruous item in Big H's office. Got that?'

Cooper was sure he had, and as a back-up, the call recorder on his phone would store a record of the conversation. 'Yeah, I got it.'

'I'll be moving soon. New location will be due east, and the number of klicks is the house number of your old flat in Hammersmith. From there, the same number of klicks north.'

That was easy. Cooper's old house number was five.

'I'll put my phone in airplane mode so it can't be tracked,' Mann said. 'I'll turn it on for a few seconds at the top of every even hour, so if you have anything to tell me, send a text message. I'll be in place for 48 hours, then I have to move.'

'No worries. Someone will be with you well before then. Take care, mate.' He didn't want to say he was on his way, just in case someone—specifically, someone Russian—was eavesdropping on the call.

The phone went dead in Cooper's hand. He opened the call recorder, then dialled Horton's number on his new phone. When the chief answered, Cooper explained what had just happened and played the entire conversation for his boss.

'I think he's using What3Words,' Cooper said when it ended. 'It's an app that pinpoints your location to within a few yards.'

'I'm familiar with it,' Horton said. 'Do you know the answers to his three clues?'

'Not the first one, but I'm gonna call Debra in a moment. The second one I'll have to look up. We saw a Gilbert

O'Sullivan tribute artist in Dublin, so it must be something to do with that.'

'You were born in January, weren't you?'

'I was,' Cooper said. 'I'm surprised you remembered.'

'I didn't, but I know my seventies music. Gilbert O'Sullivan had a hit with January Git. The word preceding Maisie is *introducing*.'

'That's two we have, then,' Cooper said. 'The last one, the incongruous item in your office, is the fishtank.'

'So speak to Debra and get the first one. Let me know where he is and we'll work up an exfil strategy.'

Horton signed off, and Cooper dialled Debra Mann's number. It was early, but he was sure she wouldn't mind if it meant her husband would be home soon.

She sounded sleepy when she answered.

'Hi,' Cooper said. 'Did I wake you?'

'Yes,' Debra replied, not attempting to hide her annoyance.

'Sorry, but I need to ask you something.'

'Roland, it's half five in the morning!'

'I know, but this is important.'

Debra sighed. 'Go on,' she said.

'What do you do every Thursday, without fail?'

'Are you serious? Because I don't find it—'

'—I'm deadly serious,' Cooper broke in. 'I really need to know. Trust me, I wouldn't call you at this hour if it wasn't important.'

Cooper heard a table lamp click on. 'Every Thursday? I wash clothes.'

'Wash clothes?'

'Yeah. I do my laundry.'

'Just a second.'

Cooper opened What3Words and entered ///laundry.introducing.fishtank. 'That can't be it. That places him in the middle of the Bering Strait.'

'What the hell are you talking about? What is this nonsense?'

Cooper knew he'd have to come clean if he wanted her co-operation. 'I just got a call from Alex. He managed to escape from prison, but now he needs help getting out of the country. He gave me clues to his whereabouts, and one of them was something you do every Thursday, but that doesn't seem to be the right answer.'

'Alex is free? When did this happen?'

The plane started boarding, and Cooper knew he didn't have time to explain it all to her. 'I'll tell you later, I promise, but right now I need to know what else you do on Thursdays.'

'Nothing,' she insisted. 'Whenever Alex asks if I want to go out or host a dinner party, I tell him not to arrange it for a Thursday because that's my laundry day. I like to get it all done before the weekend.'

'Then one of the other clues must be wrong,' Cooper mumbled aloud.

'What were they?' Debra asked.

'One was a Gilbert O'Sullivan song, and Horton got that one. The last was the item in Horton's office that looks out of place.'

'That'll probably be his fishbowl,' Debra said. 'Alex told me about that. Said it was a strange thing for the head of MI6 to have on a sideboard.'

Fishbowl, not fishtank. Cooper entered ///laundry.introducing.fishbowl. The app changed location, and when he zoomed out he saw that it was

219

showing a point just off a highway. When he enlarged the area even more, he saw Moscow appear in the bottom left corner of the screen.

'That's it!' he smiled. 'Debra, thank you so much. I'll—'

'—Where is he?'

'What? Oh, he's just outside Moscow.'

'Where exactly?' she pressed. 'A mile outside? A hundred miles?' The phone went quiet before she added, 'I need to know if he's close to friendlies, Roland.'

He checked the app. 'It's about thirty-five miles as the crow flies. As for friendlies, I'm on my way to meet him now. I'll have him home before you know it.'

'Then do me a favour, stay in touch. I want to know as soon as he's in safe hands.'

'Will do,' Cooper promised.

Debra thanked him and hung up. Cooper dialled Horton back and gave him the location. 'Remember, that's where he is now. By the time I get there, he'll be five kilometres east and five north. I checked, and there's a road there. With any luck, it'll just be a case of driving past, picking him up and finding our way to a friendly border.'

'Let's hope,' Horton said.

The airline crew put out a last call for passengers, and Cooper told his boss that he had to go.

'Stay safe over there,' the chief said. 'I'll brief the team at this end.'

* * *

Debra Mann swung her legs out of the bed and cursed. How many times did she have to tip off the Russians before they got their act together and finished off her husband?

When Roland had paid her that first visit to tell her that Alex had been captured, she'd been genuinely upset. Not because of her husband's predicament, but because the FSB had let him live. Things had improved when she'd learned that Alex wouldn't be exchanged for a Russian prisoner, but she needed finality. While there was even the smallest chance that her cheating bastard of a husband could make it home, she wouldn't be free of him. He'd denied doing anything wrong, of course, but she wasn't stupid. No man could spend so much time around beautiful women without trying something, especially when he was a thousand miles from home.

She could have filed for divorce, sure, but she wanted him to suffer. Not only was he sleeping around, but he was lying about it, too. If he'd just admit it, she could live with that and move on.

No. This was the only way. Get rid of him for good, take the insurance money, start a new life.

There was still work to do, though. Alex might have broken out of prison, but he was still in Russia. She had to make sure he didn't leave.

Debra went to her wardrobe and took the old suitcase from the top shelf. Inside was the black wig she'd used to visit the Russian Embassy a year earlier.

Time to use it again.

Chapter 29

The smell hit Sergei Belyakov the moment he walked into the café, and the aroma of food fried in three-day-old fat did nothing for his appetite. However, he wasn't here to partake of Ealing's culinary delights. He went to the counter and ordered a coffee in a takeaway cup, then looked for the man he was supposed to meet.

He was sitting at a table facing the entrance, sipping a hot drink. Next to him on the table was a well-thumbed copy of an obscure novel, a signal that they were free to make the exchange. If the man had been reading it, it would mean he'd been followed and that Belyakov should just walk away.

Belyakov walked to the table and gestured to the empty seat opposite. The man shrugged and gave a *help yourself* gesture. Belyakov sat, saying nothing. He took out his phone and started reading from a website. From the corner of his eye, he saw the man opposite reach under the table, then pick up his book and leave.

Once he was out the door, Belyakov swapped seats, sitting where his contact had just been. He reached under the table and his fingers came across the envelope that had been stuck there using double-sided tape. He tugged it free and put it in his inside pocket, then drank a little more of his coffee as he pretended to be interested in a news article. His mind was elsewhere, though. He knew that the envelope would contain a key and the address of the lock up garage where he could find the delivery vehicles.

After ten minutes, Belyakov left the café and walked a circuitous route back to the hire car that he'd left in an underground car park. He saw no sign of a tail, and when he got in the vehicle, he opened the envelope and checked the contents.

The lock up garage was across town, in Seven Kings. It took Belyakov an hour to get there, and he backed the car up to the garage door before opening the unit. Inside he saw just four plain brown cardboard boxes. Belyakov reversed the car inside, locked the garage door, then switched a light on. A fluorescent tube on the ceiling buzzed and hummed into life.

Belyakov opened the first of the boxes. Inside was his Makarov pistol, which had been brought into the country via diplomatic pouch. There was also a drone, the same model as he'd practised with in Russia. He took it out and turned it over, pleased to see that the delivery module was already in place. He unclipped it, a small plastic unit the size and shape of a cigarette packet, and put it in his pocket. In the bottom of the box was a phone. Belyakov woke it up and went to the apps. One of them was called Travel Guide. He opened it and clicked on Locations, and it displayed a list of four places in London. Belyakov clicked the first of them and a map appeared, showing a red pin in a side street three hundred yards from Nelson's Column. From that marker, a line snaked across to Trafalgar Square, halfway down Whitehall, then across to the River Thames. That was where the drone would discard the delivery module before flying on another half mile and ditching in the river.

Belyakov checked the other three locations and saw that they all had their routes pre-programmed. He removed the delivery modules from the other three drones, then locked the garage and drove back to his hotel.

All he had to do now was fill the small boxes with the items he'd brought with him from Moscow, re-attach them to the drones, then release them at the precise location. It was okay to be out by a few metres, he knew, but he'd been assured that a parking space would be waiting for him. He just had to set the drones on their way, then drive away.

The machines would follow their allotted flight paths, dispensing death as they went.

Chapter 30

Maksim Kuznetsov slammed the phone down and glared at Gurin. Why he'd listened to this young idiot was a mystery.

'They weren't there,' the second-in-command of the FSB said. 'I just sent twelve heavily-armed men in, and they almost frightened an old cleaning woman to death!'

Gurin looked terrified, and Kuznetsov did nothing to put him at ease. Instead, he walked over to the map that was pinned to the office wall and put a big cross through the albino's house in St Petersburg. He stood back and surveyed the remaining properties, all dotted around the capital. Some of them were a stone's throw from where he stood, and Gregor Belsky could be hiding in any of them.

Or none of them.

Perhaps Levchenko had foreseen this and found somewhere else for the prisoners to lie low. A building owned by a friend or acquaintance, someone unconnected to the mobster.

Kuznetsov shook that thought away as unlikely. The fewer people who knew about the escapees, the better. The albino would no doubt see things the same way. One didn't avoid arrest for so long by taking unnecessary risks.

Kuznetsov turned to see Gurin gazing at the wall map. The analyst still looked nervous, but there was a new intensity in his stare.

'What is it?'

Gurin swallowed.

'Spit it out, man!'

'I thought…I thought they would want to steer clear of Moscow, which is why I suggested St Petersburg. If that was wrong, then perhaps here.' Gurin walked to the map and pointed at a numbered pin representing one of Levchenko's houses. It was northeast of the capital.

Kuznetsov looked at the corresponding details for property number thirty-two.

'Idiot! It hasn't been built yet!'

'Actually, it just hasn't been completed yet.' Gurin returned to the desk and retrieved a photograph. 'I checked the satellite images, just in case it was a viable option and we had to send our people in. Better to know the landscape beforehand.'

Kuznetsov waived away the explanation. 'Just get to the point.'

Gurin swallowed again. 'Yes, sir. It seems that the main structure of the house has been finished. It's by no means complete but would certainly be habitable. All it would need is a generator, some bottled water and a supply of food. They could live there for weeks.'

Kuznetsov took the satellite photo from the analyst and studied it. The roof looked to be in place, so there was a chance Gurin was right. Then again, his record so far was not exactly exemplary.

'You're forgetting one thing,' he said. 'If they're still building it, the workers would notice six escaped prisoners living inside.'

'Yes, I thought that, too, but if you look at the timestamp on the photograph, it's two in the afternoon yesterday. Surely there would be some activity, but there's no sign of anyone in the picture. No vehicles, nothing.'

Kuznetsov looked again and saw that Gurin was right. It appeared the builders were no longer there.

'Get on to the planning department for that district and find out which company submitted the plans, then call them and ask why work has stopped.'

Gurin scurried off to do his bidding, and Kuznetsov called over another subordinate and told him to make fresh coffee. The drink arrived just as Gurin returned.

'There was a problem with an amendment to the application and work was halted until it can be sorted out,' Gurin said. 'There's been no one on site for the last ten days, but they did leave some equipment there, including a generator.'

It appeared to be the perfect place for Belsky to hide out, but Kuznetsov wanted further proof. He sat down at his computer and brought up the live satellite feed, then manipulated the image to focus on the dacha. He picked up the photo and compared it to the picture on the screen. They appeared identical.

'There,' Gurin said, standing over Kuznetsov and pointing to the monitor. 'A patch of earth has been disturbed.'

Kuznetsov looked from the printout to the screen and saw that the analyst was right. An area the size of a small car appeared a different colour to its surroundings. It was enough to convince him that someone had been there overnight.

Kuznetsov got on the phone to Colonel Roman Torbinski, the head of Alpha Group, and ordered him to send a team of twelve to the unbuilt dacha immediately. Although they shared the same rank, Kuznetsov's position within the FSB gave him all the authority he needed.

'Do we have confirmation that Belsky is there?'

'No,' Kuznetsov admitted, 'but it's the most likely place. If you find anyone there, wait for me to arrive before you go in.'

His boss, Dmitri Gudkov, wasn't pleased that Belsky and the Englishman had been at large for so long. If he was present when they were captured, it would go some way to restoring his good standing.

'Understood. I'll have a team on target in ninety minutes.'

Kuznetsov put the phone down. If Alpha Group stuck to that schedule, he'd have a positive ID by two o'clock.

You'd better be there, Belsky.

The more he thought about it, the more he was convinced he had the right place. He'd put surveillance on all of Levchenko's other properties and there had been no sign of Belsky or the others so far. The unfinished dacha was the only one he'd discounted.

'Get some food in here!' Kuznetsov bellowed, and one of his junior officers walked hastily out of the room to carry out his orders.

As he waited for his lunch to arrive, Kuznetsov looked at his available manpower. Most of his people were concentrated in Moscow, so it wouldn't take them long to get to the dacha if he needed them. Not that Kuznetsov imagined he would. Alpha Group were the best of the best, and a team of twelve was more than enough to overwhelm a few escaped convicts.

A phone rang. A soldier answered it, then held the receiver out. 'Colonel!'

Kuznetsov took the phone and identified himself.

'Good afternoon, Colonel. This is Kirov, London station. I understand you're heading up the search for the spy, Alex Mann.'

'I am.'

'Then I have something for you. Last year a woman came to the embassy and told us about Mann—'

'—I know that!' Kuznetsov interrupted.

'If you'd permit me to finish,' the station chief said. 'The same woman came in this morning with further information.'

That got Kuznetsov's attention. 'I'm listening.'

'She said he was at a place thirty-five miles north of central Moscow, give or take.'

Kuznetsov walked over to the map and used a ruler to measure the distance to the dacha. It was out by one mile. That was close enough for him. He held the phone to his chest. 'Gurin! Bring my car around!' He put the phone back to his ear. 'Did she say anything else?' he asked.

'Yes. Someone is flying out to meet Mann. Someone by the name of Roland Cooper.'

The name didn't ring any bells, but he wrote it down on a Post-It note. 'What else?'

'That's all she said.'

'Have you identified her?' Kuznetsov asked.

'I had someone tail her. We'll find out soon enough.'

Kuznetsov thanked him and ended the call.

'Sir,' Gurin said, 'your car is waiting.'

229

Kuznetsov handed him the note. 'This man is arriving on a flight from England today. I want him tailed.'

'Yes, sir.'

The colonel put his jacket on. 'Don't lose him, or else.'

He pushed open the door, clattering into the junior officer carrying a tray of sandwiches. The food flew in the air, but Kuznetsov barely broke stride. Down at the car, he instructed his driver to head north on the M-8. He was on his phone the moment he strapped himself in.

'Torbinski, I have confirmation that Belsky is there. I want you to hold your men back until I arrive. I'll be with you shortly.'

Chapter 31

What Gurin thought would be a straightforward task was proving to be a nightmare. He'd searched all incoming flight manifests for the name Roland Cooper, only to be told by the computer that no such passenger existed. He'd thought Cooper might be on a later flight, but nothing coming out of the UK had him listed as being on board.

Cooper had to be using an alias.

Gurin reached for the phone to call Kuznetsov, then hesitated. If he went running to the boss the moment things got a little difficult, any chance of career progression would be over before it had begun. No, he had to work through it himself.

Think. Think!

If Cooper was able to get a new identity at such short notice, he must be with the security service. At the very least, he was working for the British government in some capacity. If that was the case, his details might be in the FSB database.

He logged in and did a search.

Nothing.

Gurin cursed. How the hell was he supposed to tail someone when it could be one of hundreds of passengers arriving from London? He slumped in his chair and closed down the database window. He was left looking at the passenger manifest for the 6:05 flight from Heathrow.

Well, it won't be you, he said to himself, looking at the name of the first passenger. *Irina Grigorieva. You couldn't get more female and Russian.*

He put his head in his hands and closed his eyes, wondering how to phrase the call to Kuznetsov. It would earn him an earful at the very least. Given the colonel's current mood, he'd be lucky to get a transfer to Siberia. If he couldn't find the Englishman who would be…

Gurin opened his eyes, the answer obvious now. He looked at the manifest once more. At the top it showed the number of male and female passengers. There were three hundred and forty in total, and just under two hundred women could be discounted immediately. After taking off the infants and children, it came down to a hundred and twenty males.

Would he be travelling on a Russian passport? Gurin thought it unlikely. For the last ten years they had been biometric, and it was unlikely that the British could gain access to the database to insert a forgery. No, he could be travelling under a Western name. He scanned the list and found over thirty male passengers that fit the bill.

It's still too many!

He pored over the document, hoping to see something in the data. There was the name, the class of seat, the date the ticket was purchased, the—

Gurin's eyes flicked back to the date column. Cooper wouldn't have purchased his ticket weeks or months in advance. It would have been after the prison break. He looked for seats booked in the last forty-eight hours and found just one.

John Morgan.

Gurin looked at the time, then checked the flight details. The plane had landed ten minutes ago, so there wasn't much time to get things moving. He checked the duty roster for the team assigned to the airport. They always had at least four men on station throughout the day, and when he saw who was on duty, he called the team leader.

'A passenger named John Morgan just arrived on the London flight. Colonel Kuznetsov wants him followed. It's imperative that you don't lose him.'

'Send me a photo.'

'We don't have one,' Gurin told him. 'We only got news of this a few moments ago.'

'What do you have?' the voice asked. 'Is he trouble? Is he here to kill, to steal, what?'

'He's apparently here to help an escaped convict, that's all we know so far,' Gurin admitted.

'No problem. We'll handle it.'

Gurin hung up and called the colonel. 'There were no passengers by the name Roland Cooper, but there was one called John Morgan who booked his ticket late last night. He must be using an alias.'

'Naturally,' Kuznetsov said. 'Have someone tail him.'

'Already in motion, sir.'

'Good. Tell them to keep me updated.'

* * *

Sergeant Max Vasiliev ended the call and got on the radio to his number two, Boris Litvin. 'Head over to the car rental desks and find out if a John Morgan has booked anything. If he has, I want a tracker installed.'

'Acknowledged.'

Vasiliev had been in the game for several years, and calls like this were not uncommon. Usually, he received advance notice when a person of interest was about to land, with a full biography, threat assessment, and most importantly, photographs to identify the target. Sometimes, though, requests came in on the fly, and he'd long ago settled on a strategy for dealing with them.

With the rental cars covered, Vasiliev went to see the head of immigration. He knocked and entered Roman Mamayev's office, then told the fat man behind the desk that he needed to identify an incoming passenger.

Mamayev took the name and entered it onto a database that would show an alert to all immigration staff manning the cubicles. The moment John Morgan handed over his passport, it would take just the press of a button to send confirmation to the FSB control room. Vasiliev would be watching the monitors waiting to see which desk raised the silent alarm and he'd know which suspect to follow. Seconds later, so would the rest of his team.

'That's done,' Mamayev said. 'Who is it this time?'

'No idea,' Vasiliev admitted, and even if he knew, he wouldn't share the details with a man like Mamayev.

Vasiliev left and returned to his own office just as the queues began to form at passport control. He looked at the lines of people on his monitors, wondering which one was the target. He usually had a good eye for these things. A few of the passengers looked promising, but on closer inspection he discounted them for various reasons. Someone on a rescue mission would be young and fit.

Anyone over fifty was out of the frame, as was anyone carrying extra baggage around the waist.

He was still looking for the likely John Morgan when the screen flashed his name for cubicle four. Vasiliev was surprised to see that it was one of the people he'd easily discounted. The man had a hideous scar down one side of his face which made him stand out. Not a good attribute for a spy.

Vasiliev took a screenshot of Morgan and sent it to the messenger group in the app used by his team, then contacted Litvin.

'Did he hire a car?'

'Yes, a BMW. The tracker is in place and showing a good signal.'

'Understood. Meet me out front in five.'

Vasiliev contacted the other two members of his team and told them to hold the fort while he and Litvin were away.

He used the cameras to follow John Morgan through the airport. When he arrived at the car rental desk, Vasiliev left his office and walked to the exit of the arrivals lounge.

'He's on his way to the car,' he told the stocky Litvin, who handed him a tablet device. Vasiliev noted their current location in green and a red spot representing the BMW.

Once the red marker started to move, Vasiliev contacted headquarters and let them know he was in pursuit, and that they should assign another two-man team to the airport on a temporary basis.

'Let him get a mile ahead,' he said to Litvin. 'The tracker will do the work.'

* * *

The moment Roland Cooper stepped off the British Airways flight, he started looking for anyone who might be FSB. He didn't expect them to arrest him, but if they knew he was here—and more importantly, *why* he was here— they'd want to tail him at the very least. As he queued at immigration he looked around, trying to appear bored, but no one caught his eye. When it was his turn, he handed over his John Morgan passport. He thought it better to travel under an alias. Once the checks were complete, he retrieved his small suitcase from baggage collection and made his way to the car rental desk. He'd booked a BMW in advance, something that would get him out of a fix quickly if necessary.

After filling out several forms and taking insurance, Cooper put his luggage on the back seat and drove to the nearest petrol station, where he filled the car's tank. He'd already scoped out the area around the rendezvous point and there was another station within ten miles. He would top up again before collecting Mann and making his way to Latvia. Once across the border, they should be safe.

It was just before two in the afternoon local time when he joined the road that circled Moscow. He would leave it when he reached the exit for the M-8, then it was a straight road most of the way. Alex would be waiting just after the exit for Loza.

* * *

After the BMW pulled out of the petrol station and continued east on the MKAD, the road that ran around the capital, Vasiliev called the man who'd set the mission in motion.

'We're on Morgan's tail. What's the objective?' Vasiliev asked.

'He's going to meet an escaped prisoner. We want to catch him in the act.'

'Do you know his destination?'

Gurin read out the location of Levchenko's dacha, and Vasiliev marked it on his electronic map.

'He's approaching the exit,' Vasiliev said. 'He should turn off and head northeast on the M-8 any moment now. Wait one.' He watched the red dot take the appropriate exit. 'Yeah, he's heading in the right direction. How many units are involved?'

'Just yours,' Gurin said. 'Or two, if you count the colonel. He's on his way to the dacha as we speak. Alpha Group is also en route.'

'Is Kuznetsov on comms?' Vasiliev asked.

Gurin said he wasn't sure, and gave Vasiliev the colonel's cell phone number, just in case.

Vasiliev ended the call and dialled Kuznetsov's number. After introducing himself and giving a status update, he asked what his orders were.

'Just tail Morgan until he reaches the dacha. Once he's there, Alpha Group will move in and handle the situation.'

'Understood.'

When Kuznetsov hung up, Vasiliev held up the tablet for Litvin to see. 'That's where he's heading. Once he gets there, we inform Kuznetsov and he'll tell us when he's in custody.'

'That's it? We just tail him?'

'The colonel thought it appropriate to bring Alpha Group along,' Vasiliev told the driver. 'You really want to tackle suspects who warrant that response?'

Litvin looked straight ahead. 'I guess not.'

Vasiliev didn't think so. Alpha Group only went where no one else would go. They were armed to the teeth and well disciplined, with years of counter-terrorism training. Litvin and his service pistol didn't come close.

They followed Morgan's BMW onto the M-8, and Vasiliev chastised Litvin a couple of times for getting too close. With the tracker working properly, there was no reason to risk detection.

Thirty minutes after joining the motorway, Vasiliev called Kuznetsov.

* * *

Kuznetsov heard the approaching vehicle before he saw it. He was standing just beyond a bend half a mile along the track that led to the dacha. The ZIL Karatel—also known as The Punisher—was a sleek, armour-plated body on oversized wheels. The front windows were swept back to deflect head-on rounds, and gull-wing doors along the side allowed a swift exit for the personnel inside. It pulled up and Kuznetsov indicated for the driver to follow him. The ZIL followed as he walked to his own vehicle, which was parked out of sight in a clump of trees.

When they reached the hiding place, an officer got out of the ZIL's front passenger seat. 'Major Arshavin, sir,' the man said, saluting.

Kuznetsov returned it. 'They're down this road, maybe seven hundred metres. I took a quick look through the trees but saw nothing. They must be inside.'

The other members of Alpha Group were climbing out of the vehicle, and Arshavin called one of them over. He told the man to scout out the house and report back any sign of movement. Arshavin then opened the tablet computer he was carrying. It displayed a satellite image of the house and surrounding area.

'We're here,' the major said, pointing at the screen. 'As you can see, there's no cover for at least five hundred yards all around the building. If we go in during daylight hours, they'll see us coming. If they're armed, it could get messy.'

Kuznetsov had already foreseen this problem. 'You want to wait until dark, is that it?'

'That would be the preferred option,' Arshavin admitted.

'The other being…?'

'Set two snipers in the treeline and the rest of us mount up. Our vehicle can cover that ground in about twenty seconds. If anyone tries to engage us in that time, the snipers take them out.'

'Sounds like a good plan to me.'

'If you want them all dead, sir, it's a good plan. If you want any of them alive, we need to go with option one.'

Kuznetsov fixed Arshavin in a steely glare. 'I need them alive, but we can't wait until dark.'

In truth, he only needed Belsky and Mann alive. He didn't personally care if Mann lived or died, but the president wanted him in one piece. As for Belsky, if they could force a confession from him, Kuznetsov could finally take down that albino bastard Levchenko. It would have been nice if he could concoct charges and send him down for life, just as they had with Mann, but President Sokolov reserved judicial abuse for political opponents, not common criminals.

The major was the first to blink. 'I'll discuss it with my men,' he said. 'We'll find a way.'

'Good. I want to be moving in the next twenty minutes. In the meantime, another suspect is due to arrive shortly. Stop him before he gets to the house.'

'Dead or alive?' Arshavin asked.

'Alive. And do it quietly. I don't want to alert the others.'

He was determined to present both Mann and his rescuer to his boss, but more so to the president. Gudkov would step down at some point, and such a propaganda coup would clear the way for Kuznetsov to take over as head of the most powerful organisation in Russia. He was already next in line, but unless he came out of this shitstorm smelling of victory, taking the next rung on the ladder wasn't guaranteed.

Arshavin ran to the ZIL and barked instructions at the men standing around it. One of them took a stop stick from the rear of the futuristic-looking vehicle and the team ran to the road to take up their positions. Should any vehicles approach, they would throw the stop stick into its path and the spiked implement would shred the tyres.

Kuznetsov's phone rang.

'Yes.'

'He's about to reach the dacha,' Vasiliev said. 'Another mile and he'll be there.'

'Okay. Once he makes the turnoff, hang back. I'll call you if we need you.'

* * *

'It should be coming up on the left,' Vasiliev said to Litvin. 'Follow him when he makes the turn, then stop. Kuznetsov wants us to wait for his signal.'

Litvin just nodded, and Vasiliev watched as the marker approached the turning. Four hundred metres. Two hundred metres. One hundred.

Vasiliev tapped the screen, convinced something was wrong with it. The marker was continuing down the same road.

'Shit.'

He took out his phone and called Kuznetsov.

'We've got a problem.'

* * *

'What do you mean, he didn't take the turn?'

Kuznetsov gripped the phone as the obvious conclusion leaped to the front of his mind. Gurin had them following the wrong man!

'I don't know what else to say,' Vasiliev told him. 'He reached the turnoff for the dacha and just kept going.'

Kuznetsov swore and cut the call, then dialled Gurin's number.

'Sir, he should be nearing the dacha shortly,' the analyst said, his tone confident.

'He reached it and drove straight past it, you *idiot*! You had the men chasing the wrong passenger!'

'What? But I…I…it has to be him. He was the only one it could be.'

'Well, it wasn't. He drove straight past the house without stopping.'

The phone went quiet for a while, then Gurin found his voice. 'Maybe he missed the turn off. Or maybe—'

'—or maybe you fucked up! Find the real passenger. *Now!*'

Kuznetsov stabbed at the End Call symbol on the screen. Moments earlier he'd been imagining the praise he would receive from President Sokolov. Now, he wondered if he was about to swap his comfortable office for the gulag.

He strode over to Arshavin, who crouched behind a tree near the side of the road.

'Change of plan,' Kuznetsov said. 'Leave two men here in case he shows, but I want the rest of you to assault that house in the next ten minutes.' There was no point admitting to the major that his incompetent subordinates had been following the wrong man.

Arshavin nodded gravely and selected two soldiers to stay behind. The rest returned to the ZIL to work up an assault plan.

Kuznetsov walked to within ten metres of the treeline and stared out at the dacha. If Roland Cooper was already in the country, they would find him. Cooper wasn't here to stay, so he must have an exit plan for himself and Mann. Flights were out, which meant a land crossing.

He scrolled through the contacts list on his phone and found the number for the head of the border service. It ran under the FSB umbrella, which put it at Kuznetsov's disposal.

Kuznetsov hesitated. Cooper wouldn't head to the border until he had Mann, and the spy was holed up in the dacha that Alpha Group were about to storm. Should he lure Cooper in, or take Mann while he had the chance?

He decided to put Cooper on the back burner and deal with him once Mann was safely in custody. Hopefully in the next few hours they'd have a photograph to go with the name, which would make capturing Cooper a lot easier.

'We're ready to go,' Arshavin said.

Kuznetsov almost jumped. He spun, angry that the major had chosen to sneak up on him.

'Very well. And remember what I said. I want them alive.'

Arshavin responded with a salute and walked back to his team. A sniper walked past Kuznetsov and took up a position five metres closer to the treeline, hunkering down behind a log. Kuznetsov retreated in case the convicts inside the dacha decided to return fire on the soldier's position.

Thirty seconds passed, then Kuznetsov heard the ZIL's 730 horsepower engine roar into life. Moments later, Arshavin returned with two pairs of binoculars. He handed one to Kuznetsov just as the ZIL shot out of the trees, following the rough track to the house. Four black-clad men hung off the side of the speeding vehicle, their weapons ready to dispense death.

Kuznetsov expected gunfire to erupt from the building at any moment, but the ZIL powered on without meeting any resistance. It skidded to a halt ten metres from the dacha and the men clinging to the sides jumped off and ran to the front door. Another four men sprang from the ZIL and ran to the rear of the building. At the main entrance, one ripped the plastic sheeting off the front doorway and another immediately threw in a stun grenade. The moment it exploded, all four men rushed inside.

Kuznetsov watched the action unfold and was relieved to hear no gunfire. It sounded like the prisoners had surrendered without a fight.

Two minutes after the men of Alpha Group had rushed in, they casually strolled back out.

Alone.

'What the hell's going on?' Kuznetsov snapped at Arshavin.

The major got on the radio and asked the same question of the sergeant who had led the assault. When the reply came back, Arshavin grimaced before passing on the message to Kuznetsov.

'They're all dead.'

'Dead?' Kuznetsov barked. 'How? I heard no gunfire.'

'They've been dead for a while, at least eight hours.'

That made no sense. Why would the albino break them out of prison just to kill them? He had to see for himself. Perhaps the murder scene would offer some explanation.

Kuznetsov handed the binoculars back to Arshavin and jogged to the house. The major followed.

By the time they reached the dacha, Alpha Group had formed a perimeter, facing away from the building. Kuznetsov suspected it was because there was no threat from those inside, but whoever had killed them might still be in the area.

Kuznetsov strode past the elite troops and into the house. The stench was enough to confirm that the major had been correct: these bodies weren't fresh. He put a handkerchief over his mouth and began the process of counting and identifying the corpses.

The first he saw was the hulking figure of Gregor Belsky. On a mattress in the corner lay the body of Mikhail Berimov. Kuznetsov crossed the hallway and found two more. Yerik Asimov was lying at the end of a dried blood trail, and Kuznetsov followed it to the front door, where a dark patch showed where the man had originally fallen. Someone had dragged him inside the house and placed him next to Sacha Kokorin.

That left Konstantin Ignashevich and Alex Mann.

Kuznetsov instructed two men to climb the ladders to the upper levels and check to see if anyone was hiding up there. A couple of minutes later, the top floor was declared clear.

'We found what looks like a grave,' Arshavin said, appearing at Kuznetsov's shoulder.

'Show me.'

The major led him outside and pointed to a mound of disturbed earth.

'Is this the only one?' Kuznetsov asked.

'The only one we found.'

Of the six escaped prisoners, five were dead. But who made it out alive? Ignashevich or Mann? Only one way to find out.

'Dig it up,' he told Arshavin. 'I need to know if this is the British spy.'

A pair of shovels were conveniently resting against the side of the house, and the major instructed two of his men to pick them up and get to work.

A knot formed in his chest as he pictured Mann's face peering up at him with dead eyes. If the spy was under the soil, the president was not going to be happy. If it was Ignashevich…

The thought tailed off as he realised he already knew the answer. The British wouldn't send someone to the dacha unless they knew Mann was there, and the only person who could have told them was Mann himself.

Kuznetsov turned and took his phone from his pocket as he walked away from the grave.

'You aren't going to wait and see who it is?' Arshavin shouted after him.

'I already know,' Kuznetsov said. He called Vasiliev. 'Where's the car you were following?'

'Up ahead. It looks like it stopped at a gas station.'

'Keep on it. I'm sending more units to support you.'

Kuznetsov turned back to Arshavin. 'Leave that,' he said, pointing to the men with the shovels. 'I want everyone ready to move out in two minutes.'

Mann wouldn't be stupid enough to hang around a murder scene. He'd want to get as far away as possible, perhaps even over the border, but he could only do that if he had a vehicle. The fact that Cooper was in the area suggested Mann was on foot and planning to meet him.

Kuznetsov sensed the net closing in on the spy. All he had to do was follow Cooper and he'd lead them right to Mann.

He called Gurin.

'Send five more units to my location,' Kuznetsov said. All FSB cars had trackers installed, so there was no point wasting time telling Gurin where he was.

'Yes, sir. Immediately. And…about Cooper…'

'Don't worry, I'm sure you found the right man. He just surprised us, that's all. It looks like Mann is in this area and Cooper is going to pick him up. When he does, I'll be there to—'

Gunfire interrupted the call. It had come from the road leading to the dacha, where Arshavin had left two of his men.

Was it Mann? Kuznetsov wondered. *Was he stupid enough to take on Alpha Group on his own?*

He got the answer moments later as two black SUVs burst into view, powering towards the house. They rode side by side, and four men leaned out of the windows firing automatic rifles.

Kuznetsov threw himself to the ground behind an industrial-sized bag of gravel as Alpha Group responded. Weapons blazed from both sides, but from his hiding place Kuznetsov could only see Arshavin's men. Two of them took hits, and the SUVs kept coming.

Kuznetsov took out his service pistol. It felt tiny and useless against such heavy opposition, but it was all he had. He briefly considered running for one of the weapons dropped by the fallen Alpha Group members, but knew he'd be cut down before he got a chance to use it.

There was a sudden succession of loud thuds and the shriek of twisting metal. Kuznetsov risked a glance at the SUVs and saw one coming to rest after rolling several times. The body was battered, the occupants lifeless.

One more vehicle remained, though, and it sprinted onwards into a hail of bullets. The driver zig-zagged to make a harder target, but a volley pierced the windscreen and a large blood splatter confirmed the kill. The SUV rolled to a stop and the occupants got out, taking cover behind the open doors. It was four of them against the remaining six of Alpha Group, a mismatch if ever there was one.

One of the attackers went down screaming with a bullet to the leg. The moment he hit the ground, rounds pounded his exposed upper body, shredding his black leather jacket and turning his t-shirt crimson.

The remaining three put up a brave resistance, but the odds were never in their favour. Alpha Group had the advantages of cover, numbers and expertise.

While two from AG put down covering fire, the other four moved to the flanks to get a better angle on the attackers. One of the trio was cut down by the sniper in the trees, and as the incoming fire petered out, Kuznetsov looked around the gravel bag and saw that the remaining two had exhausted their ammunition. They threw down their weapons and raised their hands.

'Hold your fire!' Kuznetsov shouted, knowing Alpha Group's reputation for shooting first and not bothering with questions.

Arshavin repeated the order, and the scene descended into silence.

Half of Alpha Group rushed in and knocked the two men to the ground while the others covered them. The two men were aggressively frisked, then pulled up onto their knees.

Kuznetsov stood and walked towards the two prisoners. They were side by side, two metres apart, their hands clasped behind their heads.

'What are you doing here? Who sent you?'

They both looked at Kuznetsov, but neither spoke. He pointed his pistol at one of them.

'Was it Levchenko?'

Kuznetsov noticed a flicker of recognition when he mentioned the albino's name. It just confirmed his suspicion that Levchenko was behind the jail break. Why else would these men be here?

'So what are you, a security detail?'

The pair remained silent, so Kuznetsov fired, hitting one of the men in the forehead. His head shot backwards and he collapsed slowly onto his side. Kuznetsov trained his gun on the other one. 'What about you? Feel talkative?'

The man simply swallowed and closed his eyes, awaiting the inevitable.

Much as Kuznetsov wanted to oblige him, he needed someone to finger Levchenko. The prisoners being at the albino's house was circumstantial; he could claim to have no knowledge of them being there. With the prisoners dead, the only man with ties to Levchenko's involvement was kneeling in front of him, awaiting a bullet.

'Take him back to Moscow!' Kuznetsov growled, lowering his weapon. 'And make sure he's still alive when you get there!'

He left Alpha Group to tend to the prisoners and their own wounded and jogged back to his car. There was still the matter of Cooper and Mann to deal with. It would have been nice to have Alpha Group on hand to help, but that would be overkill. He had one unit on their tail and five more converging, which should be more than enough to handle two men.

Once in his vehicle, he called Gurin to find out whether the other teams were on their way.

'Yes, sir. Five units, as requested. They set off a few minutes ago, heading to your location.'

'Good. Alpha Group will be bringing a prisoner in. I want him prepped for interrogation.'

Kuznetsov explained who it was, and that he was a vital link to Nikolai Levchenko. 'I don't want him harming himself, you understand?'

'I'll ensure he has a guard watching him until you return,' Gurin promised.

'Do that. And send me the IDs of the team that are joining us. I want to be able to oversee the operation from here.'

Kuznetsov took a tablet PC from a compartment behind the driver's seat and Gurin gave him the details. He entered them into an app and saw the six green markers for the FSB units and one red one for Cooper.

Kuznetsov's next call was to Vasiliev. 'I have you on screen. What is the suspect doing?'

'He just left the gas station. We're about a mile behind him.'

Was that where he was to meet Mann? Kuznetsov wondered. If it was, and the two Brits were now together, he could pounce once the other team were in position. 'Close up and pass him. I want to know if he's still alone.'

'Yes, sir.'

Chapter 32

After topping up the tank, Cooper left the gas station and headed for Loza. He'd also purchased some snacks, thinking Mann would be hungry after a night in the open. He'd wanted to get him some warm clothes, too, but that wasn't something they stocked. Once he'd picked his friend up, they'd stop off on the way to the border to get him a new wardrobe.

Cooper glanced at his phone and saw that the rendezvous point was close, with the motorway exit just a couple of miles ahead. He signalled to get into the inside lane, and that's when he saw the powerful saloon bearing down on him. Cooper switched lanes, and the black car pulled alongside him for a moment. The front passenger stole a glance at Cooper before the car shot off down the road.

It wasn't typical behaviour, and Cooper had been trained to pick up on such incongruities. *Were they tailing him?* he wondered. Either that, or they were checking him out to see if it was worth robbing him of his car and possessions. Whatever their intentions, it got the adrenaline flowing.

Cooper made a mental note of the licence plate. If he saw the same car again, it was unlikely to be a coincidence.

He watched the car speed away, and his nerves settled a little when he saw the saloon pass the turn off and continue down the motorway. So far, he'd seen no one following him, but if he was being tailed, there would probably be a team involved, not just one vehicle. He checked his rear-view mirror and saw nothing that looked like a surveillance unit. No motorcycles, no fast cars, just a couple of lumbering trucks and a few old bangers that would be useless in a pursuit.

Satisfied that his tail was clear, he took the exit and followed the curved road as his position converged with the marker on the screen. He slowed, and once the two dots settled next to each other, he pulled over onto a dirt strip and got out.

Cooper could hear the sound of traffic passing on the nearby motorway, but that was all. The road he was on was lined with birch trees and stretched in a straight line for as far as he could see. A car was approaching, making him wish he was armed, but as it neared he saw a woman driving and kids in the back. It passed without incident.

'Glad you could make it.'

Cooper spun to see a grey-clad figure rise out of the bushes.

'Alex! Christ, you look like shit!'

'Thanks, buddy,' Mann grinned. 'Good to see you, too.'

Cooper noticed the automatic rifle Mann carried. 'Where the hell did you get that?'

'Long story,' Mann said as he climbed into the front passenger seat. 'I'll tell you on the way.'

Cooper got behind the wheel, and Mann handed over a pistol. 'The guy this belongs to doesn't need it anymore.'

Cooper stuffed the gun into his waistband, spun the car around and headed towards the Latvian border.

* * *

'Well?' Kuznetsov asked the moment Vasiliev answered.

'He's still alone, but the moment we passed him he left the motorway. Wait…he's stopped.'

'This must be where he's picking Mann up,' Kuznetsov said. He checked his tablet and saw Vasiliev's car moving away from Cooper's. 'Get back on his tail immediately and verify that Mann is with him. We'll stop them before they reach Moscow.'

Kuznetsov cut the call and dialled Gurin's number.

'It looks like Cooper found Mann and they're heading back to town.'

'I saw that,' Gurin said. 'I can order three of the five units to double back so they can set up a rolling roadblock when Cooper reaches them.'

'Do it,' Kuznetsov said.

* * *

'…then I took his rifle and scarpered.'

Mann had given Cooper the ultra-condensed version of events. The rest could wait for the unofficial debrief, which would take place in Mann's rose garden accompanied by an ice box full of cold beers.

'There is one other thing,' he told Cooper. 'Before she was picked up, Helena Federova told me I had to stop Sergei Belyakov.'

He watched Cooper search his memory and come up blank.

'Doesn't ring a bell.'

'I've never heard of him, either,' Mann said, 'but we have to get word back to London.'

'I read the reports Sloane sent in. I can't believe you used that as a bargaining chip.'

'I was desperate,' Mann said. 'Besides, I wasn't going to hold out forever, just until the last moment. I thought I had another twenty-four hours, but they came and took me during the night, so I had no chance to tell Sloane.'

'I'd better let Horton know,' Cooper said, taking his mobile out.

'Give it to me,' Mann said. 'We can't give his name out over the phone. The Russians track everything, and the moment we say Belyakov they'll be swarming all over us. I'll create a draft email and give the boss the details of the account. He can sign in and read it.'

Mann accessed a Gmail account he'd set up for this purpose. He started off with his safe word to show that he wasn't under duress, then gave Belyakov's name and instructions to find and detain him.

'And Belyakov's definitely in England?' Cooper asked.

'He might not be,' Mann admitted. 'Helena didn't give me any details, but the fact she told me suggested London was the target of whatever he's planning.' He handed the phone back to Cooper. 'Call Horton, tell him to check the Alan Brice account.'

Cooper dialled and put it on speaker. When the boss answered, Cooper told him he had his package, and that he should check the Brice email.

'Well done,' Horton said, and he sounded genuinely relieved. That soon turned to concern. 'The boys and girls at the doughnut have picked up lots of chatter in recent hours. You're not out of the woods yet.'

The doughnut was the nickname for the circular building that housed GCHQ, the government communications headquarters.

'Anything specific?' Cooper asked.

'Sadly, no, but keep your eyes peeled.'

'Ask him when back-up will be here,' Mann mouthed to Cooper.

Cooper didn't relay the question. Instead, he told Horton that he'd check in every hour, then hung up.

'There's no back-up,' Cooper said to Mann. 'The PM didn't even want to send me. He said he doesn't want to create an international incident, but if you ask me, he's just scared of standing up to Sokolov. If it wasn't for Horton, you'd be walking home.'

Mann's jaw tightened. 'Sloane told me Sokolov wanted to do an exchange but Ward refused.'

Cooper looked at him. 'That's right. A Russian who lives in London.'

'So he's had two chances to bring me home, but didn't want to take them?'

Cooper simply shrugged.

They drove in silence for a while, as anger boiled inside Mann. He'd risked his life for his country, and twice in quick succession his government had wanted to abandon him to his fate. Apparently it was only Horton's persistence that gave him a chance to get home.

The time for recriminations would come, though. Right now, getting home to his wife was Mann's priority.

'How's Debra?' he asked.

'Just about how you'd expect, mate. Worried. Anxious.'

Mann had anticipated as much. 'I never told you this before, but she's been nagging me to quit for over a year now.'

Cooper looked at him. 'Can't say I blame her. It's not exactly the safest profession, and this last couple of weeks just handed her an industrial-size tin of "I told you so".'

Mann shook his head. 'It's not the danger that worries her, it's the people I have to associate with. She's convinced I'm sleeping around.'

'Really?' Cooper looked surprised. 'She never struck me as the jealous type.'

'She's the original green-eyed monster, believe me. She wasn't at first, but since she tripped over my legend's social media accounts, she's been unbearable. She thinks I'm sleeping with everyone I'm photographed with.'

'Ouch.'

'Ouch is right,' Mann sighed.

'How come you never told me this before?' Cooper asked.

'Could you have done anything about it?'

'Not really,' Cooper admitted. 'I guess it's something you guys have to sort out for yourselves.'

'It is,' Mann said, 'and I know the perfect way to put an end to Debra's suspicions. Once we get home, the first thing I'm gonna do is hand in my resignation.'

Cooper grimaced. 'You'll probably have to.'

'What do you mean?' Mann asked.

'Alex, I know you live for spy shit, but I think I already burned that bridge.' Cooper explained how he'd leaked news of Mann's capture to the media to force the PM's hand. 'Sorry, mate. You'll have to find another line of work.'

'Don't worry about it,' Mann said. 'I'll think of something.' He had no idea what it might be, though. Cooper was right: spy work was everything. 'Maybe I'll sell luxury yachts for real.'

'Bad idea,' Cooper said. 'Too high-profile. Sokolov isn't gonna forget about you, so you'll have to lie low for a while. He probably won't come for you in England, but if you start travelling to sell your wares, it'll be open season on Alex Mann.'

He had a point, Mann conceded. Better to keep his head down for a few months, spend some quality time with Debra, then see what the job market had to offer.

'When we get back, I'll—'

Cooper stopped mid-sentence, his eyes glued on the rear-view mirror.

'What is it?' Mann asked.

'We're being tailed,' Cooper said, slowing a little to force the car behind to close the gap to within fifty yards. When it did, Cooper cursed. 'That same car eyeballed me about half an hour ago when I was heading to pick you up.'

Mann didn't bother asking whether he was sure. Cooper was a solid field agent, and if he said he'd seen the car before, Mann trusted him.

'How long were they following you?'

'They weren't,' Cooper told him. 'One minute my tail was clear, the next they did a pass and headed north.'

'Then the Russians knew you were coming. They must have put a tracker on the car.'

'If they did, we'll know who it was. We've had everyone who knew about your assignment under surveillance for the last couple of weeks. Phones, internet, movements, everything. It's probably the same person who gave you up in the first place.'

'Any idea who it could be?' Mann asked.

'My money's on FoSec's aide, Sarah Mulholland. There's a strong Russian connection. That can wait, though. How do you want to deal with this?'

'We need to switch vehicles,' Mann said, resisting the urge to turn and look at his pursuers. That would let the Russians know they'd been made. 'Or at least get rid of the tracker.'

'Agreed, but to do that we need to get rid of these guys. Get ready with the AK.'

Cooper took his foot off the accelerator and let the car slow further, then he engaged the clutch and selected second gear. When the speed dropped to thirty miles an hour, he released the clutch, then pumped it again and again. The car jerked along for a hundred yards before juddering to a halt.

'Let's hope they think we broke down,' Cooper said, his eyes on the mirror. He checked that the pistol Mann had given him was secure in his waistband and covered it with his jumper.

The Russian car pulled up ten yards behind them. Cooper saw both occupants looking straight ahead, and one of them appeared to be talking.

'He's probably calling it in,' he said to Mann. 'Let's see if we can draw them out.'

Cooper popped the bonnet and got out. He lifted the lid on the engine and leaned over, as if inspecting it.

Mann eased his door open a crack. The two Russians sat for a moment, then looked at each other before climbing out of their car. One of them was tall, the other stocky. Both wore fleece-lined leather jackets which were only zipped up a couple of inches despite the conditions.

Mann eased the safety to the single shot setting as the Russians approached the hire car. They split up, one going to each side. Both reached inside their jackets.

That was enough for Mann. They were going for weapons, and he had to get the drop on them. He kicked his door open and got out in the same movement, his rifle lined up on the target a second later.

'Don't move!' Mann shouted in Russian.

The tall one froze, his hand halfway out of his coat. Mann could see the grip of the pistol. From the corner of his eye, he saw that Cooper had drawn on the stocky one.

'Take it out nice and slowly,' Mann instructed his opponent, who eased the gun out of its holster and tossed it aside.

Cars passed them intermittently. One of them, a black SUV with tinted windows, slowed a little as it passed. For a moment Mann thought it might be the FSB, but it continued down the road. Mann relaxed a little, but the last thing he wanted was an audience. After collecting the discarded pistols, he instructed both Russians to walk into the trees that lined the road. They dawdled, but Mann hurried them up by kicking the tall one in the base of the back. He got the message. Once ten yards in, he told them to empty their pockets and roll up their trouser legs to prove they had no hidden weapons. The stocky one had a small pistol in an ankle holster, which he grudgingly handed over. On the ground lay two wallets, a couple of phones, a pack of cigarettes and a lighter.

No handcuffs.

That sealed their fate. Getting to the Latvian border was going to be hard enough; doing so with a couple of FSB men would be doubly difficult.

Mann ordered the Russians to get down on their knees, cross their ankles and clasp their hands behind their heads.

'Cover them,' Mann said to Cooper, and checked the two prisoners for comms. He found that they both wore tiny ear buds. Mann took them, along with the linked radios.

'How many more are coming?' Mann asked the stocky one.

The Russian hocked up a mouthful of phlegm and spat, his eyes never leaving Mann's.

'I only kill people if I have to,' Mann said to him. 'If you answer my questions, I won't have to kill you.'

The man continued to stare malevolently at Mann.

'Please yourself.'

Mann pulled the trigger and the stocky figure fell backwards, a neat hole in his forehead. Mann turned his gun on the other one. 'You want to answer my questions?'

'You'll kill me anyway. What else can you do? Take me with you?'

'No, but I can strip you naked and leave you here. No one's going to be in a hurry to stop and offer you a lift.'

The man weighed up his options, eventually settling for survival.

'Five more units heading this way. No, wait. Six. Kuznetsov is coming, too.'

Mann looked for signs of deceit but saw none. 'Are you the one who put the tracker on my car?'

The Russian nodded slowly. 'It's in the boot, under the carpet.'

Mann glanced at Cooper and gestured with his head to check it out. Cooper returned a minute later with a small device in his hand.

'Where exactly are the other units?' Mann asked his prisoner.

'Three are ahead of you, waiting for word that you're close so that they can block the road. The other two are a mile down the road, waiting for me to report in. Kuznetsov is on his way.'

Mann handed him an ear bud and transceiver and placed the other bud in his own ear. 'Tell them we weren't in the car. The occupants said we swapped the BMW for their old Skoda. Make up a registration number. If they ask where we are, say we were last seen heading north.'

As the Russian put the bud in his ear, Mann levelled the rifle and aimed at his chest. He listened as the man identified himself as Vasiliev and told his colleagues about the car switch. When he gave the last known heading, a familiar voice exploded in Mann's ear.

'Then get after them!'

Kuznetsov.

'Understood,' Vasiliev said, and removed the ear bud.

Mann kept the gun levelled on the Russian and order him to strip. The man had taken off his jacket and T-shirt when Kuznetsov's voice came over the air again. 'Vasiliev! Why aren't you moving?'

Mann frowned. The only way the FSB's second-in-command could know that Vasiliev's car was still stationary was if it had a tracker fitted. He ordered Vasiliev to put his bud back in and say he was taking a leak, then he'd be on his way.

'How do I disable the tracker in your car?' Mann asked Vasiliev when he'd done as instructed.

The Russian shrugged. 'I don't know, I never tried. I think it's wired into the fuse box somehow.'

Mann cursed inwardly. He'd planned to take the Russian's car, but that was now out of the question. If the tracker was one he could transfer to another car, that was one thing, but he couldn't afford to spend half an hour installing it in a decoy vehicle. However, if Vasiliev's car didn't start moving soon, Kuznetsov would soon send someone to investigate. They would know that he and Cooper were still in the BMW and they'd be right back where they started.

There was also the roadblock to consider. Vasiliev said there were two cars behind and three waiting up the road. If they took the FSB car, and came across a roadblock, they'd be in deep shit.

'Stop undressing,' Mann said to Vasiliev. 'Put your clothes back on and get in the car.'

Vasiliev looked confused, but did as he was told. Mann followed as the Russian returned to his vehicle.

'Get in and drive north,' Mann told him as he climbed in the back seat. The carriageway they were on led to Moscow, so they would have to turn around at the next junction.

Cooper joined them a minute later, sitting next to the driver.

'What took you?' Mann asked, as Vasiliev started the engine and set off.

'I started the BMW and left the doors open. Hopefully someone will steal it and get close enough to the FSB to keep them occupied for a while.'

It might buy them some time, Mann agreed, but they still needed to clear the area without tipping off Kuznetsov. They couldn't do that while this car was being tracked.

A thought struck him. 'How does Kuznetsov track you?' Mann asked Vasiliev.

The Russian gestured to the glove box. Cooper opened it and found a tablet device. He handed it to Mann.

There were seven dots on the screen, a trio close together up ahead and a pair farther north, plus two lone markers. One was between the trio and the pair, and that had to be the vehicle they were in.

How to play this? Mann wondered. He could order Vasiliev to say he was heading back to Moscow in case the suspects doubled back, or feign a puncture. That would give them long enough to find another mode of transport and clear the area. No, if he did that, Vasiliev's colleagues might drop by to help him change the tyre.

The marker was approaching the junction. The trio ahead of them had already turned north.

Mann held the tablet so that Vasiliev could see it. 'Follow them,' he said.

Vasiliev made the turn, maintaining a two-mile gap on the teams up the road. Farther back, the other two cars followed minutes later.

'Radio Kuznetsov,' Mann said. 'Tell him you're going to split off and go northwest. No point all of you looking in the same place.'

The Russian did as instructed. Kuznetsov acknowledged moments later.

At the next junction, Mann watched the first three dots continue on the R104, and Vasiliev branched off onto the

A108 when he reached the same spot. Mann kept his eyes on the remaining cars, hoping they didn't follow.

Chapter 33

Maksim Kuznetsov watched Vasiliev's marker finally start to move, then used his thumb and finger to enlarge the map. There were three main roads that snaked northwards, and Mann could be on any one of them. Expanding the view even further, Kuznetsov's eye was drawn to the border. Unless Mann was planning to drive to China, the northeast route was the least likely. He was about to order his men to split into two groups and take the other two routes when Vasiliev's voice came over the radio.

'I'm going to head northwest and expand the search.'

'Understood,' Kuznetsov replied. He checked the designators for the two cars behind Vasiliev's. 'Agapov, Turgenev, take the A108 when you get to the next junction and form up on Vasiliev.'

The two cars acknowledged the order.

'We'll go that way, too,' Kuznetsov told his driver.

* * *

'Shit!'

'What is it?' Cooper asked Mann.

'The two cars behind us have been instructed to join up with us.'

It was the last thing they needed. While Mann could crouch down in the back seat, when the other FSB cars got close, they'd spot Cooper. If Cooper stayed hidden, too, the others would wonder what had happened to Vasiliev's partner.

'Hit the gas,' Mann told Vasiliev. It was only a temporary fix, but maintaining the gap could buy them a little time to formulate a strategy.

What he eventually came up with wasn't so much a plan as a Hail Mary. He resorted to his earlier idea of feigning a puncture. He explained what he had in mind to Cooper, who agreed that it was the best option they had.

'Do you have a foot pump in the boot?' Mann asked Vasiliev.

'Foot pump?'

'To inflate a tyre,' Mann explained.

Vasiliev nodded.

'Good,' Mann said. 'I want you to call in that you have a puncture, then pull over. We'll let a tyre down, then run into the woods. If any of your colleagues stop to help, say you can do it yourself. If they ask where your stocky friend is, say he's taking a shit. I'll be listening all the time and we'll be able to see you, so don't try and warn them. Any sign of trouble, you get the first bullet.'

Vasiliev acknowledged that he understood, then pulled onto the grass that ran alongside the motorway.

Mann asked for the car keys, then told everyone to get out. He ran around the back, opened the boot and put the jack next to the rear passenger side wheel. After letting the air out of the tyre, he told Vasiliev to get the spare out and make it look like he was changing the wheel, then he ran to join Cooper, who had disappeared into the woods. They lay down close to the base of a tree trunk, peering out on the road.

'Think we can trust him?' Cooper asked.

'What choice have we got?'

'None, really. And even if this works, what next?'

'We stick him in the boot and commandeer a new vehicle.'

'You mean steal one,' Cooper smiled.

'Potato, tomato,' Mann said, looking at the tablet he'd taken from the car. The two dots were closing fast, and it wasn't long before the first of the FSB vehicles pulled up alongside Vasiliev, who was jacking up the back of the car.

The side window wound down, and though he couldn't hear what was said, Mann could see the smirk as the passenger spoke to Vasiliev. The reply was a single finger. The passenger roared with laughter, and the car pulled away, much to Mann's relief.

The driver of the second vehicle wasn't so accommodating. He pulled up behind Vasiliev's car and got out, inspecting the damage.

Mann saw Vasiliev gesture extravagantly for his colleague to clear off, but the other Russian took off his jacket and rolled up his sleeves.

'Not good,' Cooper whispered.

Not good at all, Mann thought. It wouldn't take long to discover that there was no damage to the tyre, and then things would get interesting.

Events took a turn for the worse when another car pulled up and Maksim Kuznetsov climbed out of the back seat. He immediately began gesticulating and barking orders, and

Vasiliev and the other FSB officer rushed to change the wheel.

Kuznetsov looked around, then asked Vasiliev something. He responded with a thumb over his shoulder, indicating the trees. A moment later, Mann heard Kuznetsov's voice over the earpiece: 'Litvin, what's taking you so long?'

Mann knew he had to answer, but as he didn't know what Litvin sounded like, he kept it short. 'Coming,' he said gruffly, before turning to Cooper. 'We have to make a move.' As they couldn't escape the area on foot, that meant eliminating the threat in front of them.

Cooper was on the same wavelength. 'You take out the two drivers. I'll take the ones out in the open.'

That was the sensible move. Mann's AK would be more effective against the car windows than the pistol Cooper was carrying.

'Okay. On my signal.'

Mann got Kuznetsov's driver in his sights, knowing that the moment he took the shot, all hell would break loose. He squeezed the trigger and watched as his target slumped sideways. Cooper fired a split second later, and the three Russians standing near Vasiliev's car scattered like cockroaches. Mann saw one of them take a hit, but it wasn't a kill shot. He managed to scramble behind Vasiliev's car and returned fire.

Mann turned his attention to the driver of the other car, but the Russian was already out of his vehicle. He crouched behind the bonnet, his legs obscured by the wheel, leaving Mann no clear shot.

Mann's earpiece roared into life, and he heard Kuznetsov call in reinforcements.

'Spread out,' Mann said to Cooper, while moving to his left. 'Try and get around the side. We have to finish this before their backup arrives.'

Bullets slammed into the trees as Mann ran past them, and he replied with a volley of fire until his magazine ran dry. He threw himself behind a large trunk, ejected the old mag and switched it for a new one. The tree shuddered as the Russians concentrated their fire on it, but respite came when Cooper joined in, pinning the enemy down and giving Mann a chance to move.

He got ten yards before he saw another car skid to a halt, and two men jumped out, their weapons already in their hands. Seconds later, another car joined the fray. It was two against eight, and the newcomers already had positioned themselves to counter Mann's flanking manoeuvre, either by design or accident.

Mann fired at a head that had popped into view from behind a car bonnet, but the target was gone a split second later. It was like a grown-up game of whack-a-mole, and the prize was his life.

He almost jumped out of his skin when Cooper hit the ground next to him.

'What are you doing here? You're supposed to be flanking them!'

'I got a phone call,' Cooper said, handing over his mobile before taking a shot at the Russians.

Taking a call during a firefight that they were destined to lose was as surreal as it got. Mann frowned, then put the phone to his ear.

'Hello?'

'When we engage them,' a stern voice said in a thick Yorkshire accent, 'keep your heads down until the firing stops.'

'Who is this?'

The phone went dead in his hand, and Mann dropped it in front of Cooper. 'Who the hell was that?' he asked as he let off a few more bursts.

'No idea, but it sounds like we're gonna get some help.'

It came moments later. Mann saw a black SUV with blacked-out windows approach. It was the same one he'd seen earlier, and as it neared the procession of parked FSB cars, the side windows opened and it slowed to a crawl. Two stubby rifles appeared and the muzzles flashed. Mann saw two bodies jerk and spin before collapsing to the ground. The occupants of the SUV went along the line of cars, dispensing death without receiving so much as a single bullet in reply.

The SUV stopped, and the front passenger waved for Mann and Cooper to shift their arses.

Mann grabbed Cooper's collar and hauled him to his feet, and they both ran for the SUV. As they came around the back of one of the FSB vehicles, Mann saw a trail of bodies lining the side of the road. All were dead, apart from one. Kuznetsov lay on the ground, moaning, with three red patches on his torso. Mann was tempted to let him bleed out, but there was a chance a passing motorist might stop and take him to a hospital.

Mann couldn't let that happen, not after what Kuznetsov had done to both him and Helena. Mann took out the pistol he'd taken from Vasiliev and aimed it at Kuznetsov.

'This is for Helena Federova,' he said, and shot the Russian in the knee. He was pleased to see the pain register. 'This is from me.'

He put a bullet in Kuznetsov's head, then ran to the SUV.

The rear door was open and Cooper was already on the back seat, along with two others. Mann jumped in and had to lie across bodies.

When the driver took off and Cooper slammed the door shut, Mann looked up at the guy he was resting on.

'I'll ask again: who are you guys?'

'The official line is,' a tough-looking Yorkshireman said, 'we're concerned citizens on holiday. We saw someone being attacked and helped them out.'

'And unofficially?'

'E Squadron.'

Mann knew of them, but had never met them. They were specialists chosen from the SAS ranks, tasked with carrying out clandestine military actions on behalf of MI6.

'Horton told me the PM refused to sanction your use,' Cooper said.

'That's right, but H sent us anyway. Our brief was to observe and only get involved if your lives were at risk.'

'But how did you find us?' Mann asked.

'Cooper's new phone,' the soldier said, holding up an iPad. 'It's not an ordinary mobile. It has a tracker installed, plus it can be accessed remotely so we can hear every word you say.'

That's how they knew we were in trouble, Mann thought.

'It would have been nice if Horton had told me,' Cooper grumbled.

'We were last resort, only to help out if your lives were in danger. Up until then, you were doing okay. If you'd known we were available, always three miles behind you, you might have relied on us to get you out of the country. H didn't want us to get involved at all, if we could help it, but it sounded like the shit was flying.'

'It was,' Mann agreed. 'Speaking of exfils, what's the plan?'

Everyone held their breath as the sound of wailing sirens filled the air, but the emergency vehicles flashed past and quickly disappeared in the opposite direction.

'We'll be switching vehicles in the next few minutes, then taking you to a remote location where you'll catch your ride to Estonia. It won't be pleasant, but it'll get you there.'

Mann had been through so much in the last couple of weeks, another day or so wouldn't make much difference.

There was still one outstanding issue to resolve, though.

'How secure are your comms to London?' he asked the Yorkshireman.

'As secure as they get. You need to call home?'

'Yeah, I have to get a message to Horton.'

The soldier took a phone from his jacket. It was chunkier than a standard mobile, but the functionality was the same. Mann entered Horton's number and had to wait around ten seconds for the software to go through the security protocols before he heard it connect.

'H,' the boss said, obviously recognising the number.

'It's Mann. Thanks for sending the cavalry.'

'Alex! So good to hear your voice! How's the weather?'

Again, Mann answered in a way that would confirm he wasn't under duress. 'Can't complain. Have you checked the Brice email account?'

Horton confirmed that he had.

'You need to find and detain Sergei Belyakov. I have no idea who he is or what he's planning, but Helena Federova risked her life to give me his name.'

'I've got people checking the files to see if we have anything on him,' Horton said. There was a pause. 'How are you holding up?'

'I've been better,' Mann conceded. 'I just wanna get home.'

'Understood. You're in safe hands with Sergeant Daniels and his men. I'll see you in a couple of days.'

Horton ended the call, and Mann handed the phone back to the soldier.

'Which of you is Daniels?'

'That's me,' the Yorkshireman said.

'Let me know the next time you're back home,' Mann said. 'I owe you guys a pint.'

'Too fuckin' right!' a Geordie laughed from the front seat.

Chapter 34

Sergeant Daniels had been right about the journey to the Estonian border: it was a nightmare.

Mann and Cooper spent nineteen hours in a cramped compartment hidden in the floor of a pig transporter. Apart from the smell, urine from a hundred animals seeped through minute cracks in the wood, leaving them both soaked by the time they reached the outskirts of Tallinn.

An official from the British embassy met them with toiletry bags and changes of clothes. It clearly wasn't the first time the live animal transporter had been used to spirit people out of Russia. Once they cleaned up, they were taken to the embassy and fed while their travel documents were prepared.

FSB officers were known to frequent the airport terminal, so they took a charter flight from a military airport for the short hop to Helsinki. From there, they caught a British Airways flight home.

Mann was exhausted. He'd taken a physical and emotional battering over the last two weeks, and all he wanted was to get home to Debra, take a hot shower, and slide into bed.

It wasn't to be.

Horton met them when the plane landed, and the debrief started the moment the pool car left Heathrow.

'I know you've been through a lot,' the chief said, 'but we need to do this as soon as possible.'

'I understand,' Mann told him, sipping from a bottle of water and wishing it was vodka. 'But before we do that, what did you find on Belyakov?'

'He's low-ranking FSB. We had nothing on him, but our American friends had his name and a surveillance photo. We've run it through facial recognition at all ports, but there have been no hits from passengers arriving in the last three days.'

'Then maybe Helena's warning came in time,' Mann said, recalling the sacrifice she'd made to pass him the information.

'Perhaps,' Horton agreed. 'I've asked Box to look further back, just in case.'

Mann thought about suggesting they check all passenger manifests in the last few months, but it was doubtful Belyakov would enter the country using his real identity. No, if he was coming, it would be up to the security services to spot him.

Horton woke his phone up and started the voice recorder. 'In your own time.'

With the events still fresh in his mind, Mann had no difficulty recalling every detail of his ordeal. Horton interjected with questions a couple of times, but for the most part he let Mann recount his experiences without interruption.

Twenty minutes later, Mann was finished.

Horton turned off the recorder. 'That was quite an adventure,' he said. 'I'll arrange for you to meet with someone to discuss the impact.'

'You mean a shrink?' Mann asked. 'No, thanks. All I need is a couple of days off, then I'll be back in the office to get my affairs in order.'

Horton frowned. 'What do you mean?'

'I mean I'm out,' Mann said. 'Throughout my career I'd always thought that if I got into a scrape, my government would be there to bail me out. Now I know that's not the case. Why should I risk my life for people who willingly abandon me the moment things get a little hairy?'

'It's never that simple,' Horton said. 'The PM has so many things to consider that decisions like this are rarely black and white. That aside, your days as a field operative are effectively over. You were named in a leak, so you can't go back out, no matter where the assignment. That said, we don't want to lose your expertise. You still have so much to offer the service.'

'Thanks,' Mann said, 'but I need a clean break. I couldn't prepare others to go through the same thing knowing it was a coin toss whether they ever made it home.'

They rode in silence for a while, until Mann spoke again.

'I want to thank you,' he told Horton. 'Cooper says you stuck your neck out to get us home. If you hadn't sent E Squadron to keep an eye on us, we'd be dead by now. I appreciate that.'

Horton said nothing, and Mann guessed the chief was contemplating his own future.

'How will this leave you?' Mann asked him.

Horton shrugged. 'I don't know. Once the PM hears that I disobeyed him, I'll either get early retirement, or he'll throw the book at me.'

'Won't that depend on the real account of my escape?' Mann asked.

'What do you mean?'

Mann twisted in his seat. 'Cooper and I were pinned down by Kuznetsov and his men when the black SUV showed up. I'm pretty sure the occupants worked for Nikolai Levchenko. Fortunately, we were able to overpower them and make our way to the border with help from some locals.' Cooper was in the front seat, and Mann tapped him on the shoulder. 'Isn't that right?'

'Sounds accurate as hell to me,' Cooper said.

'That's nice of you, but it won't hold up to scrutiny.'

'It will if we get our stories straight,' Mann insisted. 'Give me and Cooper a couple of hours and we'll have a watertight story.'

Horton looked unconvinced.

'It's the least we can do,' Mann pressed. 'Besides, what's the worst they can do if they don't believe me? Fire me? I'm leaving anyway.'

'What about Cooper?' Horton asked. 'It could spell the end of his career if the truth ever comes out.'

'Then make sure it doesn't,' Cooper said without turning around. 'Send Sergeant Daniels and his boys in to take Levchenko out and, hey presto, no one can disprove our account.'

'How did you get across the border?' Horton asked.

'Hitched a ride in the back of a pig truck,' Mann said. 'I was already privy to that method of escape, and I arranged for someone from the embassy to meet us and help us from that point on.'

'And did you make those arrangements, or was it Daniels?'

'It was me,' Mann said truthfully. 'The sarge said the less involvement he had, the better.'

Horton digested the idea for a while, then took his phone from his pocket and deleted the recording of the initial debrief.

'I think you two should get some rest. You're clearly too traumatised to face another interrogation right now. My driver will drop you off at Cooper's place. Be in my office at nine tomorrow morning.'

That suited Mann. They'd spend an hour or two getting their stories aligned, then he'd borrow Cooper's mini and drive home to see Debra.

Chapter 35

Cooper was walking to the entrance to the SIS building when he heard a whistle. He turned to see Mann strolling towards him.

'All set?' Mann asked, handing over the keys to Cooper's mini.

'Ready as I'll ever be. How's Debra?'

'She was shocked to see me,' Mann said.

'I did tell you to call ahead.'

'And spoil the surprise? You've got no romance in your soul, that's your problem.'

'Yeah, well, getting this story straight is our problem, so concentrate. Put last night's bedroom gymnastics out of your mind and focus.'

'Yes, sir,' Mann quipped, flicking off a mock salute.

Sharon Williams met them at reception at exactly eight o'clock. She threw her arms around Mann and hugged him like a long-lost lover.

'Good to see you home,' she said when she peeled herself off him.

'Good to be home,' Mann smiled.

'Let's see if you feel that way after the debrief. They brought in a couple of top civil servants to lead it.'

Her statement set Cooper on edge. 'Why the change in protocol?'

'I think it had something to do with Kuznetsov being killed. That stirred up a whole shitstorm, and the PM is keeping a keen eye on this.'

Cooper and Mann exchanged glances, but neither spoke. They had their story, and as long as they stuck to it, there shouldn't be any problems.

So it turned out.

Mann was the first to give his account, while Cooper sat in a waiting room nursing a coffee. He'd been over the story in his head countless times, and he knew which questions they were likely to ask. How many men did Levchenko send in the black SUV? How did those men know where to find them? How did he and Mann disable them? How did they contact the embassy in Tallinn?

They'd settled on concise answers, making sure the wording was varied enough that their stories didn't sound rehearsed.

Mann emerged after almost an hour. The corner of his mouth lifted in a brief smile, then he was gone.

Cooper was shown into the office, which had been set up like the movie version of a police interview room. A single table sat in the middle of the room, with two chairs on one side and one opposite.

The session lasted barely thirty minutes, his interrogators focusing only on Cooper's involvement. They didn't ask all the questions he was expecting, nor did they throw in any new ones. It was almost as if his testimony was a box-ticking exercise.

When he was done, Cooper went down to the canteen and found Mann tucking into a full English breakfast. He got himself a coffee and sat opposite him.

'That was easier than I'd imagined,' Cooper said.

'Same here.' Mann popped a slice of sausage into his mouth and chewed.

Cooper sipped his drink, and the nagging thought that had struck him the previous night jumped into his head again.

'What is it?' Mann asked.

'What?'

'You look like something's weighing heavily.'

'Just something that didn't strike me at the time,' Cooper said, 'but it came up in the debrief. How did the FSB know I was coming?'

'What did you tell them?' Mann asked.

'Nothing. I said I had no idea, but I think that whoever tipped off the Russians about you also told them I was on my way.'

Mann chewed slowly as he digested the information. 'Did you travel under a legend?'

'Of course.'

'Then not many people will have had that information. That should narrow down your search.'

It would indeed, Cooper thought. It could wait, though. He was due to meet Aaron Duffield at ten, and hopefully Five would have picked up any tell-tale communications.

'So, what's the plan?' Cooper asked. 'You still quitting?'

Mann swallowed. 'I am. And before you ask, no, I don't know what I'm gonna do. I've got a couple of options that I'm weighing up.'

Cooper helped himself to a slice of Mann's buttered toast. 'I'm moving on, too.'

Mann put his knife and fork down. 'Why?'

'Because, one, logistical support bores the arse off me, and two, I'm also fed up with the government treating operatives like…like…'

'…like pieces on a chess board?'

'I was going to say, like nappies,' Cooper said. 'Once the shit starts flowing, they toss you aside and find a replacement.'

'Mine was more refined,' Mann smiled. 'Seriously, though, you should have something in place before you quit. Don't make any rash decisions.'

'I've been thinking about it since you first told me you were getting out. I know how much I miss spy shit, and you would, too. So, I was thinking, why don't we go freelance?'

Mann frowned. 'You mean become mercenaries?'

'No, nothing like that,' Cooper said, waving his toast in the air. 'We'd be…consultants.'

'The difference being?'

Cooper grinned. 'Fewer gunfights, more cash.'

Mann looked thoughtful as he chewed another mouthful. When he swallowed, he said, 'That could work.'

Cooper dipped the last of his stolen toast in Mann's baked beans. 'I can't believe you told Sloane about my dog,' he said.

'What? He told you about that?'

'He sent transcripts of every conversation he had with you,' Cooper told Mann. 'Seriously, you think I'm that insensitive?'

'Mate, I was just about to be sent down for life!'

Cooper smiled. 'I know, I'm just fucking with you.' He drummed a brief tattoo on the table with his fingers, then stood. 'I've got to head across the river to see what progress they've made finding the person who ratted us out.'

'Want an extra set of eyes?'

'Nah, you get home and spend some time with the missus. I'll let you know if I find anything.'

Mann saluted with his knife, and Cooper zipped his leather jacket up before walking out of the canteen.

* * *

The streets were packed as Cooper made his way to Thames House. The protest march against the government's stealthy dismantling of the National Health Service wasn't due to start for another couple of hours, but the crowds were already gathering. A large variety of placards and banners decrying the government's actions were on show, with many participants dressed as either doctors or patients.

The journey to the MI5 building took twice as long as usual, and Cooper found Aaron Duffield waiting for him at reception. He looked like a kid who'd just been given a puppy.

'Tell me you've got something,' Cooper said.

'I think we have.'

They jogged up the stairs to Duffield's office on the third floor. Once inside, Duffield sat at his computer and gestured for Cooper to bring a chair around.

'We got nothing on elint,' Duffield said as he tapped at the keyboard, 'but we did get a hit at the Russian Embassy.'

He brought up a picture on the screen and sat back so that Cooper could study it.

'I've seen this before,' Cooper said, looking at the woman wearing the tan overcoat and wide-brimmed hat. 'I remember the black hair and sunglasses. She was an unknown.'

'Check the date,' Duffield said, and Cooper looked at the photographs metadata.

'Friday morning.' The original photo of the mystery woman had been taken a year earlier, and now here she was, returning to the Russian Embassy just as he'd been about to land in Moscow. Had she gone there to tell the Russians that he was on his way? Most importantly, who the hell was she? 'Please tell me you identified her.'

'Fortunately, we did. We had a surplus of trainees, so I allocated two to the embassy. When facial recognition failed to find a match, the team sent a newbie to follow her and get some proper photos.' Duffield hit a couple of keys and the picture on the screen changed.

Cooper stared at it, unable to believe what he was seeing. The woman was sitting in a coffee shop and had taken off the sunglasses and hat. She'd been in the process of removing the black wig when the photo was taken.

Cooper prided himself on having a wide and varied vocabulary, but only one word seemed appropriate for a moment like this.

'Fuck.'

'That's what I thought,' Duffield said. He handed Cooper a manila folder. 'I prepared a report containing photos, dates and times—'

Duffield's phone rang, and he picked it up. The conversation was brief, but it left Duffield with a smile on his face. He was quick to explain why.

'We found Belyakov.'

Chapter 36

Dmitri Gudkov knocked on the president's door with trepidation. As head of the FSB, it was his responsibility to bring the killers of Maksim Kuznetsov to justice. Not only that, but with his second-in-command dead, the blame for failing to apprehend the British spy would fall squarely on his own shoulders.

'Come!'

Gudkov walked in to find Sokolov sitting behind his expansive desk. Igor was normally a difficult man to read, but today his fury was on full display. Gudkov came to attention in front of the president.

'Where is Mann?' Sokolov barked.

'Sir, we have been unable to locate him. I've tripled our men at every port, searching every vehicle, no matter how small. Their presence alone should be enough to deter him from attempting to leave the country. Internally, every police force from here to the Bering Strait is on the lookout for him.'

'And what if he's already gone?'

'Highly unlikely. The men at the borders were put on alert ten minutes after Mann was rescued.'

Sokolov lit a cigarette and blew a grey cloud towards Gudkov. 'Did you at least find out who was helping him? Do you know who killed Kuznetsov?'

'Nothing concrete, but it has all the hallmarks of Nikolai Levchenko. The albino is the only one audacious enough to try such a thing. I believe he found out that Mann had killed his men and escaped from his dacha, and he wanted his revenge.'

'What does Levchenko have to say for himself?'

Gudkov squirmed. 'We haven't been able to locate him. I've sent men to every property he owns, leases or recently sold, but there's no sign of him. He's clearly hiding, and it must be because of his involvement in Maksim's murder.'

'Then find him,' Sokolov growled. 'Find the albino and you'll find the Englishman.'

The president took a long drag on his cigarette, stubbed it out, then waved a dismissive hand at Gudkov.

The head of the FSB stood firm. 'Sir, there's something else we must discuss.'

'What?' Sokolov asked, not even attempting to hide his irritation.

'Belyakov.'

Sokolov's eyes narrowed. 'What of him?'

'Do you think it is wise to continue with the test, given the circumstances?'

'What circumstances? Stop talking in riddles!'

Gudkov swallowed. 'Of course, sir. I mean, until we can confirm that Helena Federova didn't pass information about Belyakov's mission to Mann, shouldn't we postpone the test?'

Sokolov glared at him for a moment, then his face contorted in anger. He sprang from his chair and violently swept his coffee mug off the desk before banging his fists on the sturdy oak top. 'You assured me that Federova didn't say anything to Mann about Belyakov's mission!'

Gudkov had been expecting an outburst, but not one this ferocious. It was extreme, even for Igor.

'I did, though to be fair, I simply passed on Kuznetsov's assessment,' Gudkov said.

'Kuznetsov, who is conveniently dead?' Sokolov mocked. 'That won't wash with me. It's your department, your responsibility.'

'I understand that, and I believe Maksim was correct. However, I think it would be wise to exercise…caution. Perhaps postpone the test for a few months.'

Sokolov lit another cigarette and stepped out from behind his desk. He ambled around the expansive office slowly, deep in concentration. The president stopped in front of a picture of Vladimir Ilyich Lenin that was hanging on the wall.

'We continue as scheduled,' he eventually said. 'If we delay, then Operation Lightning Spear will have to be pushed back. We can't afford to do that.'

Gudkov knew the president was right. Lightning Spear was the plan to topple the regimes in Azerbaijan, Moldova, Georgia and Armenia and install sympathetic pro-Russian governments before reassimilating them into a new Soviet Union. There would be severe push back from the United States, so it was vital that America was crippled before the plan was implemented. The four countries were seeking membership in NATO, and to delay action brought the risk of them succeeding. If that were to happen, then Russia would face taking on the world's powerhouses, not simply a few ill-equipped armies.

Gudkov could only hope that Kuznetsov had been as thorough in his interrogation of Federova as he had been with all his other prisoners. The man had no equal when it came to extracting the truth.

He prayed Kuznetsov had done so this time. If not, and the world discovered the truth behind Belyakov's mission, the West would do more than freeze Russian assets and add a few people to no-fly lists. What they planned was nothing short of crimes against humanity. It was not something they could spin their way out of with propaganda and misinformation.

'As you wish,' Gudkov told the president.

He turned to leave, relieved to have escaped the meeting intact, but Igor Sokolov was quick to hand him a reality check.

'Dmitri, find Mann and Levchenko. I want them both in custody today. Your future depends on it.'

Chapter 37

Sergei Belyakov felt strangely calm as he climbed into his hire car. He was about to unleash an agent—chemical or biological, he didn't know—on the people of London. Men, women, children would all be affected. Yet he felt nothing. No trepidation or doubt, no remorse, no guilt. He was a soldier first, and as his president had explained, this was war. His was only a small yet vital part in a global plan, and if it wasn't carried out, Russia's role as a world superpower would be over. Belyakov didn't know why, nor did he ask.

It was just before nine, and he'd been instructed to launch the attack at midday, just as the march got underway. That gave him three hours to get to the lockup garage, fit the delivery systems to the drones, drive them to the launch site, and let them loose.

He took a circuitous route to the garage. It added half an hour to his journey time, but he'd been warned that traffic would be snarled around Trafalgar Square due to the march.

Belyakov checked his watch when he reached his destination. He'd taken ten minutes longer than anticipated due to roadworks, but he'd factored in a little extra. He backed into the garage, closed the doors and squeezed out of the car. The boxes were where he'd left them, and the tell-tale markers were still in place. He'd stuck tiny slips of paper between the boxes, so if any had been moved, he'd know about it.

It took Belyakov ten minutes to install the delivery pods, check the batteries, and ensure the phone was still paired to the drones, then he placed them in his boot. He drove out of the garage and locked up before heading back into London.

* * *

Cooper got on the phone and told Horton about the discovery.

'Facial recognition picked up Belyakov travelling into Heathrow thirteen days ago under the name Anatoly Volkov. A credit card under that name shows he's staying in a hotel in Earl's Court.'

'That's great news,' the chief replied.

'Maybe, maybe not. He's booked on a plane to Moscow late this evening, so whatever he has planned, he's either done it, or about to do it.'

'Then let's hope the police get to him in time.'

'The DG is liaising with them as we speak,' Cooper told him.

'Okay. Get back here in case we can offer any support.'

'On my way.' Cooper ended the call and glanced down at the report on the desk. It contained the name of the person who had betrayed Mann, and it was only right that his friend should know about it before anyone else.

He read through the thin file to make sure the evidence was irrefutable. The timings all added up, and it even contained a motive.

Cooper dialled Mann's number and asked where he was.

'Just about to get in my car and head home,' Mann said.

'Do me a favour and hang around a few minutes. There's something you need to know.' Cooper nodded his thanks to Duffield and left his office.

'Can't it wait? I want to get back and see Debra.'

'Trust me, you want to hear this.'

'Then tell me now,' Mann insisted.

Cooper wasn't about to relent. 'I'll meet you at your car in ten minutes.'

He hung up before Mann could object, then jogged back across the river.

Cooper found Mann sitting in his car, a sporty Mercedes convertible. The top was down, and a classic Bowie track filled the underground car park. Cooper got in beside him.

'What's so urgent?' Mann asked him.

Cooper hesitated. What he was about to reveal would devastate his friend. Years of trust, betrayed. There was no easy way to break the news, so he simply handed Mann the report Duffield had put together.

'What's this?'

'The person who shopped you to the Russians,' Cooper said, and watched as Mann opened the file.

On the front page was a photograph of the mole, and Mann's jaw clenched as he stared at the woman on the page.

'Is this some kind of joke?'

'I'm afraid not,' Cooper said. 'She put on a disguise and visited the Russian Embassy a year ago. It's likely the FSB have been watching you since then. She went back a few days ago, on the morning I flew to pick you up. That's how the Russians knew I was coming and were able to plant a tracker on my hire car.'

Mann stared at the photograph of his wife, his hands trembling almost imperceptibly.

'How did she know?'

'I told her,' Cooper said. 'I called her from the airport to ask about her Thursday ritual and she wanted to know exactly where you were. I gave her a rough location, and she must have passed that on to the Russians.'

Mann's head moved slowly from side to side, a clear sign of denial.

'I told you we got transcripts of all the conversations you had with Sloane. In one of them you joked about Debra taking out life insurance on you, but MI5 checked it out, and a policy was signed the day before she went to the embassy for the first time.'

Mann continued to study the face of the woman he'd spent the last nine years with, seven as husband and wife.

'You can say "fuck" if you want,' Cooper deadpanned. 'I did.'

His attempt to lighten the mood fell flat.

'Why?' Mann asked the photo. 'I mean…why?'

'You said yourself, she's a jealous woman. Maybe she just convinced herself you were having an affair and couldn't bear to be with you anymore.'

'If that was the case, she could have divorced me,' Mann said. 'Why set me up like that?'

'Revenge for cheating on her…the money…who knows.'

Mann flicked through the pages of the report. 'It explains her reaction when I turned up unannounced last night. I thought she was just shocked to see me, but looking back, she didn't seem genuinely thrilled to see me. She was…cold…distant…'

Cooper felt for his friend. To be betrayed was one thing, but to know it was someone so close to him must be tearing Mann apart. Cooper gave him some time to digest it, then asked, 'How do you want to play this?'

'I don't know. I need to think.'

Cooper understood. 'I haven't told Horton about this yet. I wanted you to be the first to know.'

Mann thanked Cooper. He turned the radio off, took the key from the ignition, and got out of the car. 'I'm gonna take a walk.'

'Roger that. I have to report to H, anyway. We found Belyakov, and—'

'Where?' Mann interrupted.

'A hotel in Earl's Court. The chief wants us to provide backup if it's needed. I shouldn't think it will be, though. The police are on their way to pick him up as we speak.'

Mann got back in the car. 'What's the name of the hotel?' he asked as he jabbed the key in the ignition. The engine roared as he backed out of the parking space and headed for the exit.

'The Majestic on Trebovir Road.'

Mann stopped at the barrier and punched the destination into his satnav.

'There's not much point going there,' Cooper argued. 'The police will probably already have him in custody.'

'I need to see him,' Mann said. 'A brave woman risked her life to warn me about him. It's the least I can do for her.'

* * *

293

Mann's mind was racing faster than his sports car as he weaved his way through the streets of London.

How could she do that to me? he wondered as he overtook a bus. He'd given Debra the best years of his life and remained faithful throughout. They'd fought a handful of times over trivial matters, but they always made up the same day. He'd been a good husband. Attentive, caring, selfless. Yet her baseless suspicions had driven Debra to do the unthinkable.

He tried to push thoughts of his wife aside. Her fate was sealed, and the time for reflection would come. Right now, he wanted to confront the man who had cost Helena Federova her life.

Cooper was on the phone to Horton, asking him to smooth the way with the police. If they just turned up asking questions, they wouldn't get far. MI6 personnel didn't carry identification, so in situations like this it was always better to give the other party advance notice.

They reached the entrance to Trebivor Road and found that the street had been cordoned off with police tape. Several emergency vehicles were parked up around the Majestic Hotel.

Mann and Cooper got out and walked to the nearest constable.

'Where's Commander Collins?' Mann asked the cop.

The officer looked him up and down. 'And you are?'

'Morgan and Davenport,' Mann said. 'He's expecting us.'

The cop got on the radio. A minute later, an officer wearing commander insignia approached the cordon and signalled for the constable to let Mann and Cooper through.

'Where's Volkov?' Mann asked after Collins introduced himself.

'You've had a wasted journey,' Collins said. 'There's no sign of your man.'

'He checked out?' Cooper asked.

'No. The receptionist said he left the hotel at about nine this morning, as he usually does. A forensics team has given his room a cursory examination but found nothing suspicious, and I'm about to pull my men back. I'll station plain-clothed ARVs at each end of the street, so if he comes back, we'll pick him up.'

'You're not going to look for him?' Mann asked, amazed at the policeman's blasé attitude.

'I wish I could, but leaving two armed response vehicles here is stretching resources to the limit. Intel from Five suggests a right-wing group is planning to infiltrate the NHS march this afternoon, so that's where we're concentrating our efforts.'

Mann's demeanour darkened. 'I don't think you appreciate the severity of the situation, Commander.'

'Then perhaps you could enlighten me,' Collins replied. 'All I was told was that Volkov *may* be armed and dangerous and *may* be about to engage in an act of terrorism. As you can imagine, my superiors are finding it hard to justify classifying him as a priority.'

'I can tell you that a brave woman died to give us his name,' Mann growled, 'and he plans to leave the country tonight. If he's going to do anything, it'll be in the next few hours.'

'Then I suggest you get your boss to speak to my boss, because my hands are tied.'

Mann wanted to argue, but knew it would be fruitless. Collins was just following orders, not issuing them. He was right in that the men at the top should speak to each other.

'Come on,' he said to Cooper, and walked back to his car, taking his phone out. He dialled Horton's number.

'No sign of Belyakov,' Mann told the chief. 'He's in London somewhere, but the police don't have enough spare men to search for him. Something about a right-wing threat to today's NHS mar...wait. That could be his target!'

'If he's booked on a flight home this evening, that makes sense,' Horton agreed. 'I'll have a word with the police. In the meantime, get back here—no, better still, get over to Box and see if you can help with a search. I'll let them know you're coming.'

Mann jumped into the car and was moving the second Cooper got in. They raced back to Thames House, and as promised they were met at reception.

'The control room is fully staffed,' Aaron Duffield said as he walked them to the underground car park. 'If you want to make yourselves useful, we need feet on the ground.'

That suited Mann. Anything was better than sitting in the office waiting for the bad news to come in.

'We've got facial recognition searching the gathering crowds for him,' Duffield continued, 'and we know that he hired a silver Skoda using his Volkov credit card. The police have been told to contact us immediately if his car is spotted on the ANPR network. I'll be co-ordinating the ground troops from Mobile One.'

'What's our role?' Cooper asked, as they reached the surveillance van that was disguised with the British Telecom livery.

'Walk the crowd, see if you can spot him.'

They climbed in the back, and Duffield handed them comms units. They looked like the ear buds that Mann used with his phone when he was exercising. As Mann and

Cooper put the devices in their ears, Duffield opened a laptop and showed them a map with several pulsing green dots.

'They act as trackers as well as radios, so I'll know where you are at any given time. Just speak normally; the buds will pick up everything you say. Alex, you're Bravo Six-One. Roland, Bravo Six-Two.'

'Now we just need to know what he looks like,' Mann said.

Duffield remedied that. He asked for their phone numbers, then sent them both a picture of Belyakov that MI5 had received from the CIA.

Mann studied the face. Belyakov was forty, his hair cut close to his scalp. His face was plain, nondescript, neither ugly nor particularly handsome.

'CCTV from Heathrow suggests he's grown his hair,' Duffield said. 'It's now a couple of inches long, cut in a side parting. He might have changed it since, we don't yet know. The team are searching CCTV from around his hotel to see if he's altered his appearance again recently. If he has, I'll update you.'

'Then it looks like we're all set,' Cooper said. 'Where do you want us?'

'Trafalgar Square for now,' Duffield said. 'That's where the march is due to kick off in…' He checked his watch. '…ninety minutes.' He banged on the panel that separated them from the driver. The van's engine roared into life and they moved off.

Not long after, they came to a stop. A screen in the back displayed the feed from a camera mounted in the cab. Mann saw that they were outside the Palace of Westminster, and traffic was at a standstill ahead of them.

'We'll get out here,' Mann said. 'It'll be quicker to walk.'

Duffield opened the back doors and the two men climbed out. As they walked towards Whitehall, they could see uniformed police trying to unravel a snarl of traffic caused by a shunt between a van and a bus.

'Bravo Six-One, radio check,' Mann said.

'This is Alpha One. Loud and clear, Bravo Six-One,' Duffield replied.

Cooper repeated the process, and he, too, was giving off a good signal.

They passed the Cenotaph, and the police presence increased dramatically as they approached Downing Street. Concrete barriers blocked the entrance to the prime minister's office and residence, and almost forty uniformed officers stood behind the temporary fortifications. That was in addition to the armed police contingent guarding the gates to Number Ten.

'Ward's taking no chances,' Cooper mused.

'I don't blame him. He won the election promising to protect the NHS and increase funding, then gave all that extra money to private providers. That's made a lot of people angry. He's bound to come in for some stick today.'

'Yeah, well, we're not here to help the PM with his political woes. Let's split up and find this bastard.'

Mann agreed that was the best approach.

When they reached Trafalgar Square, the sheer number of people was astonishing. The crowd filled every inch of pavement and spilled out onto the road. Some wore NHS uniforms, while others were dressed as patients. Most carried placards or banners. The air was filled with the low hum of tens of thousands of conversations.

Spotting Belyakov was going to be nigh-on impossible.

Mann offered Cooper a piece of gum and stuck one in his own mouth. 'You go that way,' he said to Cooper, pointing east.

As his friend peeled off, Mann began making his way through the throng. It was tough going. The protesters were packed together, and the only way he could make progress was to nudge people aside, which earned him a few rebukes and hard stares.

After a few minutes he managed to get to the equestrian statue of Charles I. A banner hung from the horse's head, reading *Save the NHS*. Mann scrambled up the plinth and looked out over the crowd.

Belyakov was a shade over six feet tall, so it was unlikely his head would be obscured. However, many of the people below him were wearing hats of varying styles. Many were NHS-issue surgical head coverings, others were caps and bobble hats to fight off the late autumn chill.

Mann felt deflated at the enormity of the task, but he forced himself to concentrate.

What's his goal? He asked himself. If the march was indeed Belyakov's target, what was the best way to inflict maximum damage? Suicide bombings were not part of the FSB's playbook, and even if he was carrying such a device, how many people could he kill? Fifty? A hundred? No, that would be a waste of effort. To do real damage to such a large gathering, it would have to be something else.

Chemical.

Biological.

President Sokolov had used such attacks before, though never on a scale this grand. They were usually directed at individual defectors or dissidents who had fled Moscow for England. One had been attacked in Salisbury with a

Novichok nerve agent, while another had been poisoned with polonium.

Were they looking in the wrong place? Was Belyakov just here to assassinate another of Sokolov's critics? That seemed the likely option, but then why was Belyakov booked on a flight for this evening? Was it just coincidence that he was leaving immediately after the protest?

Mann took out his phone to call Horton and pass on his thoughts. He'd just hit the Dial button when a shout went up next to him.

'Hi, Mum!'

Mann looked round to see a teenager smiling and waving at the sky. Mann followed the kid's gaze and saw a black object hovering a couple of hundred feet above the crowd.

A police surveillance drone.

Police forces often used drones to monitor large protests, recording the participants in case any turned to criminal activities. Their live feeds were also patched into facial recognition systems that could spot known troublemakers.

'Yes, Alex?'

Horton's voice interrupted Mann's thoughts. He'd made the call to suggest the march might not be Belyakov's target, but now he wasn't so sure. Mann recalled the sound of terror in Helena's voice when she'd given him Belyakov's name. She wouldn't have been so concerned if it was just a single Russian in the firing line. With the Russian penchant for poisonings and the ideal delivery vehicle hovering above his head, Mann knew he was in the right place.

'Chief, what counter-drone technology do we have in our arsenal?'

'What kind of drones are we talking about?' Horton asked. 'Reapers, or off-the-shelf toys?'

Reapers were the huge unmanned aerial vehicles deployed in the Middle East, capable of performing both reconnaissance and assault. They would never be deployed in the UK. Even if they were, they would be easy to spot on radar. 'The ones you can buy in the shops,' Mann said.

'Six don't have any, but Box and the Met both have access to Iron Sky.'

'That's operational?'

Mann was aware of the project, but the last he'd heard it had been years in the planning with little actual progress to show for it. The issue had been which method to employ. Some companies had offered RF solutions, which jam the radio frequencies being sent by the controller to the drone, while others had suggested their HPM systems. These used high power microwave devices to generate an electromagnetic pulse capable of disrupting electronics. Both methods had their plus sides, but also their drawbacks. Deploying RF defences could lead the target drone to behave erratically by masking the controller signal, but automated drones with pre-set flight paths were unaffected. HPM was more effective, but came at a high price. It would also destroy other electronic devices in the area. These included not only smart phones and computers, but pacemakers. Deploying them near hospitals or other components of the country's critical infrastructure was a no-no.

'As of three months ago,' Horton said. 'Why do you ask?'

Mann let him know what he was thinking, and the chief chewed it over.

'Sounds plausible,' Horton eventually said. 'I'll get on to the relevant parties.'

301

Mann hung up. 'Rollie,' he said over comms, 'meet me outside Tesco Express. Change of plan.'

* * *

Roland Cooper wandered the periphery of the crowd. It would be pointless trying to navigate his way through the tightly packed throng.

When the message from Mann came through his earpiece, he looked around for the shop and saw it across the road from him.

'Two minutes.'

After fighting his way through the sea of people, Cooper saw Mann standing outside the store.

'He won't be here,' Mann told him. He explained his theory that Russians preferred chemical attacks rather than explosives, and how drones would be the perfect delivery vehicle in these circumstances.

'If you're right, he's got to be close,' Cooper said. 'Those things don't have much of a range.'

'Agreed.' Mann opened comms to Duffield. 'Alpha One, he's unlikely to be in the crowd, but he has to be nearby. Get some men in the adjoining streets. We're looking for anyone who might be remote piloting a drone, and he won't want an audience.'

'Roger that. I'll tell control to concentrate CCTV surveillance on the immediate area.'

Mann took out his phone and checked a map of the local vicinity, then tapped Cooper on the arm. 'Come on.' To Duffield, he said, 'We'll head down Whitehall and check out Whitehall Place and Whitehall Court.'

'Affirmative.'

The crowd had spilled down the street that led past the prime minister's residence and on to the Palace of Westminster, the march's destination. 'It'll take forever to get through them,' Mann said. 'Let's take Northumberland Avenue.'

They turned just as a driver leaned on his horn just feet from them. The long, loud blast was deafening. A couple of protesters were standing in front of a silver Skoda saloon, gesturing angrily at the man behind the wheel.

'We're walking here!' one shouted.

The driver beeped his horn again, then wound down his window and stuck his head out, shouting for the protester to get the fuck out of his way.

The Russian accent grabbed Mann's attention. He got a good look at the driver, and immediately nudged Cooper with his elbow. Mann clicked the button on his transceiver.

'Alpha One, target spotted at my location.'

As Duffield acknowledged his transmission, Mann instinctively wanted to confront Belyakov. He managed one step towards the car, but Cooper grabbed his elbow.

'Wait. We don't know if he's armed.'

Cooper was right. They had no weapons of their own, and if Belyakov was packing, things could get ugly.

'Bravo Six-One, an ARV is five minutes out,' Duffield said.

Mann and Cooper looked at each other. It didn't sound like a long time, but Belyakov could do a lot of damage in that time, especially if they lost sight of him. If the Russian's intention was to detonate a car bomb, he wouldn't be in such a hurry to leave the area. That meant the threat wasn't immediate.

'We have to stall him,' Mann said.

Belyakov was still leaning on his horn, only now he was inching his vehicle forward, forcing the protesters into a choice: stand their ground, or back off and avoid injury. Before they could choose the latter, Cooper ran to join them, shouting angrily at Belyakov and banging on the bonnet of his car.

It appeared to be working. Belyakov applied the handbrake, but Mann's heart almost stopped when he saw the Russian put his hand inside his jacket.

Shit! He's reaching…

* * *

Sergei Belyakov made good time until he got to within a mile of Trafalgar Square, at which point traffic slowed to a crawl. The clock on the dashboard told him he still had over an hour to reach the parking space that had been reserved for him, but for every minute that ticked by, he only managed to move a couple of yards. Though the deadline wasn't set in stone, he was still determined to make it. Ten minutes late and the effects of the weapon he was about to unleash might be diminished, and he didn't fancy explaining any tardiness to Colonel Kuznetsov.

Twenty minutes after creeping past St. Paul's Cathedral, Belyakov was relieved to see traffic thinning out. The hold-up had been caused by a nasty collision between a truck and a car, which several emergency vehicles were attending to. A cop directed traffic, and Belyakov waited patiently for his turn. When he was waved through, he managed to get the car up to thirty miles an hour, but only briefly. Once on Strand, he looked for the turning onto Adam Street.

When he found it, his heart almost stopped. The junction had been closed off. Several men in high-visibility jackets were digging up the road, and detour signs pointed down Strand towards Trafalgar Square. Belyakov cursed and thumped the wheel. Traffic was stop-start once more, so he took the opportunity to plot a different route to his destination.

Come on, he urged, as the cars ahead inched forward. *Come on.*

It was 11:25 before he saw Nelson's Column in the distance, and he knew he was close. From there, it was a left onto Northumberland Avenue, then through back streets to the parking space. A few minutes later, he was about to make his turn when two pedestrians walked out in front of his car. He leaned on the horn, but rather than clearing out of the way, they stood and berated him as if he were in the wrong.

If this had happened in Moscow, he would have run them over, then arrested them for hampering an FSB officer. That wouldn't wash here. Instead, he could only behave like a typical Londoner, so he wound his window down and leaned out.

'Get out of the fucking way!'

His words had no effect, so he closed his window again and eased out the clutch, making his intentions clear: move or get hit.

A third man joined the protesters. This one slammed his fists on the bonnet of the car. 'What are you playing at?'

Belyakov suspected that if he didn't clear the area soon, things could quickly escalate. Tempting as it was to shoot the lot of them, it would jeopardise his mission. Instead, he decided to bluff them. He reached to take out his phone, so that he could pretend to call the police, but before he could free it from his jacket pocket, another man appeared. He said something to the trio that upset one of them, and he was shoved violently against the bonnet of Belyakov's Skoda. The newcomer crumpled to the ground, but a moment later he was back on his feet and pushing the three protesters back onto the pavement.

Belyakov wondered if perhaps he was a plain-clothed cop, or just someone who didn't want to see three people splattered under the wheels of a car, but the road was now clear. Belyakov drove on, and a minute later he took a left turn into an underpass.

* * *

Seeing Belyakov reach for a weapon, Mann had to act fast. There was no telling what the Russian would do if he felt his mission was under threat, but at the same time he didn't want to lose Belyakov.

'ARV four minutes out,' Duffield said in Mann's ear. 'Bravo Six-One, is he still at your position?'

'Affirmative,' Mann replied instinctively, and as he said the word, a thought struck him. He took the bud from his ear and the gum from his mouth and ran over to Cooper, standing between him and the Skoda.

'Push me, hard!' he hissed.

Cooper looked confused for a second, but when Mann gave him a 'hurry up' look, Cooper shoved him in the chest.

Mann threw himself backwards, landing hard on the bonnet, then slithered down to the ground. Once he was out of sight of the driver, he wedged the gum and earpiece into the car's grille, then got back to his feet.

'Get out of the road!' Mann yelled. 'You'll get the police involved and they'll close the march down before it's even begun.'

To emphasise his point, Mann pushed Cooper towards the pavement. He was about to do the same to the other two, but they'd got the message.

The Skoda moved off, and as it drove down Northumberland Avenue, Cooper grabbed Mann's elbow.

'What the hell are you doing?' Cooper growled. 'You just let him get away!'

'He looked to be reaching for a weapon,' Mann said. 'I couldn't risk letting him use it. Anyway, I stuck my earpiece to his car. Tell Alpha One and ask for constant updates on Belyakov's location.

Cooper managed a sly grin. 'Sneaky bastard.'

'Just tell Duffield,' Mann urged him.

Cooper relayed the message and waited for a response.

'He took a left on Embankment Place and is now on Villiers Street…wait…John Adam Street.'

Mann was looking at the map on his phone as Cooper relayed the directions.

'Let's go this way,' Mann said, pointing down Strand. 'It's quicker.'

They moved as fast as the conditions allowed, but the march organisers were now in full cry, herding everyone together to spell out the schedule, route and conditions imposed by the police.

It took Mann and Cooper a couple of minutes to clear a way to Strand, by which time Duffield had an update.

'He's stationary on the corner of Adam Street and Adelphi Terrace.'

Mann asked how long it would take the ARV to get there and was told they were still four minutes away due to heavy traffic. He checked his map and indicated to Cooper that they should turn right. When they did, they saw that Belyakov was already out of the car and leaning into the boot. He was sixty yards from them.

'Now what?' Cooper asked.

Mann's jaw clenched. 'We take him out.'

'And if he's carrying?'

'Then we're fucked,' Mann said.

Cooper slipped off his leather jacket. 'I have an idea. If I click my fingers, draw his fire.'

* * *

'Get out of the fucking way!'

Despite its flashing lights and siren, the armed response vehicle was going nowhere. Cars edged to the side of the road, but there was simply no gap for Officer Stuart Dunn to aim for. Certainly not one large enough to accommodate his BMW X5.

'They want to know how long,' Officer Ken Wright said from the back seat.

'Still four minutes,' the sergeant in the front seat said.

Dunn looked for a way out of the jam, but he couldn't even take to the pavement. For one, it wasn't wide enough, and even if it had been, there were simply too many pedestrians to allow him to take that route.

Dunn opened his door and got out, standing on the sill so that he could get a clear view down the road. Nothing was moving. He climbed back inside and slammed the door shut.

'Plan B,' he said, and eased the car to the side of the road. He got the passenger side wheels onto the pavement, then pulled the handbrake, turned off the siren, and cut the engine. He left the lights flashing. 'We have to go on foot. There's no way we're clearing this mess.'

The four men got out and ran to the back of the BMW. Sergeant Joel Hicks keyed in a code to unlock the gun safe, and they each grabbed their weapons.

* * *

Belyakov took the first of the drones from the boot and switched it on before placing it on the ground. He opened the app on the phone and saw that the machine was showing a paired signal. He'd been instructed to get all four airborne at the same time, which meant turning them all on, ensuring they were mated with the phone, then clicking the Start button on each icon in the app.

If you put them into flight one at a time, someone might see you and raise the alarm before you can get them all into the air. If that happens, the mission will be compromised and you will have failed. We cannot allow that.

With Kuznetsov's words ringing in his ear, Belyakov reached into the boot for the second unit. As he did, he heard footsteps behind him.

They were approaching fast.

He spun around and immediately recognised them as two of the people who had been remonstrating in front of his car minutes earlier. Not the original two, but the other pair.

What the hell do they want? he wondered.

As they got closer, Belyakov saw that they were both smiling.

'Hi,' said the one carrying an old leather jacket across his arm. 'Glad we found you. We just wanted to apologise for hitting your car earlier.'

They were now roughly ten yards away and still walking towards him, and something about them didn't seem right. For one, it was far too cold to be walking around without a jacket on. His training taught him to pick up on such incongruities, as well as identifying when people were likely to be friend or foe. These two definitely fell into the latter category.

'Don't mention it,' Belyakov said. He straightened and placed his hands on his hips, his fingers inches from the Makarov tucked into the back of his waistband.

'What you got there?' the second man asked.

They were still closing, now just five yards from him. Belyakov had to make a decision. If he turned the gun on them, he would be forced to use it. That would blow the mission. He might be able to launch the drones, but success would only be guaranteed if he got out of the country without drawing attention to himself. If the British police and security services were able to link him and the mission to Moscow, the result would be devastating. Perhaps not for President Sokolov, who could spin his way out of it, but certainly for Belyakov.

The two men had closed to within three yards, and they had moved slightly apart, as if meaning to attack on two fronts.

Belyakov was forced to act.

* * *

Sergeant Joel Hicks was the first to admit that he wasn't the fittest man on the planet, and it was pure adrenaline that kept him going. The pavement was packed with people, tourists mixed with protesters, but the ARV team was still able to maintain a decent pace through a combination of shouting and jostling.

A mile never seemed so far. Most of the pedestrians scattered when they saw the heavily armed police officers running towards them, but others were slow to move. The crowd ahead parted, but an elderly couple carried on their casual stroll as if they either hadn't heard the commotion or didn't care. The team had to skirt around them, wasting valuable seconds.

Enough of this shit!

Hicks took to the road, dodging between cars. He glanced behind him to see the others were following his lead, and the pace picked up dramatically.

They were within four hundred yards of Adam Street when a woman in an SUV decided to get out and see what was causing the hold-up. She opened her door just as Hicks drew level with her car, and he had no time to stop. He slammed into the edge of the door, his face and right knee taking the full force of the impact. Hicks went down hard, his head banging against the side of a van.

'Sarge, you okay?'

Dunn stood over him, panting and looking concerned.

Hicks waved him away and tried to stand, but pain shot from his kneecap. He fell back down and checked for damage. There was no blood, but his leg hurt like a bitch.

Dunn was staring at Hicks' head. 'That looks nasty.'

Hicks felt his forehead and his glove came back wet. 'I'll live. Help me up.'

Dunn got the sergeant to his feet, and Hicks took a few tender steps to test his knee. It screamed with each step.

'Wait here,' Dunn said. 'We'll go on without you.'

'No.' There was no way Hicks was going to stand down just because some stupid cow didn't know how to check her mirrors. He hobbled around for a few seconds, and the pain eventually receded enough that he could put his full weight on his leg. He wiped his forehead with his sleeve, then took his glove off and touched the wound. It didn't feel too bad.

'Let's go,' he said to Dunn. 'You take the lead this time.'

* * *

Belyakov whipped out his Makarov and pointed it at the one carrying the jacket. 'That's close enough.'

The pair stopped dead, and Belyakov moved to his side so that he could cover them both with the weapon.

The one with the leather jacket was closest to him. 'Whoa, mate! No need for that! We just wanted to say sorry, that's all.'

'Yeah, we didn't wanna cause any trouble,' the other one said, spreading his arms out wide.

Conscious that they could be seen from the street, Belyakov let the gun fall to his side, out of view, but with the barrel still pointed at the target. Having acted, he now faced a dilemma. If he were to release the drones now, the two men would know about it. If he sent them on their way, they would no doubt tell the police about the pistol he was carrying.

'Over to the wall,' he said. 'Both of you.'

He made up his mind to release the drones, then force the two men into his car, where he would shoot them before driving out of the city to dispose of their bodies. He wouldn't have time to bury them properly, and their remains would soon be found, but by that time he'd be back home in Moscow.

That plan relied on his two captors complying, and it fell apart moments later. The one carrying the leather jacket followed his instructions, but then he clicked his fingers. Instantly, the other one made a run for it. Belyakov raised the pistol, got a lead on the fleeing figure, and squeezed the trigger.

* * *

The faint yet unmistakeable sound of gunfire reached Hicks just as he was about to throw in the towel. Dunn was already thirty yards ahead of him, and he must have heard it, too, because he spurted away. Hicks chased after him, newfound strength pushing him on.

* * *

'Over to the wall. Both of you.'

Cooper did as instructed, crabbing slowly sideways so that he was always facing Belyakov. After giving Mann the signal, he would have to act quickly and decisively. There would be no margin for error.

With his left hand, Cooper clicked his fingers. The moment he did so, Mann made a run for it. He sprinted away from Cooper, who saw Belyakov raise his weapon. As the Russian got Mann in his sights, Cooper threw his heavy leather jacket at him. It hit Belyakov's gun hand just as a bullet left the chamber.

Not stopping to see the result of the shot, Cooper charged Belyakov. He got to within striking range as the Russian brought his gun around, batting the hand holding the Makarov to one side before delivering a punch to Belyakov's throat. The Russian twisted and leaned backwards, rendering the blow ineffective. The move left Cooper off balance, and Belyakov brought his knee up into Cooper's thigh. The combination of dead leg and his own momentum sent Cooper tumbling to the ground in a flailing heap. The side of his head slammed into the road, and as he lay on his back, dazed, Cooper saw Belyakov aim the pistol at him. From two yards, there was no way he could miss.

Mann came from nowhere. Cooper saw his friend launch himself through the air, tackling Belyakov high in the chest. Both men went sprawling, and the gun flew from Belyakov's grasp. As his vision blurred, Cooper could just make out the two men scrambling for the weapon. Mann looked favourite to reach it, but Belyakov grabbed his ankle and twisted, pulling Mann backwards. Mann kicked out, scraping the sole of his shoe down Belyakov's fingers, forcing him to release his grip. It seemed to do the trick, but when Mann got back to his feet, the Russian rugby-tackled him around the waist. He rammed Mann into the side of a parked car, then took a step back and started laying into Mann with his fists.

Cooper struggled to his feet, his head swimming and his legs reacting like set custard.

Mann was in trouble. He was doing what he could to fend off Belyakov's blows, but Cooper could see his defences crumbling. Cooper staggered over to intervene, but Belyakov swept Mann's legs away and watched him fall to the ground. The Russian walked over to the Makarov and picked it up, then caught sight of Cooper.

He raised the weapon and pointed it at Cooper's head.

Cooper looked down the barrel, knowing his time had come. He was surprised to discover that he wasn't scared. He was angry that he hadn't been strong enough to stop Belyakov, that he'd failed to protect his friend, but there was no fear.

Cooper closed his eyes and waited for the shot, knowing he'd be dead before he heard it.

That wasn't the case.

The sound rang out, but Cooper was still standing. He opened his eyes and saw Belyakov lying on the ground, convulsing. The pistol was lying next to the Russian, and a pool of blood was forming beneath him. Cooper stumbled towards the Russian on shaky legs and saw a red patch growing over Belyakov's heart.

'Stay back!'

A rough hand grabbed Cooper's arm and dragged him away from the dying Belyakov.

Cooper turned his head to see a panting uniformed cop wearing a black baseball cap, three more heavily armed behind him. He looked like he'd been in a war himself, with blood streaming down his face.

'Check my friend,' Cooper said. At least, that was what he tried to say. The words sounded in his own ears like he was talking with a mouth full of treacle.

'Let's get the medics to look at you,' the cop said, gulping in air while guiding Cooper away from the scene of the shooting.

One of the other officers jogged to Mann, while the other two attended to the Russian.

The injured cop gently sat Cooper on the kerb before giving him a once-over.

'You've got a nasty head wound,' he said.

'So have you,' Cooper replied.

'I know. Just try to stay still. An ambulance is on its way.'

The words swam in Cooper's ears. He put his hand to his head and his fingers came back covered in blood.

At least Alex was okay. Cooper saw his friend being helped to his feet, and although there was blood on Mann's face, he seemed to be walking without any problem.

Cooper wiped his fingers on his trousers, and when he looked up, Mann was standing over him.

'You okay?'

Cooper nodded, then winced as he wished he hadn't. 'I'll live.'

'Good.' Mann turned to the cop. 'Don't let anyone touch that drone. It most likely contains a chemical or biological weapon. Get a HASMAT team in to secure it. There are more in the boot of the car, too.'

The police officer got on the radio, and Mann sat next to Cooper.

'You don't look too good.'

'I don't feel too good,' Cooper replied. As the adrenaline of the fight wore off, his head was beginning to pound. He looked up at the cop. 'What the hell took you so long? And what happened to your face?'

The officer offered a semblance of a smile. 'Car trouble.'

Chapter 38

'Listen to the experts,' Mann said. 'They know what they're talking about.'

'I feel fine, really.'

Cooper tried to sit up, but the nurse pushed him back down onto the bed. 'You've got a concussion,' she said, tucking him in. 'Twenty-four hours' observation, that's the rule.'

'She's right,' Mann said from the chair next to Cooper's bed. 'You don't want to take any chances.'

Cooper sighed. 'How long have I got left?'

'Twenty-three and a half hours,' the nurse smiled. 'And if I hear one more complaint, I'll stick your bed pan in the freezer for an hour. That'll really give you something to moan about.'

'You're bluffing,' Cooper said with a grin.

'Try me. On my salary, I can't afford Netflix. I have to make my own entertainment.'

The nurse left, and Cooper sighed again. 'It's not fair. I should be out getting drunk, not lying here listening to threats from an underpaid matron.'

'No alcohol for a few days, either,' Mann said. He unplugged Cooper's phone and handed it to him. 'There. Fully charged. Watch a few movies, listen to some music, whatever. You'll be home before you know it.'

The door to the private room opened, and Aaron Duffield stuck his head inside.

'Not disturbing anything, am I?'

'No, mate. Come on in,' Mann told him.

Duffield stood over Cooper's bed with his hands on his hips. 'How are you doing?'

'He's bored and miserable, but otherwise in perfect health,' Mann said. 'They're just keeping him in for observation.'

Duffield nodded thoughtfully at Cooper, then turned to Mann. 'It's actually you that I came to see.'

'Oh, yeah?'

Duffield opened his phone and entered a long code to wake it up. He handed the mobile to Mann, who looked at a picture on the screen. He'd seen one just like it earlier that day.

Debra, in disguise, walking into the Russian Embassy.

'I know all about that,' Mann said. 'Rollie filled me in.'

'Actually, this was taken this morning,' Duffield said. 'Can you think of any reason she'd still be in contact with the Russians?'

Mann could only think of one. Her initial attempts to get Moscow to dispose of him had failed, and she was doubling down. Any doubts he'd had about her guilt had just been dispelled. 'She's telling the Russians where I am.'

'That's what I suspected,' Duffield said. 'I thought it might be prudent to warn you.'

'Thanks, but she has no idea where I really am.' He still hadn't decided how to confront her about her treachery, and having her turn up at the hospital wasn't part of his plan. Mann had spoken to Horton about it, and the chief had agreed that picking Debra up wasn't a priority right now. They would move on her once Mann was ready. 'I told her I was involved in an incident and was receiving treatment, but didn't say where. The staff here have been instructed not to reveal my location. Same goes for Rollie.'

'That covers you for now, but you'll have to go home eventually.'

Duffield was right. Assuming President Sokolov had the appetite to send someone all the way to England to kill him—which Mann thought highly unlikely—they would probably act when he was at home, relaxed, off his guard.

'Thanks for letting me know,' Mann said to Duffield. 'I'll take it from here.'

The man from Five thanked them both for their help in taking Belyakov down, then left. Once he was gone, Mann took out his phone and called Horton.

After once again assuring the boss that he and Cooper would be fine, Mann asked the chief if there was any progress in identifying the agent the drones had been carrying.

'It doesn't appear to be chemical or biological,' Horton said. 'The bods at Porton Down think it's some kind of nanotechnology.'

'Nanobots? Those things are real?'

'It seems so. Companies have been working on their development for the past twenty years at least. It looks like Sokolov has found a way to make them work.'

'But what do they do?' Mann asked.

'That, we don't know. Tests are being conducted as we speak.'

Whatever the capabilities of the tiny robots, Mann doubted they were designed for anything other than nefarious purposes.

'What's the Russian response?' Mann asked.

'The usual, so far. Flat denials of any involvement.'

That was always the way. Even after being presented with irrefutable evidence of the Russian security service being involved in the assassination attempt of a London-based Sokolov critic, the Kremlin had denied being behind it.

'What have the Russians been told?' Mann asked.

'Only that we suspect they planned an attack, and that more details would be forthcoming.'

That was how the game was played. The Russians would offer staunch denials, and Britain would drip feed details to refute each statement Sokolov made. The frustrating aspect was that, to date, all investigations into Russian hits had been reactive. Someone had been killed or targeted, and by the time it was linked to the Kremlin, the perpetrators were long gone.

Sokolov wouldn't be able to deny it if his man was caught in the act.

'How would you like concrete proof that Sokolov is behind this?' Mann asked.

'I'm listening.'

* * *

'Where are you?' Debra asked. 'What the hell's going on?'

'They've moved me to a place called Parkland,' Mann replied. 'It's a private hospital near Horsham.'

'But why are they keeping you in? Are you hurt?'

'I took a bit of a beating,' Mann replied. 'They said I have a concussion and a few cracked ribs. I should be home in a couple of days.'

'I'm coming to see you.'

'There's no point. We've also got a Russian suspect here, recovering from a gunshot wound. They're not allowing anyone in except the staff and police. No friends, no family, no one.'

'That's ridiculous! I'm your wife!'

Yeah, some wife. 'I know, darling, but it's a high-profile investigation. We're building a strong case against Sokolov, and if he manages to get to our prisoner, the entire thing will collapse. I shouldn't even be telling you where I am.'

There was silence for a moment. 'Well, as long as you're safe.'

'I am,' Mann assured her, doing his best to sound upbeat. 'I'll be home in a couple of days. Get the champagne on ice.'

'I will,' Debra promised. 'Love you.'

Lying bitch! 'Love you, too.'

* * *

Dmitri Gudkov handed Sokolov the report he'd compiled and stood to attention in front of the president's desk.

As if writing it down is going to lessen the blow, Gudkov thought.

It couldn't possibly have been worse. In the last twelve hours, it had been established that the woman who had informed them about Alex Mann's true profession over a year earlier was none other than his wife, Debra. She had been back to the embassy in London to tell them that Alex Mann was now back in England and was being treated for minor injuries at a private hospital in Sussex, despite Gudkov's efforts to seal the borders. To cap it all off, the BBC had announced that a terrorist plot to attack the NHS march with drones had been foiled. A suspect had been wounded during the police operation and was now recovering in hospital. Senior officers were waiting to question him.

Gudkov knew he had failed on every level: Mann was free, and Project Nightfall, the means with which they planned to cripple America, was probably being dissected in a British laboratory at that very moment. He couldn't even offer Nikolai Levchenko's head to soften the blow. The albino had disappeared off the face of the planet.

Sokolov finished reading the report, then squeezed his eyes closed, as if fighting off a headache. He opened them and blinked twice, then read from the single sheet of paper again, prolonging Gudkov's misery.

Please let it be a firing squad, Gudkov thought. He knew the end was near, but after all his years of loyal service, he felt he deserved a quick death. The alternative was hanging. It wasn't something the head of the FSB relished.

Sokolov slapped the paper with the back of his hand, interrupting Gudkov's macabre thoughts.

'I want them dead.'

It wasn't what Gudkov had been expecting to hear. 'I'm sorry, who?'

Sokolov tossed the report back at him. 'Mann and Belyakov. It says here that they're being treated at the same hospital. Send someone to kill them both. Belyakov can't be allowed to say a word.'

Gudkov's relief was palpable. 'Of course, sir. I'll arrange it immediately.'

He almost ran from the office, wanting to escape before the president could change his mind.

He'd been handed a reprieve. At the moment it was probably temporary, but if he could pull this off and restore some deniability, he might escape with his life.

Chapter 39

Wassily Levin strolled through customs at Heathrow airport and stood with his hands behind his back, looking at one of the arrivals boards. A moment later, he felt someone brush past him. He touched the side of his jacket and felt the small case that had been dropped in his pocket. It had been brought to England via diplomatic pouch on an earlier flight from Moscow.

It wasn't the kind of thing he wanted border agents to find on his person.

Levin followed the signs to the car park, where he found the rented BMW on the third level, as arranged. He took the key fob from the wheel well and got in.

The small case contained two hypodermic needles, both filled with a clear liquid. He took them from the case and made sure the protective plastic caps were firmly in place before putting them on the seat next to him. Using a wet wipe from the glove box, he cleaned his prints from the case. He would toss it from the window on the drive to the hospital. Also in the glove box was a uniform complete with ID card, and a Makarov pistol. He'd been warned that the weapon was only to be used in case of extreme emergency.

When he pushed for clarification, he'd been told that he couldn't be taken alive.

The message was clear: complete the mission, or don't come back.

Levin took off his jacket and put the blue uniform on over his own clothes. He tucked the gun into his waistband before setting off.

Levin had memorised the route on the flight over. He'd specified that he'd wanted a car with no satnav, as he knew a competent forensics team could extract a vehicle's travel history from them. For that same reason, he never carried a cell phone on a mission.

Parkland Hospital was a private institution on the outskirts of Horsham in Sussex. As he approached it, Levin still had misgivings. When plans were thrown together at the eleventh hour, it was easy for errors to slip in. He had been fed details of the operation while on his way to Sheremetyevo Airport, such was the urgency to get things in motion.

He was to pose as a staff member to gain access to the facility. Security was certain to be tight, with few allowed in, so pretending to work there was his best chance of getting close to the targets. The ID card bore the name Marius Barbu, a Romanian cleaner working for the facilities management company that serviced the hospital.

It was time to discover whether his ruse would work.

Levin parked a couple of hundred yards from the hospital—it would look odd for a low-paid worker to roll up in an expensive vehicle. He put the needles in his trouser pocket and walked the rest of the way.

The researchers who had helped to put the mission together had spoken to a Ukrainian cleaner who worked at the hospital. From him, they had learned the layout of the building, and that there was a staff entrance around the back of the hospital. Levin walked past a shed containing rubbish bins and found the door he was looking for.

The moment of truth.

He held his breath and pressed his ID card against the reader on the side of the door frame. A red light appeared.

Shit!

Levin tried again, and this time he was rewarded with a green light and an audible click. Exhaling, he pushed the door open and found himself face to face with an armed policeman.

'Can I help you?'

Levin had been prepared to encounter such security. 'I Marius. Work…' He made circular motions with his hand. Levin's English was excellent, but it wouldn't be in keeping with his role.

'You're a cleaner,' the policeman said.

Levin nodded happily. 'Yes. Cleaner.'

The officer looked at the badge, then at Levin, and finally handed it back. 'Okay, in you go.'

Levin smiled and took his badge back, clipping it to his tunic. He walked down a short corridor before opening a door on his right. As he'd been briefed, it was the cleaning cupboard. He wheeled out a trolley loaded with cleaning products and pretended to check that he had everything he needed, conscious that the policeman was keeping a sharp eye on him. He went into the cupboard and added a few extra rags and a couple of bottles of disinfectant to the trolley, just to make it look like he knew what he was doing.

Through the red door, take the service lift to the second floor.

The first floor of the building was a day clinic, while the second housed the in-patient wards and operating theatre. When the lift *dinged* to a halt, Levin pushed his trolley into an expansive hallway. The wheels of his cart glided over the linoleum flooring as he followed the signs to Shakespeare Ward, which was Parkland's intensive care unit. That was the most likely place to find a gunshot victim.

This was where things got tricky. To be sure of disposing of Belyakov, Levin could take out everyone in the vicinity and put a bullet in his compatriot's head, but the orders had been that it had to look like natural causes. The drug in the hypodermics was slow-acting, which would give him time to clear the area before Belyakov took his final breath. Toxicology reports would not detect the slightest trace.

All he had to do was administer it without being detected.

Fortune appeared to be on his side. After entering the ward and having his ID checked once more by another armed police officer, Levin pushed his trolley around a corner and past several doors, each with patient details handwritten on a panel. On the fifth door, he found the first name he was looking for. Alex Mann. Next to it was Sergei Belyakov.

Levin had been instructed to deal with Belyakov first. He was the more important target, and because of his injuries, the least likely to put up any resistance.

Checking that no one was watching, Levin twisted the door handle on Belyakov's room and slipped inside. The room was dark except for the array of monitoring machines that stood next to the single bed. From that faint light, Levin could clearly make out the face of Sergei Belyakov.

Levin took one of the needles from his pocket and removed the plastic cap as he approached the bed. He was glad to see a drip feeding into Belyakov's arm, which was how he'd planned to administer the drug. Better to do it that way than to inject it straight into the patient, which would wake him and arouse suspicion. Levin unscrewed the needle and pumped the contents of the syringe into the Luer lock port, all the time keeping an eye on Belyakov to make sure he didn't stir.

That was when he noticed something strange. Belyakov didn't appear to be breathing. Levin thought perhaps it might just be the light playing tricks, but when he leaned in close there was no sound coming from Belyakov's mouth. Levin touched Belyakov's cheek, just to be sure, and the cold skin confirmed his fears.

Belyakov was dead, and had been for some time.

'Turn around slowly, Levin. Hands in the air.'

Levin was stunned. How did they know his name? Had Moscow set him up? No, they wouldn't do that. There were much easier ways of getting rid of him.

'We've been tracking you since you landed three hours ago,' the voice said. 'We know why you're here.'

Levin remembered the warning he'd received from his superiors. *Don't let them take you alive.* He had no intention of doing so.

He straightened up and slowly turned, letting his right arm sneak behind his back. He'd just got his fingers on the grip of the Makarov when his entire body was wracked with pain.

* * *

Mann watched Levin freeze like a statue, then drop to the floor. He kept his finger on the trigger of the taser for another five seconds, just to be sure, then released it. Levin's gun had fallen from his grasp, and the armed officer standing next to Mann kicked it out of reach before applying handcuffs to Levin's wrists. Three more cops ran into the room, and they applied restraints to Levin's ankles before frisking him. After emptying the Russian's pockets, they carried him out of the room.

Moments after Levin's departure, Willoughby Horton appeared in the doorway.

'I think we can safely say that went well,' the chief smiled.

It had indeed. With the surveillance photographs, the drug Levin intended to kill with, and a suspect to parade in front of the cameras, not even Sokolov could talk his way out of this one.

It was just a shame that it wouldn't have worked without Debra's treachery.

Horton seemed to know what he was thinking.

'I guess there's just one thing left to do,' he said.

There was, and it wasn't something Mann was looking forward to.

'Have you decided how you want to do this? Obviously, we'd like it taken care of sooner rather than later.'

'Yeah, I know.'

Chapter 40

Roland Cooper knocked on the door to Mann's home and waited for Debra to answer. He hadn't phoned ahead, but as it was Thursday, he knew she'd be home doing the laundry.

Debra opened the door, and when she looked beyond Cooper and saw two uniformed police officers, a smile briefly played on her face before disappearing as quickly as it had come.

'Where's Alex?' she asked, with what sounded to Cooper like genuine concern. She was a good actress, he'd give her that.

'Can we come in?' Cooper asked her. 'I'm afraid it's bad news.'

'What do you mean, bad news? Where's my husband?'

'I think it's best if we talk inside.'

Debra relented and let them in, closing the door behind the trio before leading them to the living room. The French windows were open, and Cooper could see a marguerita glass on the garden table.

Debra sat on the sofa, her hands clasped tightly together. 'Where's Alex?' she repeated.

'There was…an incident at the hospital…'

'What do you mean, an incident? Is Alex okay?'

'It appears the Russian president sent someone to kill a prisoner we were holding. I believe they were also tasked with killing Alex.'

Debra's hand shot to her mouth. 'Oh, my God!'

She's overdoing it now, Cooper thought. Time to put her out of her misery. 'Yeah. Fortunately, we knew they were coming. We managed to capture the assassin and no one was hurt.'

Debra leapt to her feet, her despair swiftly turning to anger. 'Is this some kind of sick joke?'

'No,' Mann said, stepping in from the garden. 'These officers aren't here to inform you of my death, despite how hard you tried. They're here to arrest you for treason.'

Debra ran to her husband, but Mann grabbed her by the shoulders and held her at arms' length.

'Don't even bother trying to deny it,' he told her. 'You visited the Russian Embassy four times. Once a year ago, then again when Rollie told you I'd escaped from the Widow Maker, again when I arrived back home, and then two days ago, to tell them that I was staying in Parkland Hospital.'

'Darling, I don't know what you're talking about. I love you. I always have.'

Mann pushed her onto the sofa and took two photographs from his pocket. One was of Debra in disguise, walking into the embassy. The other was of her in the coffee shop, removing her wig. He tossed them onto her lap.

Debra looked at them, and all pretence evaporated. 'Well, what did you expect me to do?' she spat. 'Sit here and play the doting wife while you're in Russia shagging everything that moves?'

'That's just it,' Mann said. 'I wasn't shagging anyone. I've been faithful throughout our marriage, but you just wouldn't believe me. You should have just left once the trust had gone, but no, you had to take things to the extreme.' He looked at the two police officers. 'You can take her away now.'

Debra got to her feet to protest, but her slim frame was no match for the burly cops. They had her cuffed in seconds, and one read Debra her rights.

'Alex!' she pleaded. 'Please don't do this!'

The tears were genuine this time, but Mann was unmoved. He watched as the two uniforms marched his wife through the front door. Cooper followed them and closed it once they were gone. When he walked back into the living room, he clapped his hands together. 'Fancy a cuppa?'

'What? You...I just lost my wife of seven years, and you're asking if I want a cup of tea?'

'Yeah, sorry, mate. Bit insensitive.' He stood, thoughtful, then added, 'Beer?'

Mann sighed. From the scuffed leather jacket he was wearing to his lack of tact, Cooper would always be Cooper.

'Make it vodka.'

Chapter 41

'The story dominating the front pages this morning is the news that MI5 and MI6, in an unprecedented co-ordinated effort, have foiled what they call a Russian state-backed terror plot. With me, I have Julia Hart, chief political editor of the Guardian, and Royston Kearns from The Times. Julia, I'll start with you. The level of detail we've been given is unheard of, isn't it?'

'That's right, Kim. The government are usually tight-lipped when it comes to security operations such as this, but we've been given access to some pretty chilling stuff here. I think the fact that the suspected terrorist was killed is part of the reason, because as you know, if this were to go to trial, the defence team could call these revelations prejudicial, but that's not the case here.'

'But, still, we've never been privy to such detail before. We have the name of the suspect who was shot dead, we have a copy of his FSB file photograph, pictures of the drones he was trying to launch, there's just so much more than we'd expect. Royston, what's your take on this?'

'We mustn't forget that this government has been pilloried in the house in recent weeks because of the rising crime figures, and with a general election less than a year away, it could be nothing more than a stunt to enhance their pretty dreadful polling figures, if I'm honest.'

Cooper turned the TV off and finished his morning coffee. 'Shall we?'

Mann stood and put on his jacket. 'Ready when you are.'

They drove to Vauxhall Cross in Cooper's mini. Rain lashed at the windscreen, but for Mann it couldn't be a more glorious day. He'd come to terms with Debra's actions, and now he was about to embark on a new episode in his life.

Inside the building, they strolled to Horton's office. *For the last time*, Mann realised. He looked at Cooper, who appeared equally at ease. 'You sure you wanna do this?' Mann asked.

'Never been surer.'

They knocked and waited for the chief to call them in, then stood in front of Horton's desk.

Mann couldn't help but steal a glance at the fish tank on the sideboard. *Fishbowl*, he reminded himself.

Horton leaned back in his chair. 'Gentlemen. To what do I owe the pleasure?'

'I think you know, Chief,' Mann smiled.

They both took sealed envelopes from their pockets and placed them on Horton's desk.

'And there's no way I can make you change your minds?'

'I'm afraid not,' Cooper told him.

Horton gave them a resigned look. 'I didn't think so.' He stood and walked over to his small aquarium, where he took a pinch of flakes and dropped them into the water. The two guppies raced to the surface to feed greedily. 'It's a shame. Things are really hotting up right now. Interesting times, as someone once said.'

'News from Moscow?' Mann asked.

Horton put the lid back on the food container. 'Sokolov denied everything, naturally. He blamed it on rogue elements within the FSB. Elements that have apparently admitted their guilt and been appropriately punished.'

'Who did he blame?' Cooper asked.

'Gudkov. Had him tried and executed within a couple of days. Hanged, by all accounts.'

'So even with all that proof, Sokolov gets away with it?' Mann didn't even try to hide his disgust.

'For now, yes. But, for want of a better phrase, karma can be a real bitch.'

Cooper was confused. 'Care to elaborate?'

Horton smiled. 'No, I wouldn't. What I can tell you is that you did your country a great service in preventing the attack. Our people have analysed the cargo in the drones, and it's pretty nasty stuff.'

'Nanobots, you said.'

'Actually, Alex, they're microbots. Early tests suggest these ones were designed to induce cancer.'

'Induce it?'

'So the scientists say. We'll need to study it in a lot more depth, but that's their preliminary judgement.'

'Then this could be a mixed blessing,' Cooper said. 'If they can induce cancer, is there a chance they could be altered to cure it instead?'

'We have people working on that as we speak. What I do know is that this technology is far in advance of our own. It could take years to decipher it, never mind alter it.'

'Well at least some good came of all this.'

'Perhaps,' Horton conceded. 'Perhaps.' He returned to his seat. 'Anyway, I've already had a word with HR. There's no need to work your full notice, so hand over anything you think relevant by the end of the week and you're free to go.'

'Thanks, Chief,' Cooper said. 'That's much appreciated.'

Horton waved it away. 'Have you decided what you're going to do?'

Mann and Cooper looked at each other. Mann spoke for them. 'We're going to become security consultants.'

'You mean mercenaries.'

'Similar,' Mann smiled, 'but with more cash.'

'And hopefully fewer gunfights,' Cooper added.

Horton chuckled, then waved a hand towards the door. 'Get out of here.'

They turned to leave, but Mann stopped. 'What about you? Did our debrief work?'

'Like a charm,' Horton said. 'The PM was satisfied that we hadn't overstepped the mark, and word from Moscow station is that Sokolov has some very final and permanent plans for Levchenko, so he won't be round long enough to contradict your stories.'

'Can't say I'm disappointed,' Mann told him. 'I'm glad it worked out for you.'

'I wish I could say the same. Now, scoot. Go and say your goodbyes. And no stealing office supplies on your way out.'

'Scout's honour,' Cooper said, making a three-fingered salute.

They walked to the door, but Horton had one last request.

'Once you're set up in your new venture, let me know. We need good freelancers from time to time.'

Mann promised to stay in touch, and they closed the door on the way out.

'And just like that, we become masters of our own destiny.'

'Yeah,' Cooper grimaced. 'Scary, isn't it?'

'Scary as hell. Let's go get a drink.'

Epilogue

Igor Sokolov sucked in the crisp morning air as he pounded the pavement on his regular morning jog. His security detail kept pace with him, three of them fifteen yards ahead, the other five fifteen yards behind him. Weak sunlight filtered through the fir trees as he neared the end of the first of two laps.

Although he was approaching fifty-five, Sokolov prided himself on having the physique and stamina of a much younger man. His daily exercise routine consisted of a three-mile run, followed by an hour in his private gym. Not only did it keep him fit, it also served as a circuit breaker, allowing him time to put aside the pressures of running the greatest country on the planet and just be at one with nature.

Today, however, that luxury eluded him once again.

As had been the case for the last two months, every waking moment had been spent dealing with the fallout from the bitter failure of Project Nightfall. Years of research and development had been wasted. The technology could never be used for fear it would point the blame squarely at him. The British might not have publicly revealed the true intent behind Nightfall, but they were sure to have shared details with their Western counterparts.

Sokolov had repeatedly assured Prime Minister Ward that he had no knowledge of the plot, and that the culprits had been properly punished, but that hadn't been enough. Ward was talking of increased sanctions, including removing access to the Swift financial system again. Such a move would devastate Russia's already fragile economy. He could counter such a move by threatening to limit natural gas supplies to Europe, but after the invasion of Ukraine, Britain and the EU had secured deals with Algeria and Qatar to make up any potential shortfall.

As Sokolov started his second circuit of the park, his mind once again turned to the problem of bringing America to heel. With the failure of Nightfall—and by extension, Operation Lightning Spear—it would be years before he could make another move.

That was, if he got the chance. Protests in the streets had been a daily occurrence. Despite cracking down on dissent, opposition parties had been vociferous in denouncing him for his alleged involvement in the British 'terror attack'. Even his closest ally, China, had been highly critical. President Wang might hate the West as much as Sokolov, but he wasn't about to lose out on trillions in trade to stand shoulder to shoulder with the man accused of such a heinous plot.

Sokolov was forced to admit that, at best, he had a tenuous hold on his leadership. He would have to come up with something soon if he was to achieve his goal of remaining the Russian president for the remainder of his life.

* * *

Sergeant Ben Daniels was in the café across from the park, waiting for Igor Sokolov to reach his marker. He'd sat in the same seat for the last three days, watching the president and getting the timing just right.

A week earlier, he'd shimmied up one of the trees on Sokolov's route and attached the delivery unit to an upper branch, one exactly fifteen feet above the path. The device looked like a pine cone, even when viewed up close. Hanging from a pine tree in the park across the road, it would never raise suspicion.

Daniels had timed Sokolov's runs, and they had always been consistent. The conditions were finally right. Tests back home showed that in cold weather, with no breeze, the microbots would fall at a rate of 0.3 feet per second. To drop nine feet and be level with Sokolov's mouth and nose would take twenty-seven seconds. Sokolov would be twenty-seven seconds from the drop zone when he reached the second of three park benches.

Daniels had his phone in his hand, his thumb over the green button on the screen. There was a lag of two seconds between pressing it and the fake cone opening to release its contents. Daniels had factored that in.

Sokolov was nearing the bench, his rhythm still strong, his gait assured.

Five…

Four…

Three…

Two…

Daniels looked down and pressed the button. The green circle was replaced by a timer that counted down from twenty-nine. He looked back out to the park, counting silently in his head as Sokolov neared the drop zone. The phone in his hand vibrated once to let him know the timer had reached zero. One second later, Sokolov ran underneath the cone.

Bullseye.

Daniels deleted the app he'd been using and did a factory reset on the phone before putting it in his coat pocket. After finishing his coffee, he walked out into the cold. Two blocks later, he took the phone out, removed the battery and SIM card and tossed the handset into a rubbish bin. He threw the battery into another five minutes later, and finally dropped the SIM card down a drain as he crossed a street. All that remained was to retrieve the fake cone, a task he would complete that evening.

It was the first time Daniels had been asked to kill a world leader, and he had no regrets. Sokolov had planned to do the same to millions of people in England, and this was no more than he deserved.

At this moment, around fifty million microbots would be beginning the slow yet relentless journey towards Sokolov's pancreas, and that sat just fine with Sergeant Ben Daniels.

THE END

AUTHOR'S NOTE

If you would like to be informed of new releases, simply send an email with 'Agenda' in the subject line to jambalian@outlook.com to be added to the mailing list. Alan only sends two or three emails a year, so you won't be bombarded with spam.

About the Author

Alan McDermott is a husband, father to beautiful twin girls and a full-time author from the south of England.

Born in West Germany of Scottish parents, Alan spent his early years moving from town to town as his father was posted to different Army units around the United Kingdom. Alan had a number of jobs after leaving school, including working on cruise ships in Hong Kong and Singapore, where he met his wife.

Alan's writing career began in 2011 and *Gray Justice* was his first full-length novel.

Printed in Great Britain
by Amazon

28971707R00199